CANNIBAL

DREAMS

HADENA JAMES

Acknowledgments

For everyone that reads and loves Aislinn Cain as much as I do.

Thanks to my hometown for supplying me with great pizza and subs. Seriously, you gotta try them.

Hmmm, about the ending… Yes, that really is the way this book is going to end. Now, do not skip ahead!

ALSO BY HADENA JAMES

The Dreams & Reality Series
Tortured Dreams (Book 1)
Elysium Dreams (Book 2)
Mercurial Dreams (Book 3)
Explosive Dreams (Book 4)
Cannibal Dreams (Book 5)

The Brenna Strachan Series (Urban Fantasy)
Dark Cotillion (Book 1)
Dark Illumination (Book 2)
Dark Resurrections (Book 3)
Dark Legacies (Book 4)

The Dysfunctional Chronicles
The Dysfunctional Affair (Book 1)
The Dysfunctional Valentine (Book 2)
The Dysfunctional Honeymoon (Book 3)
The Dysfunctional Proposal (Book 4)

Short Story Collection
Tales to Read Before the End of the World

PROLOGUE

He put on the clean room gear. The helmet, jumpsuit, gloves, and boots were connected together with Velcro. The clean room was a nice model. He'd ordered it off the internet over a year ago. It worked to keep the mess out of the house and it was easy to clean when he finished.

The body was already on the table. Rigor had come and gone. Most of the blood had congealed and settled, leaving dark spots visible through the skin. The wounds on the boy's body had scabbed over.

August plugged in the Sawzall. It whirred to life with a high pitched hum. The pitch became deeper as the blade bit into the first piece of flesh. The blade shredded the skin, severed the ligaments, nerves and tendons. The teeth ate through the windpipe with ease. Even when it hit the spine there was very little resistance. It sheared through the bone quickly and effectively. The boy's head fell to the floor with a thud that couldn't be heard over the motor of the saw. Dark, almost black, fluid oozed from the wound.

He moved to the arms next. These required bracing. Straps hung from the ceiling. He took his time securing each wrist into its designated strap. If he didn't, the arm might move and the saw would get into a bind, causing it to not cut through the bone.

The legs were the hardest. He started at the ankles, cutting just above the joint. He repeated the procedure just above the knee. Getting through the femur was always tricky. It dulled the blade. He had to cut it twice on each leg. The saw made a loud whine and the blade broke.

Under his mask, he swore vehemently. It took him a few minutes to replace the blade. The gloves were great for protection, not so great for manipulating small parts.

After he replaced the blade, he went back to cutting off the legs at the hip. He shoved everything except the feet inside a large, heavy duty bag.

Now, he had to work on the torso. He still hadn't figured out the best way to do it. He knew he had to remove the organs, which was always disgusting.

The saw tore into the chest. Bone dust flew up. Miniature bone slivers filled the air. The flesh was shredded as the saw yanked it away from the body. This is why the body sat for a day before being cut apart, there was less blood to be strewn about the room.

He removed the organs and put them in the bag. He took the saw and began cutting through the ribs. The torso was tedious work. It had to be cut five or six times, in different directions, before it would fit inside.

When he finished, he zipped the bag closed. Everything was inside except the feet. He used a sprayer hose to rinse the table. The water splashed and flung droplets cascading across the room as the stainless steel table was cleaned. Drains built into the table, carried away the messy leftovers of his dismemberment. Next, he dried it with a plush, soft dark blue towel.

The feet he put on the table and began examining them. They were dirty; caked with mud and blood. This would never do. He turned the water back on, making sure it was warm, and began to clean the feet.

He'd been very careful to remove them about an inch above the ankle joint. Ensuring to cut the tibia and fibula with the precision that would have made a doctor proud. The feet were mostly just scratched and cut. The result of being barefoot when forced to walk across the property into the barn. However, one wound caught his eye. It was bigger than the others, deeper.

August reached for the filet knife that he kept close by. Very carefully, he began to scrape at the wound, removing the tissue in layers and chunks until the bone was visible. This done, he washed the foot again. It was ready for the final step.

A package of tube socks, protected by a zip lock bag, set on a counter top in the room. He dried his hands and made sure they were clean before opening the package. The socks were bright white and brand new. He took them over to the feet.

Moving with ease, that was only learned through experience, he put the severed left foot into a sock. He did the same with the right. Using the extra material, he tied the socks together, ensuring that the feet dangled in them like sausages.

It took both hands to carry the duffle bag full of dismembered body parts out to his truck. He returned to his barn and grabbed the socks. Outside the clean room, he now disrobed from his clean suit. He picked up the socks and headed back outside.

He drove the twenty-one miles to the river and tossed the duffle bag into the black water. It gurgled as it sank. Even on the best days, the visibility was practically zero here. At night, only the nocturnal creatures could see his deed. He got back into the truck and drove into town.

It was late when he arrived. The bars had all closed. A few drunks loitered in the streets, talking loudly or stumbling, as they went wherever they went. He turned into a residential neighborhood. It had once been one of those fancy ones, the kind where everyone with money wanted to live, but those days were gone. It had become lower class, filled with starter homes for young families. The streets had become crowded. The small yards unappealing. It had been replaced by bigger houses in better neighborhoods. He drove slowly down the street. No lights shown from windows. No security lights flashed on. A few houses had left their outside lights burning through the night, more out of forgetfulness than anything else.

He stopped the truck in the middle of the road and tossed the socks. They wrapped neatly around a utility wire. He tried not to giggle as he got back inside, pulling his door shut very quietly, ensuring not to wake the neighborhood. Slamming doors would be unusual here at this time of night.

With the feet now safely out of his possession, he turned the truck around. He drove out of the neighborhood and was gone, disappearing into the night on an old highway that was hardly ever used. He headed east, homebound. The night was clear and cold. It had snowed a few days earlier and cinders had turned the snow black. His headlights reflected off the blackened mounds of dirty ice and onto clean, undisturbed fields of snow. He'd used his tractor to clear his driveway a few days earlier.

His tires crunched over frozen gravel as he returned. He got out of the truck and walked to the old barn. Inside, the clean room still needed to be cleaned and dismantled. He set to work. By sunrise, his muscles were starting to ache, but the room was clean. All the pieces were stacked against the wall, looking like cubicles from an abandoned office building. He left the heat running in the building and went to the house.

The house was colder. A chill had crept in as the fireplace had slowly begun to die out. He piled wood in it, bringing it back from the brink of death. The new wood hissed and popped as it soaked in the heat and flames and fueled the fire back to a roaring inferno.

August was about to sit down when he remembered he hadn't put the meat up. He sighed heavily and put his coat back on. He trekked back out to the barn and hung the meat he'd fileted off the back and ribs of the boy he'd just dumped in the river, into an old section of the barn. It had once been used to cure pork, but those days were long gone. Something growled, he turned and caught a glint of light from Genevieve, his pet jaguar. Her cage took up the largest part of the barn and cost a fortune to heat, but it was worth it.

"Genny," he cooed at her. She gave a low, guttural growl in response. A second, higher pitched growl followed. It came from the darkness behind Genny. Vera, his other pet, was hiding, but didn't want to go completely unnoticed. "Good girls," he cooed at them again before leaving.

ONE

The guy in overalls rushed me. His shoulder slammed into my gut, lifting me off the ground. The air was forced from my lungs as we hit the wall behind us. I had a gun and could hit my attacker in the back of the head with it or shoot him, but killing a serial killer on the job, produced a lot of paperwork and death was always a possibility when a gun was involved. My other option was to rip off his ear.

My fingernails dug into the cartilage at the top of the serial killer's ear. I yanked. Blood gushed into my hand, running down my arm in a crimson line. The flesh between the tips of my fingers became spongier. I pulled harder. The suspect let out a yell and pushed against my mid-section.

Gabriel and Xavier had guns drawn. John Bryant, our newest member, was holding a Taser. None of them were firing. I was too close to use either weapon safely. I'd feel the jolt of the Taser, even though it wasn't set to high.

My ribs began to hurt. If I didn't do something soon, the brut would break a rib just using his shoulder and the wall behind me.

"Now?" John asked.

"Um," Gabriel seemed to waiver for a moment. I took the moment to finish the damage I had started. The ring of the ear, including the lobe, completely came off. I dropped it to the ground and grabbed the other ear with my other hand. As soon as my fingers touched it, the killer moved back, letting me fall to my feet. I kicked him in the knee with the heavy work boots I always wore on the job. The steel-plate in the toe connected with his knee cap. The steel-plate in the bottom of the boot connected a little lower. The monster went down to one knee.

He growled at me.

"Well?" I asked the men in the room, wondering what the hell they were waiting for. John fired his Taser. The man in front of me took the voltage and began trying to stand, despite the electricity and the dislocated knee. "Jesus Christ," I muttered, kicking him again, in the other knee. There wasn't a pop, it didn't dislocate, but he grunted louder. I was running out of options and time. I really didn't want to shoot him.

"John, stop," Gabriel commanded. John took his finger off the trigger of his Taser. Gabriel moved in. He began to put cuffs on the serial killer. The monster moved like Flash Gordon, turning, he managed to grab Gabriel and swing him over his knee. His hands clutched at Gabriel's throat.

"Let him go, now," I put my gun to his forehead. Gabriel's face was turning the same shade of red as his hair. Now, I wanted to shoot him. Instead, I hit him in the forehead with the butt of my gun. He crumpled to the floor, his hand spasming and releasing Gabriel. Gabriel gagged and coughed.

"Thanks," he croaked. "You could have done it a few seconds earlier."

"I was trying to convince myself not to execute him."

"This is better," Gabriel agreed. "There would have been a lot of paperwork if you had shot him at point blank range in the forehead."

"Hey, I offered him the chance to surrender twice before he rushed me and then, I only removed his ear instead of busting open his head. I think it showed a lot of restraint." Restraint wasn't exactly my strong-point on a good day. Lately, I hadn't had many good days. Lucas was still off work. Michael was still dead. His killer was still out there. He'd gone dormant and every killer we'd caught in the last two months was a surrogate for the one that had got away.

However, while waiting for our first case in December, I had taken the initiative to use our Killer's Database to track his work. He'd been killing fair queens for years, all over the country. Until three years ago, then he'd stopped. Our sniper had re-emerged after the carnival bombings began in June of last year. He'd gone dormant again after killing Michael.

It was late January. We had at least four months until fair season began again. That didn't stop me from checking the database for his MO weekly.

The new guy, John Bryant, seemed to be working. He hesitated more than I liked and he still made some mistakes, like Tasering a suspect a few weeks earlier while Gabriel was tousling with him, but there was a steep learning curve. He'd either figure it out really quick or he'd die. So far, it didn't matter to me either way, unless it effected one of the others.

"Xavier, check her over. John, help me with the suspect," Gabriel ordered.

"I'm fine," I said before Xavier could reach me.

"You just had four hundred pounds crushing your ribs. You might be tough as nails, but you are going to be looked at before we leave this house," Gabriel informed me. "And get the crime scene people in here. There are at least parts of seven victims in the guest bedroom."

"I'll call the techs," a uniformed officer who had made entry with us said from the doorway that led to the kitchen. He was ashen and shaking. We had told him not to come in, but he had insisted. It wasn't just the body parts in the other room or the fact that the entire place smelled like road kill. He had lost some blood from a bite mark and watching me pull off a serial killer's ear seemed to disturb him.

"Arms up," Xavier told me. His fingers instantly went under my shirt and began prodding my ribs. They were bruised, his touch was akin to being stabbed, but nothing felt out of place, loose or broken. "She's good," Xavier told Gabriel.

"Are you ready for this?" Gabriel asked John. John nodded, but looked a little unsure. The press was outside. This was the first time he'd be face to face with them as we took a suspect out of a house.

This killer wasn't really special by our standards, but living in a town of only 400 people in Pennsylvania seemed interesting. The fact that he was Amish made it newsworthy. Add to it that no one knew there was a serial killer until a tornado left body parts strung across three miles of Pennsylvania and it was worthy of national news. It was also the reason we were here. The tornado had destroyed his barn where he'd been storing the dismembered corpses.

"Am I bleeding?" I asked.

"No," Xavier told me.

That was a plus, it meant my battered body wouldn't end up being broadcast across the country. As long as I could walk, upright and unassisted, without blood gushing from some part of my body, my cell phone wouldn't ring constantly. Besides, Lucas tended to freak out when it did, blaming himself for not being there.

"Shall we?" Gabriel pointed towards the door.

"Xavier or me first?" I asked.

"Xavier," Gabriel answered. I stepped aside, taking a position at the rear of the group. If our killer attempted to escape, I could shoot him on TV. That would be interesting. I was willing to bet the live broadcast would be interrupted.

Noise washed over us first. Evening was starting to set in, not yet dusk, but almost. There was still enough sun that most of the cameras didn't require extra lights. Some reporters were shouting our names; others were busy giving their spiel to their cameras as we walked past.

None of us made eye contact. We focused our gazes on the vehicle borrowed from the Marshals' Service in Pittsburgh that would be transporting our suspect. The back was an enclosed cage. The doors were already open. Several men in tactical gear with large weapons stood at the back of the doors. Xavier walked with determination, a good gait that didn't require me to walk fast to keep up, but kept us all moving past the crowds that lined our way.

"Marshal Cain, is he missing an ear?" Some reporter asked, trying to shove a microphone in my face. I walked past, unwilling to make a comment. Losing an ear was a lot better than being dead in most people's opinions.

"Nice," one of the Marshals' standing guard at the van said to us as we handed our suspect to him.

"He should have known better," Gabriel shrugged. We were out of ear shot of the cameras and reporters. This area was sealed for their protection.

"By the blood on her hands, I'd guess it was her work," one of them smirked.

"Better than a bullet to the back of the skull," Xavier answered. "The ear will heal. Most bullets in the head don't."

"Are we using your plane to get him to KC?" Someone who looked to be in charge asked.

"No, they have something lined up for him in Pittsburgh. We'll follow you into the city," Gabriel answered.

We may not get invited to other Marshals' parties very often, but we were respected by our fellow officers. They might yank our chain once in a while, but the death of Michael had proved we were just as much a part of the Marshals' as anyone else with the badge. Every Marshal with a day off out of the eight states that touched Missouri had shown up for his funeral. All of them had given their condolences to both his family and us. Michael had been buried with the full rights and rituals due to a fallen Marshal.

After handing off the Amish serial killer, we got into our SUV. There was a collective groan. It was my turn to pick the music. I hooked up my iPhone to the stereo. *Angry Johnny* by Poe instantly began to blare from the speakers when Gabriel turned the ignition. This was a new thing we were trying for long car rides. None of us agreed on music, so we each took a turn playing music for an hour. I had built a playlist with the intent of annoying my fellow passengers. They made me listen to Johnny Cash and Nelly, I could make them suffer through girl grunge bands and German industrial.

Just for the record, I am not a fan of "The Man in Black." I like my music hard, Rob Zombie and Rammstein were the chart toppers, along with Nine Inch Nails, Garbage and Ozzy Osbourne. They didn't need to know that in private, I listened to Carrie Underwood, Lady Gaga or Simon and Garfunkle. Nor did they need to know that I liked the song *The Highway Man* which featured Johnny Cash or that I had over 48,000 mp3s in my music collection. There were some things that were still private.

Two

It was night, but not dark. Cities like Pittsburgh are plagued with light pollution that keeps night time from ever being truly dark. The Marshals' Building was in a rundown part of the city. I had been told to watch myself, it was a high crime neighborhood. The Marshal that had told me had smiled while saying it.

Now, leaning against the building, having a cigarette, I could see a group of young men coming down the street. They crossed the road after making eye contact, but flashed gang signs or some other nonsense as they passed me. I watched them until they disappeared. Occasionally, a member of the group looked back, but they always whipped their head around quickly. Being around me, even during the daylight, was unsettling for most.

The group of hoodlums gone, I returned to thinking. My ribs hurt. The giant oaf hadn't broken anything, just bruised me, that didn't stop it from hurting. My back also hurt, but the pain was less determined to be noticed.

My family could be proof that violence was a genetic condition. Few of my relatives, on either side, had died natural deaths. Most had died violently. My dad and sister were just the tip of the iceberg. We had generations of Clachans and Connors that had died prematurely, most cut down in their prime, shortly after producing someone to carry on the family name. One of my great grandfathers had been hung by an angry mob after he robbed a bank. A great aunt had been killed by a drifter around the turn of the century. Her body had been carved up like a jack-o-lantern.

Perhaps, if my parents had married other people, it would have been different. My siblings and I wouldn't have been born, but maybe the cycle of violence would have been broken.

They hadn't. They had been attracted to each other, possibly because they shared a bond of violence. My paternal grandfather had disappeared when my dad was only five and the day my paternal grandmother was murdered. My dad and his brothers had been raised by different aunts and uncles.

My maternal grandparents had both died in a house fire set by a niece. My mother had lost her parents and a baby brother in the fire. She had been just nine. My mother and surviving siblings had been raised by an aunt because her grandfather had been hung. The aunt lived to be in her seventies, but died of cancer and from what I had been told, it had been a slow, painful death. Finally, the aunt overdosed on morphine just to end the suffering.

The cycle went back further. Its impact was wide and reaching, like the Reaper swinging his scythe at the branches of my family tree. Three hundred years of mostly unnatural deaths on both sides of my family. Not for the first time, I wonder if we were paying for the sins of some long dead ancestors.

Gabriel came outside. He lit his own cigarette. His lips were turned down and frown lines were deep set in his forehead and around his mouth.

"What's with the scowl, Kemosabe?" I asked, flicking my cigarette into the street. The city of Pittsburgh could fine me for littering if they wanted. There wasn't an ashtray where we stood.

"Snow storm in Kansas City," Gabriel replied. "We can't land there. We are going to have to fly into Columbia and drive home."

"With an Amish serial killer?" I looked for evidence that he was joking and found none.

"What's with the label? You don't call serial killers that happen to be Baptist, Baptist Serial Killers."

"He's Amish," I gave my boss a blank look. "In the history of the US, how many Amish serial killers can you think of?"

"None come to mind immediately," Gabriel said these words slowly, as if chewing on them.

"Me either," I answered. "It's interesting."

"We'll agree to disagree there," Gabriel said. "But no, not with the Amish serial killer. He is going to stay in a penitentiary here for a few days. We, on the other hand, do not have the luxury of not flying while the Midwest is ass deep in snow and places that don't normally get snow are having blizzards. We have to go home because your buddy has a lead."

"A lead on what?" I asked, then realized I needed more clarification. "What buddy?"

"Malachi Blake has a lead for us."

"On?"

"I don't know," Gabriel answered. "I just know that ten minutes ago, I was told we needed to get our asses on the plane and get home, come hell or high water."

"Or ass deep snow," I giggled.

"Or ass deep snow."

"Well, I've seen enough of Pittsburgh."

"You've seen like three blocks unless you count car rides."

"And discovered the hoodlums here are not much different than the hoodlums in other cities."

"Don't use the word hoodlum."

"Why? It's a good word."

"No one uses it, except you and old men. Try the word thug."

"So, I should just assume that every juvenile or young adult on the street is a cult member and serial killer?"

"Why does thug imply that they are all killers?"

"Because general wisdom says the word is derived from the word Thugee. The Thugee were a cult that practiced human sacrifice in India. One leader was said to have..."

"Stop," Gabriel held up his hand. "Never mind. I do not want to know."

"It's really rather interesting."

"I'm sure it is, but we should be leaving and we'll never get there if you start in on a history lecture that involves death, cults, and serial killers."

"I'll tell you on the plane," I followed him into the building.

I didn't tell him on the plane. I didn't tell anyone on the plane. Everyone but me slept. I was concerned about the weather. They had closed

Interstate 70 from Highway 65 west into Kansas. There would be no travelling by car from Columbia to Kansas City. Some places were reporting three feet of snow.

This was the second storm to sweep through the Midwest. The first had come a few days earlier and been much milder. We had been in Pennsylvania for it and it had surprisingly dissipated before reaching the Eastern Coast.

My concern was that it was almost 1 a.m. in Central Missouri and the Columbia Regional Airport was not an all hours airport. Either we were landing at an airport with no personnel in the face of a serious winter storm or they were paying someone to open the airport specifically for our landing.

Land we did, with runway lights and a scattering of snow piles along the tarmac. Two people, dressed in bright orange vests met us as the pilot opened the door. One seemed to be a supervisor. The other was obviously not happy, but was probably getting double time for this unexpected inconvenience.

"Sir," the first guy said to Gabriel as Gabriel descended the steps. "You have hotel arrangements in town. We have an SUV rental for your use while in Columbia. The storm is expected to hit about dawn. You won't be able to travel any further west though until the interstate gets opened back up."

I gave Xavier a look, wondering why this guy knew our hotel information. Xavier gave a slight nod and I looked at him closer. Under the bright orange vest, the outline of a badge could vaguely be made out. I nodded.

The others lagged behind as I raced for the waiting SUV. It was running and the windows were clean, so I was betting the heat was on inside. Moving slowly through the cold, in the wee hours of the morning was not my idea of a good time. I threw my two bags into the back and climbed into the driver's seat.

"What the..." Gabriel asked.

"I grew up here," I reminded him. "Who better to drive?"

"Where are we going?" Gabriel asked.

"That depends on what hotel we are staying at," I told him.

"You're staying at the Hampton Inn at Clark Lane," the guy with the badge told us.

"I know where that is," I told Gabriel. "So, I'll drive."

Most people were of the mindset that I hadn't been back to my hometown in ten years or so. This was incorrect. I had driven through it several times and planned my trips to coincidence with meal times. Despite all my travel, I had never found a better pizza than the Masterpiece at Shakespeare's or a better sub than the veggie at Sub Shop. There were competitors to be sure, but they always fell a little short. I hoped that since I was in town, I would get to enjoy both.

The team loaded into the SUV. John Bryant, our newest member, climbed in back with Xavier. It felt strange to not have Lucas also climbing into the vehicle, but he was at home, buried under snow and watching our progress on the news. Scalp grafts are more difficult than back grafts as it turns out. He was still not cleared for duty.

However, this meant we were all getting our own rooms. Gabriel still hadn't made a decision about the new guy and Xavier would not share a room with anyone but Lucas. It made travel more expensive, but I believed Gabriel was paying for his own room. This didn't really affect me, as the only girl, I always got a room to myself.

"Where'd you grow up?" Xavier asked as I started towards the exit of the airport.

"Here," I frowned at his reflection in the mirror.

"No, I mean, what house?" Xavier said. "I'm curious where Aislinn Cain got her start."

"Oh," I thought for a few moments before turning onto Highway 63 Northbound. "You want to see the house where I grew up?"

"Yes," Xavier said.

"Only if we don't get snowed in," I answered.

THREE

Columbia is climatically charmed. Storms that were terrible tended to go around the city. During my lifetime, I could remember five snow storms. Daylight brought the realization that the storm that had hammered everything west of the city, had somehow missed Columbia. There was maybe four inches of snow on the ground and the sun was shining.

It also meant that I would be enjoying food from my favorite Columbia places. While my favorite foods were pizza, subs, and Mexican; there was a place for everything in the college-oriented city.

A knock on my door reminded me of my tentative agreement to show my team where I had grown up. A part of me hoped the house had burnt to the ground. I knew it hadn't, at least it hadn't last time I had checked three years ago. It was more likely that aliens had invaded and replaced most of the citizens with pod people. This was not because house fires didn't happen, they did, more often than people wanted to admit. It was because Xavier wanted to see where I had passed my childhood. The tiny little inconvenience would ensure that the universe had preserved my home.

I climbed from bed. The digital clock told me it was almost noon. I had slept for about seven hours. The last time I had slept for that long at one time, I'd been in a medically induced coma. I'd taken the time to change into pajamas, it was a matching flannel set. The pants were purple with blue and green hearts. The top was green with blue and purple hearts. I had no idea where I had gotten such an outfit, but it was warm.

The knocking continued, becoming louder. I groaned, hoping they would hear me and stop. They didn't, instead they began beating a rhythm on the door. It had to be Xavier.

I never used the peep holes, I was convinced that someone would shove an icepick through my eye if I did. The very idea of sticking my face against the door filled me with dread. Instead, I unlocked it and opened it fully.

Needless to say, I was not surprised to see Xavier on the other side. I was surprised by the brown bag he had in his hands. If we had been anywhere else, I would have wondered what was inside, but the white receipt taped to the bag told me I had a warm, extremely cheesy veggie sub in my very near future.

"The bag may come in," I took it from him. "You may not."

"Nice jammies," Xavier came in anyway and shut the door behind him. "I'm still not used to Lucas not being here. I ordered him a sub too."

"It is very strange," I agreed, opening the bag and pulling out the full sized sub wrapped in foil. It was still hot to the touch. "Did you have them fly it by helicopter?"

"No, they were just hot when they showed up," Xavier said.

"How long ago was that?" I asked.

"Three minutes, maybe four."

"Where's yours?" I asked.

"In the bag you snatched from me."

I looked in the bag and saw a brownie and another foil wrapped sandwich.

"I call dibs on the top of that brownie," I told him.

"You don't eat brownies and why do you want just the top? Why not half of it?"

"I only like the top of the brownie and then, I only like them from Sub Shop," I answered. "They make the tops crunchy, for lack of a better term.

The inside is gooey. I don't know how they do it. But I only like the crunchy top."

"I guess I don't have a choice in this, do I?"

"That would be correct," I pulled the brownie out and peeled off the top. I put the top of the brownie on a napkin and handed the rest to Xavier. "Where's everyone else?"

"John is still sleeping. Gabriel is on the phone, arguing with Malachi and someone of significance."

"One of our mysterious committee bosses," I raised an eyebrow.

"That would be my guess."

"What are they arguing over?"

"Road conditions. It didn't sound very interesting, so I dropped off his sub and came here instead."

"I see," I bit into my sub. Mayo dribbled out the side. Xavier had ordered extra. This was at least ten million calories, but it was a small price to pay. There were three types of cheese, a ton of veggies, thick mayo, and all toasted to perfection on Italian style bread. Few things made me happy, this was one of them.

"You're smiling," Xavier said.

"It is yummy," I answered. "So, about the trip to my house."

"You aren't getting out of it. The snow disappeared around the river and we only got a couple of inches. Interstate 70 is a disaster though. Even after it was cleaned and then cleaned again, there have been three or four dozen wrecks. Gabriel thinks it's unsafe to drive on. Malachi disagrees. I don't know what the other person on the phone thinks."

I nodded and wrapped my sandwich back in the foil. I grabbed my brownie top, my sandwich and my keycard and left Xavier sitting at my table. Using my foot, I knocked as gently as I could at Gabriel's door. After a few seconds, it opened. His cell phone was still glued to his ear. I set my stuff down on his table, yanked the phone away from him and hung up.

"Uh, I was on the phone," Gabriel gave me a look.

"I know, but it's rude to talk on cell phones while eating at a table with others. It's rude when there isn't anyone else there, but it's ruder when there is. Besides, it was Malachi and one of our eight billion bosses. The worst that can happen is that they can chew you out for your phone going dead. And Malachi can't do that, he can only get cranky about it."

"That was the head of the US Marshals and Malachi," Gabriel said. "Malachi thinks he has a lead on The Butcher."

"Do you think this is the first time Malachi has thought he had a lead on The Butcher?" I sat down and opened my sandwich again. "What'd you get?"

"It doesn't bother you at all that you did that, does it?" Xavier sat down.

"Nope, not in the least," I answered. Gabriel's cell phone rang. I willed it to disappear, but it didn't.

Gabriel answered it. He was quiet as the voice on the other end spoke. It wasn't loud enough for me to hear, but I was sure he was getting his ass handed to him.

"It's for you," Gabriel handed me the phone. His face had a quizzical look. Perhaps I had pushed the boundaries a little far by hanging up on the director of the US Marshals.

"Marshal Cain," I said taking the phone.

"I've heard you are eccentric, but hanging up on me while I talked to your team leader was unexpected," the voice on the other end of the line had a Bostonian accent. It was rich and cultured, reminding me of speeches I'd heard from the Kennedy's during high school history classes.

"Sir, it wasn't," I started.

"I am aware that Marshal Hendricks was not responsible for hanging up on me. Special Agent Blake informed me that you had a pet-peeve about phones during meal times," he paused and I didn't know whether to say something or not, so I held my tongue. "My wife has the same rule. Usually, it only applies to our children, but she has given me looks when my work phone has rang during meals. This means I understand how important you consider meal times with your team and I admire that. Since you aren't working a case, we'll ignore it this time. But if you ever do that while working, you can bet your ass that I will become your worst enemy."

"Thank you, sir," I handed the phone back quickly to Gabriel. The urge to argue that there was no way the director of the US Marshals could become my worst enemy was boiling below the surface. I had enemies. Most of them were a whole lot scarier than the director.

Gabriel said a few things and hung up the phone. He set it down between Xavier and himself. For several minutes, he said nothing. He stared at his sandwich, waiting for his own temper to settle down before jumping my case.

"You are so lucky," Gabriel finally spoke. A wide smile appeared on his face. "And somehow, managed to keep my ass out of the sling. I'm guessing this is partially Malachi's doing, so I'll thank him later."

"Good plan," I unwrapped the sub and began eating again.

"After lunch, we head to the house where you grew up," Xavier said.

"John isn't feeling well, so he can stay here and sleep," Gabriel informed me.

"Ill?" I raised an eyebrow. I had a flash of something, remembering Michael who seemed constantly on the mend from some injury or illness. Inexplicably, Michael seemed more important now that he was dead. I found myself thinking of him more often than I had when he was alive. I didn't know how to explain this, so I ignored it.

"Sleep deprivation," Xavier clarified. "It would appear the Secret Service kept more stable hours than us."

I shrugged. We'd been up about thirty hours when we went head on with our Amish serial killer. It had taken us another eight to get away from the Marshals' office in Pittsburgh and get to our hotel in Columbia. It probably did require some getting used to, unless you just didn't really sleep much to begin with.

"I'm stuffed," I pushed back from the table. A stray mushroom was all that remained in the foil. I debated picking it up and eating it. A mushroom was a terrible thing to waste, a mushroom with cheese stuck to it was even worse. Eating it would probably mean that my pants wouldn't want to button. Not eating it would be wasting food. I snatched it up and tossed it into my mouth. I chewed quickly, resolved to eat it before I exploded like Mr. Creosote from *The Meaning of Life*.

"Then go get dressed, we have places to go," Xavier took another bite. I was stuck. I went and got dressed.

FOUR

Being in my hometown didn't create feelings
of nostalgia. I'd grown up in Columbia, but I had
also been kidnapped once and nearly killed several
times. Despite these incidents, the city had rather
low crime figures. For me, it had always seemed
like crime came in waves. There'd be a serial killer
or something and it would rage for a year or so,
then it would go back to simple, petty crimes. Then
the rate would soar again as another violent
criminal went on the loose.

I jumped on the highway and headed south.
The roads were mostly clear, a sprinkling of snow
and ice had been blackened by cinders and road
salts. Driving there was easy, I remembered the
address and the location. It didn't matter that
things had changed in the last twelve years or so.

The SUV turned into the subdivision.
Gabriel sat next to me. Xavier was straining against
the seatbelt in the back to get a better view.

The subdivision was like a thousand others. It was too old to be made of cookie cutter houses, but that was its only distinguishing feature. The houses had once been considered spacious and the neighborhood swanky, inhabited by the wealthy. However, that had been long before I was born. The wealthy had moved on to better areas, leaving this one to the working classes.

I turned onto a side road and stopped next to the curb. Across the road was a one-story ranch-style house with a brick front, a one car garage and a front yard only slightly bigger than a postcard. The snow in the front yard was untouched. The drive had been shoveled. I frowned at it.

"Is this the childhood home of the infamous Aislinn Cain?" Xavier had slipped out of his seat belt.

"It is," I frowned harder.

I wasn't a big fan of change. The house had definitely changed though. Light blue vinyl trim had been put on the sides, replacing the muted pink clapboard siding that had been on it when I was young. The shutters were now painted a dark brown. They had been burgundy. The snow wasn't deep enough to hide the missing brick-ringed flowerbeds that my mother had created and cultivated. My brother's basketball hoop was gone from over the garage door. A feat to be sure since my father had not only screwed it in with about a hundred screws, but then siliconed it to make sure that it couldn't break loose if one of us decided to be stupid and hang from it.

"We should go," I said. "We look like stalkers."

"We look like cops," Gabriel told me. "Weird cops, but cops all the same."

"Knowing Ace's luck, the house is probably a meth lab now and they are currently arming themselves for a full on assault," Xavier gave one of his inappropriate giggles.

"Or that," Gabriel agreed. I started the car and turned around. Half way down the block, I stopped again. My attention drawn above the road. My frown deepened and I could feel it tugging at my ears. I tried to relax my face and failed.

"What?" Xavier asked.

"I've seen tennis shoes thrown over power lines before, but never socks," I told him, slipping the car into park and getting out. I heard the other doors of the SUV open and shut. The three of us stood in the cold in front of the running vehicle and stared up.

"There's something in them," Gabriel said.

"Yeah and it's foot shaped," Xavier sounded weird. I looked at him. He was frowning. A faint scent caught my nose, like frozen meat being taken out of the freezer.

"What's the temp?" I asked.

"What?" Both men said in unison, turning to look at me. I meet their gaze and held it.

"What is the temperature?" I said the words slowly.

"About forty," Xavier answered. "Why?"

"I smell," I shrugged. It was hard to explain what meat smelled like when it thawed. It was slightly greasy smelling. "I smell..." I shrugged.

"You smell what?" Gabriel prodded.

"Meat," I finally answered. "I smell meat, like someone took a roast out of the freezer to let thaw. It's sort of a sickly, greasy smell."

"Great," Xavier said. "You know, you could pretend you don't have a super nose and we could just drive on, go back to Kansas City."

"I don't have a super nose," I informed him.

"You can smell decay better than a vulture," Gabriel quipped. "We all have to shower after sex or risk you making a comment about it because you can smell it on us."

"That sounds creepy," I told him. "I have never done that."

"It is creepy," Xavier answered. "And you have done it. Hell, sometimes showering doesn't even work."

"Try using soap," I retorted. "Everyone can smell sex."

"No, Ace, they can't. That's what we've been trying to tell you," Xavier said. "It took us a while to figure out how you knew, then you commented about something none of us could smell one time. We put the pieces together after that and agreed to shower from then on."

"Ok, fine, I have weird olfactory abilities. I still smell meat. It's very faint. So, either something is dead and starting to thaw in a front yard nearby or those feet shaped things in those socks are probably feet."

"You're call, Gabriel. We can get in the SUV and drive back to the hotel or we can call the police and fire department and get someone down here to investigate Ace's nose." Xavier wrapped his arms around himself.

"Why would someone tie up feet in socks and throw them over a power line?" I asked.

"Because the world is full of sick and twisted people," Gabriel was digging for his cell phone.

"No, that's extreme, even for a world of sick and twisted people. They will freeze, thaw, freeze, thaw, in a cycle that will slow decomp while terrorizing the people of the neighborhood because there are weird things hanging from a power line. In a few weeks, they'll have a break from the cold that lasts more than a few days and the decay smell will spread like fires in a dry corn field." Something nagged at me. I ignored it.

"We have people coming to investigate," Gabriel hung up the phone. "We should block off the street and wait for them in the SUV."

"I'll wait in the SUV," I didn't wait for a reply. I turned and walked back to the warmth of the running vehicle. Perhaps the neighborhood hadn't changed all that much. We'd never found a pair of feet hanging from a utility line, but we had lived a few blocks from a serial killer. The nagging became more intense. The memory associated with it appeared to be missing. There was just the nagging sense that I knew something about the feet on the wire.

Sirens became louder. A fire truck responded first. Gabriel talked to the men as they climbed from the massive red truck that flashed and made too much noise. A handful of squad cars pulled up within seconds of the fire truck. That was unexpected. Socks on a line didn't require multiple squad cars. A final car pulled up. This one was unmarked and two men, wearing suits, stepped out. One was older, greying with a paunch that was beginning to make his waistband disappear. The other was younger, his face didn't have the lines and marks that the older man's had. They had to be detectives. This meant that this wasn't the first time they had found feet in socks thrown over a wire.

The older man looked vaguely familiar. I searched the database in my brain for names and faces but came up blank. Gabriel motioned to me. Reluctantly, I exited the vehicle as if walking towards a guillotine ready for use.

"Aislinn Cain, my you've really grown up," the older detective said to me.

"This is Aislinn Cain?" The younger man asked. "The Aislinn Cain?"

"It's just Aislinn Cain, no 'the' required," I informed the younger man. "I'm sorry, but I don't remember you."

"It's been a long time," the older man said. "I started the force with your dad. He was a good man. I helped work your disappearance. I was actually one of the officers that interviewed Callow when we did the door to door search."

"My apologies, but I don't remember much from that," I lied.

"Oh, yeah, sorry," the older man looked embarrassed. "Detective Troy Russell." He extended his hand out for shaking. I squashed the repulsion it brought on and shook his hand. He'd known my father, I could at least show him some courtesy. Gabriel looked like he'd been bitten by a plague-carrying prairie dog. "It appears that you've stumbled into a hornet's nest."

"How so?" I asked.

"This is the sixth set of socks we've found. They always contain a pair of feet," Detective Russell informed me. His partner scowled. Russell ignored him.

"Xavier, this is all your fault," I informed my cohort.

"How is it my fault?" Xavier protested.

"You wanted to see where I grew up." I didn't add the duh that formed at the end of the sentence. "We didn't find a meth lab, we found a serial killer. So, thank you, thank you so very much."

"Who said anything about a serial killer?" The younger partner asked. The quickest flash of a smile appeared on Russell's face. If I hadn't been watching him, I might have missed it.

"The Aislinn Cain grew up to work the US Marshals Serial Crimes Tracking Unit," Russell told him. "If you need an expert on serial killers, you're looking at them." Russell had a moment when he looked confused. "However, I thought there were more of you."

"We're a five-person unit," Gabriel confirmed. "But one is recovering from injuries sustained on another case, the other is jet-lagged.

Since we didn't intend to find a serial killer looking at Ace's old house, we left him at the hotel to sleep."

"Which house used to be yours?" The younger man asked.

"The pink one," I stopped. "No, it's blue now." I corrected myself.

"You grew up in a pink house?" Xavier raised an eyebrow.

"It was a dusty pink, not hot pink and back then, it was kind of cool." I answered.

"It was never cool," Xavier informed me.

SEARCHING

Patterson Clachan was here on personal business to see his sister. He wanted his knife back. He wanted his life back. She'd been trying to act like his puppeteer for far too long. It was time she learned her place.

Of course, he'd lost all semblance of a normal life years ago. He couldn't get it back, but he could get revenge. All those years ago, Gertrude had tried to convince him to take the boy and raise him as his own. He had his own children to think about and when she'd failed to manage talking him into it, she'd turned his wife against him. He'd never forgiven his sister.

The fight that night about the young bastard child that belonged to his sister. It had raged into the night. Lila had been all for taking the child in, raising him with their own children, doing what was best for him. Gertrude and Lee couldn't provide for him, especially with the amputated foot.

The following day, after lunch, while the children were all at school, the fight had resumed. Lila had even hinted that the accident had been his fault.

It was his fault, but it wasn't an accident. He'd tried to explain his reasons to her, but she'd been so damned stubborn and then, Gertrude had called. Lila and her had talked for a while and when they hung up, Lila laid into him like never before. The normally respectful woman he'd married had been replaced by a harpie of his sister's creating.

In the beginning, he hadn't meant to kill her. It had just happened. They'd been fighting in the kitchen and he'd grabbed the knife. Next thing he knew, he was chasing Lila around the house.

This led to his children being raised by his brother, Fritz who was better known by the nickname, Chub. The only good thing was that they hadn't gone to live with Gertrude and her horrid son.

August had been damaged from birth. He could see that. He'd caught the toddler masturbating over a dead chicken. A few days later, the family dog had gone missing and August had been found covered in its blood. At the time, he couldn't think of anything else to do, he'd tried to feed August to the hogs. He hadn't planned on

Lee being within ear shot. He'd had to kill the hog and save the boy.

That led up to the incident with Lila only a week later. He'd been living under assumed names ever since. He didn't mind so much. He did miss his family, but he watched his granddaughters from afar and tried to keep them safe. Not that either needed much guardian angel bullshit, they were tough as nails those two, able to take care of themselves.

Now, one of them was in town, looking into the murders of her deranged cousin and didn't know it. He tried to warn her off, but the message was intercepted by someone on her team named John. He'd tried to tell her it was August Clachan doing the killings, but that was also foiled by the 911 dispatcher. After all, August Clachan was listed as dead.

Since, his granddaughter, Aislinn Cain, was working the case of a voraphiliac, he felt the need to stick around. If he could find the location of August's lair, he'd kill him and save her the trouble.

So, he sat in a cold car in January, waiting for his sister to slip up and lead the way to the bastard son whom she was protecting.

As the hours slipped by, memories fluttered in and out of his mind. It wasn't Gertrude's fault that she and Nina had been raped. It had been

Lee's. Lee was supposed to have been there, escorting them to that stupid party where someone had been spiking drinks with LSD. He'd found the host a few months after the party and slit him like the pig he was, after he confessed to being the one dosing the women.

Nearly forty years had passed before he'd had a chance to kill the son of a bitch that had fathered the monster. And that had been pure luck, thanks mostly in part to his granddaughter Aislinn and her friendship with Malachi Blake. The moment he laid eyes on Malachi Blake, he knew someone in that family was responsible for creating August Clachan. They each had deep green eyes, greener and darker than any prized emerald. So green, they nearly glowed in the dark. After that, it had just been a process of elimination.

Elimination had led to Tennyson Unger, Malachi Blake's maternal grandfather. The old man had died an undignified death. Begging and pleading for forgiveness, willing to do whatever to make up for creating August. However, the only redemption was death and they had both known it. He'd broken Tennyson's legs and let the mongrel dog that Tennyson abused have at it. It was poetic, considering August liked to watch people be eaten alive.

He'd meant to go after August a few years ago, after finding out he'd faked his own death. However, Aislinn had kept him hopping. Her night time visitors were a pain in the ass. Then she'd joined the Marshals and it was even harder to keep track of her. Years ago, he'd managed to get a GPS tracker and install it in her Charger, but she rarely drove it, so it was nearly pointless.

With Patterson's grandchildren, there was always something. He'd been quietly hiding in the house of a killer when Eric had climbed on top of a building and started shooting people. While he was proud of his grandson's ambition, if he'd just waited a few hours, Patterson would have taken care of the miscarriage of justice. His plan had been to wait for the family to come home and go to sleep, then he was going to kill everyone quickly except the actual man that had brutally murdered his granddaughter and son. He'd planned a slow, agonizing death for him. But Eric had beaten him to the job, putting a bullet in his head instead. The death had been too quick for Patterson's taste.

He shook himself from his memories. The house he watched was going dark. The occupants headed to bed. If Aislinn hadn't been in town, he would have slipped inside and tortured the information out of them.

However, with Aislinn and the Marshals in town poking around, that would raise more questions and possibly, more ghosts. Instead, he wrote a note stating that August was alive and Gertrude knew how to find him. He drove back into town.

Maybe he could get the Marshals out of town quickly. He reached their hotel and, pulling on an older suit jacket, walked inside. His age was never a hindrance. Most people thought of him as a harmless old man, if a bit eccentric. They didn't realize he could overpower most healthy, young adult males.

"May I help you?" The woman at the desk asked.

"Yes, I'd like to leave a note for Aislinn Cain," he said.

"I believe she's in, sir, if you'd like I can call her."

"No, it's just a note, no need to wake her. If you could just give it to her in the morning that would be fine." He slipped the envelop across the desk. He'd printed Aislinn Cain in large, flowing letters on the front and sealed it.

Tomorrow, this would all be over. She'd get the note, they'd go track down August and take him into custody.

FIVE

I had never been in a morgue in Columbia. I was sitting in one now at the University of Missouri. The chief medical examiner hadn't been happy to have Xavier stroll in and request a room, but he hadn't said much, just scowled. I wasn't known for my ability to be diplomatic, but sometimes, Xavier was worse than me. This was one of those times.

Like every other large morgue in the country, this one was stainless steel. It was cold, not just the steel, but the air itself was chilled. My behind was planted on a stool that rotated. There were times when I was capable of spinning slowly and carefully on one without setting off vertigo. Today, I was doing my best to keep it from moving at all.

"You're very pale," Xavier said as a technician brought in a bag. The bag held the feet we'd found frozen and slung over the wire earlier in the day. Of all the things we had endured together, those feet brought me dread. The technician left and returned a few minutes later with a few more bags.

"Do those all contain severed feet?" I asked.

"Six sets," Xavier said. "The others were stored because the case is ongoing."

"I need to go do anything but this," I left the room. The memory was still nagging at me. My mind couldn't quite capture it. It was like the memory needed a reboot to retrieve it. I walked away from the building and lit a cigarette in a secluded alcove. For as long as I could remember, feet had bothered me. I didn't want to see them, touch them, or anything else. I didn't even like it when people wore sandals in my presence. The memory had something to do with it.

Unfortunately, I couldn't remember it. I'd been trying since we saw the socks on the line. Proving that the thought was important was a different story, I was willing to bet it wasn't, but stranger things had happened.

"What's up?" Xavier asked.

"I just have a thing about feet," I answered.

"I know, but it seems to be more pronounced at the moment."

"Severed feet are worse than attached feet."

"Well, I have something interesting if you think you can get over your foot phobia."

"How interesting?" My curiosity peeked.

"Incredibly interesting."

I stubbed out my cigarette and put the butt in my pocket. Xavier led the way back in. I followed at a slower pace, trying not to shuffle my feet like an obstinate child.

"Well?" I asked once we were back inside the cold, stainless steel room.

Xavier pointed to all the feet. To my untrained eye, they were just feet. I didn't see his interesting revelation. I raised an eyebrow at him.

"You don't see it?" Xavier frowned.

"Um, no," I answered.

"This one has an injury, none of the others do. I examined it a little closer and I found something twisted inside the wound. Look here," he pointed at a monitor. The wound had been enlarged. The wound was a gaping hole where the tissue had been removed. Small nicks were visible on the bone where the flesh had once been.

"Ok, I see the marks, but wouldn't they be caused by removing the tissue?"

"That was my first thought, then I really started looking at them. There are two in particular that are deeper than the others."

I examined these marks. The nicks were deeper into the bone and conical shaped. I looked at Xavier.

"Are you an expert on the teeth marks of predators?" I asked him.

"No, but I've called one," Xavier was grinning. "I think he's feeding them to something large and scary."

"Then why leave the feet behind?" I asked.

"I don't know."

The memory slammed into me. I sucked in air, suddenly unable to breathe. My eyes closed as vertigo washed over me. The table was hard beneath my hands.

"They're jaguar teeth marks," I told Xavier. "Columbia has seen it before."

"What?"

"I was young, very young, this was before Callow kidnapped me. I might have been four, I wasn't in school yet. They found a set of feet next to the river. No body, just the feet, something had gnawed on them. My dad occasionally brought home work and I found the pictures by accident." I stopped talking and tried to push the feeling of vertigo away. The feet had been horribly mangled. Next to it, my father had written the word "jaguar" in bold lettering. As far as I knew, they had never solved it. However, that had been a one-time incident. It hadn't been a serial killer.

Her body was found a year or so later. It had been dismembered and shoved into a grain silo. It had also been gnawed upon by the predator. It hadn't been decomposed. My brain found her name among the details I had peeked at in my father's folder, Sarah Anderson. She'd lived across town, in a poorer section. That was all I knew about the girl in the silo.

"Gabriel and a zoologist from the University are on their way here," Xavier informed me. I nodded slowly and got up. My legs felt unsteady. After twenty-four years, why would the killer strike again?

"The feet look a little large for a young girl," I said as I exited the morgue.

"That's because they belong to a boy, all of them do," Xavier entered the hall with me. "Teens by the looks of it. The feet aren't fully developed, indicating the person hasn't finished puberty yet, but they aren't consistent with girl feet. Unless our killer is specifically targeting girls with very large, masculine feet."

"So, our killer from a life time ago hasn't returned," I sighed, feeling a sense of relief.

"I didn't say that," Xavier said. "While it is unusual for a killer to change his victim preference, it isn't unprecedented. The disposal of the feet raises some red flags. If the bite is from a jaguar it will raise even more. So, how did you get exposed to the severed feet that traumatized you into adulthood?"

"As I said, my dad occasionally brought home work that wasn't really his, this case was one of them," I answered. "I'm not sure why it bothered me, but seeing them, in little dress shoes, with pink socks and part of the severed leg sticking out of them horrified me. Somehow, I forgot the memory, but not the feelings associated with it."

"Defense mechanism because you were young?"

"I don't think so," I answered. "There's more, but I haven't remembered it. I'm sure it's in the case files though."

"More little girl feet in dress shoes and pink socks?"

"No," I answered quickly. "It was a one-off. Her body was found a year or so later, shoved in a grain silo and not decomposed. She was held somewhere for a time. Aside from the animal bites, she was healthy when she died."

"Did she die of the animal bites?"

"Yes. The jaguar crushed her skull, its teeth piercing the brain."

"Jaguars are the only cat to do that," a man said as he walked down the hall. "I'm Doctor Bob Ritter, I specialize in predatory cats."

"Doctor Xavier Reece and Doctor Aislinn Cain with the US Marshals Serial Crimes Tracking Unit," Xavier held out his hand. Dr. Ritter shook it. I did not extend the same courtesy. "You'll have to excuse my colleague, she doesn't like to touch people."

"I know, I was in seventh grade with her," Dr. Ritter answered. "Her name was Clachan back then."

"Sorry, I'm terrible at remembering people," I told him.

"I know that too," Dr. Ritter smiled at me. "I sat behind you in seventh grade science. I was pretty shy and you were even more introverted."

"Still am," I gave him a fake smile. "So, do you remember the case of Sarah Anderson?" I was young in seventh grade. I imagined Dr. Ritter was three, possibly four years older than myself.

"It was my uncle's silo," Dr. Ritter answered. "It's why I became a zoologist."

"Well," Xavier led the way into the room. "We need an expert opinion on some very unclear evidence."

"I'll see what I can do," Dr. Ritter began his examination of the feet with the missing tissue. I stood back, leaning against a counter. Gabriel came in and stood next to me, he was very quiet, not even introducing himself to the expert. John was conspicuously absent. I was dying to ask, but didn't.

After an hour of silence on our part and muttering on the part of Dr. Ritter, he stood up and rubbed his eyes. His spine popped as he moved. He looked older than he had when he first arrived. It was probably my imagination.

"All I can tell you is that they might be teeth marks of a large predator. I can't tell you it was a jaguar or any other cat, I can't even rule out it being a dog. Whoever extracted the tissue, scraped the bone to try and hide the marks." Dr. Ritter spoke to Gabriel despite the lack of introduction. "They are teeth marks though."

"Ok," Gabriel sighed. "So, it could also be a psycho with dental implants."

"It could, but," Dr. Ritter frowned. "I'm not sure dental implants would hold up chewing through bone. The human jaw just doesn't have the strength. While the marks look like the teeth just nicked them, the bone was drastically altered by the scraping. I'd bet the teeth didn't just graze it. They pierced and crushed it. Several dog breeds would have the strength, as would any predatory cat native to North America and any imported cat."

"Why would a large predator eat the feet?" I asked.

"I'm sorry?" Dr. Ritter turned his attention to me.

"Assuming it is a predator, even if it isn't a jaguar, don't they usually go for the softer, fleshier areas first, like the unprotected areas of the torso?"

"They do," Dr. Ritter agreed. "I'm speculating here, but I'd guess it was to move the person."

"I thought they carried prey by the throat," Gabriel spoke for the first time.

"Usually they do," Dr. Ritter frowned so hard I thought his face would break.

"Unless something already has hold of the other end," I said. "Hence the piercing of the bone. The predator would want a firm hold and a foot isn't a good place for that."

"That would be the best explanation. Not the only one though," Dr. Ritter answered. "It is possible that the animal was just toying with it."

"The foot was alive when it was bitten," Xavier added this detail. He'd been playing that particular card close to his vest, probably out of respect for me.

"Then the theory of the person being a plaything becomes more likely," Dr. Ritter said. "Cats will play with their food before killing and eating it, if they know they are in a secure location.

We see the behavior in partially domesticated predatory cats as well as housecats."

"Like a cat playing with a cornered mouse," I didn't bother to hide the disgust.

"Yes and if the cat has a partner that they share with, it is even more likely. However, the majority of predatory cats are solitary. Canines though don't really play with their food unless training offspring to hunt."

"Thanks, Doctor," Gabriel held out his hand. "We'll be in touch."

"Any time," Dr. Ritter left the three of us.

"Don't ask," Gabriel stopped me from asking about John. "So, what becomes a companion for a large cat?"

"In captivity? Anything it decides not to eat," I answered.

"Are you an expert?" Xavier asked.

"Not in the least," I answered. "But a predatory cat isn't much different than a predatory human." I looked at the feet and shivered, "good grief, why couldn't he be leaving severed heads or something?"

Six

The folder was dark brown. A corner of a sheet of paper stuck out the edge, yellowing with age. Black ink in a familiar scribble was on the front of the folder as well as the tab. The folder had once belonged to my father. This kept me from opening it.

Ten minutes earlier, I had discovered that this case had broken my father. Until then, I had always believed he was just a cop with a squad car. This was not the case. He'd been a detective, a detective that had turned in his shiny detective's shield and gone back to being a cop with a squad car because of Sarah Anderson's case.

There was a genetic component to Anti-Social Personality Disorder. It was what made a sociopath or psychopath with ASPD different than one with Borderline Personality Disorder. ASPD meant a person was born with it while Borderline

Personality Disorders were created. Nature versus nurture at its best, meaning my type ran in families.

My mother was a warm, caring individual who could love easily and readily. My father had been more aloof. While my siblings would argue that I was his favorite, I couldn't actually say that I had ever heard my father tell me that he loved me. He'd been a distant man, hard to know and even harder to understand. Sometimes, I wondered if he had been a sociopath as well. If so, he was more functional than I was, but there were different levels of sociopathic tendencies.

"Hey," Gabriel said quietly, "if you don't want to do it, I will."

"I'm fine," I countered, determined to learn the secrets within the folder, like if my father ever had a suspect. My eyes scanned the lines of handwritten notes, my brain processing the information as fast as I could read it.

There had only been one suspect. A store owner in town with a penchant for exotic animals. At the time, he'd owned a jaguar, a black bear, and a wolverine. Unfortunately, he'd died during the investigation when the wolverine attacked him from a tree branch and suffocated him. No evidence had been found at his house to link him to Sarah Anderson. And aside from owning a candy store, there was no real reason to think he'd ever crossed paths with the little girl. While Columbia wasn't the size of Kansas City, it did have a population over 100,000, meaning it certainly wasn't an "everyone knows everyone" kind of town.

Besides the permanent residents, the city housed the main branch of the University of Missouri, plus two other, smaller colleges; Columbia College and Stephens College. This made for a mobile population of students. My own experience in college had proven that serial killers existed even among the young and hip crowd of college attendees.

However, there wasn't a zoo in the city. There was a wildlife refuge north of town that housed a variety of different animals, although I had never heard of them housing a jaguar. I had seen and heard lions there before, as well as less dangerous animals like camels and zebras. It wasn't open to the public and access was restricted. I had only seen the animals because I'd had a relative that lived close to the sanctuary.

"There are currently no registered jaguars near here," John Bryan informed us. "There are a few other feline predators though. I have permits for four tigers, three lions, six mountain lions, two lynxes, a caracal, an ocelot, and perhaps most terrifying, a clouded leopard."

"That's one of the most endangered cats in the world, why is there one here?" I asked.

"Some sanctuary," John frowned. "About half the permits are registered to it."

"North of town," I sighed. "It's a good sized refuge, but they must have expanded, because they wouldn't have had the room for all those cats at the old location."

"It says they have over 100 acres," John informed me.

"They've expanded a lot," I tried not to sigh again. I didn't know the owners. I knew they'd been in trouble once or twice when I was a kid for poor enclosures and things, but if they had expanded, they had obviously fixed that problem.

"How sure are you that it was a jaguar the first time?" Gabriel asked.

"Sarah Anderson's skull was crushed, but more importantly, there were four puncture marks and some other teeth impressions on the bone," I answered. "I may not be a wildlife expert, but I know jaguars are the only cat that does that."

"Why do you know that?" Xavier asked.

"My dad bought a huge book on wild cats when the body was discovered."

"And you read it," Gabriel answered.

"It was a book, what was I supposed to do with it?" I raised an eyebrow at him.

"It doesn't mean this attack and the Sarah Anderson attack are related, it's been how many years?" John Bryan asked.

"Twenty-four or twenty-five," I answered. "However, it's the feet. Sarah's feet were found a few days after she went missing. They'd been severed just above the ankle bones, shoved into a pair of white socks, then Mary Jane's and left by the river. They didn't know how she died until they found her body. People do not randomly cut off feet and leave them places. Especially not dressed feet. It would be an astronomical coincidence if they weren't connected."

My mind kicked into overdrive. My brain searched for the memories of my childhood. They were easy enough to find. I had been a boring child and had grown up to be a boring adult, with the exception of serial killers, rapists, and mass murders sending me flowers, candy, severed fingers, dead prairie dogs, love letters, and occasionally, following me home. Although, since moving into the Federal Guard Neighborhood, I hadn't had one follow me home, which was nice, but made for quiet nights.

I found no memories of feet being discovered, with or without their body. The file said something about missing children, but they had all happened before Sarah Anderson and their bodies, including their feet, had never been found. Of course, that had stopped by the time I was old enough to walk to school and started again a few years later when Callow began preying on children. Despite being a pedophile and a serial killer of children, Callow hadn't owned a jaguar. He'd lived two streets from my house. Our yards were barely big enough for medium sized dogs. There was also the matter of him being dead, he couldn't be tying feet into tube socks and throwing them over utility wires.

"We have a pattern," John suddenly announced, breaking my concentration. Gabriel looked at him expectantly. John cleared his throat, suddenly feeling the weight of all our eyes on him. "So, there are a handful of teen boys listed as runaways. They all fit into Xavier's age range of twelve to sixteen and none have been found."

"Are they DNA testing the feet and comparing them to samples from the runaways," Gabriel asked.

"No, that costs money," John answered. "And getting a DNA test takes a lot of time and money when you aren't a US Marshal."

"I'm on it," Xavier jumped from his chair. Aside from being borderline nutjobs, we had access to resources that police departments didn't. As much as I liked to think that our capture rate was because we were just that damn good, the truth was, we had an entire forensics unit dedicated to serial killers. We could get DNA in a few days, sometimes less. Crime scene techs collected evidence and it was overnighted to Kansas City to our special lab. The work was done and the report magically appeared on all our computers. I'd never met our dedicated crime fighting forensics unit, but I was willing to bet they were extremely good at their jobs and possibly, a little crazy.

The only downside was that we had to share the forensics unit with the FBI's VCU. However, we had never jockeyed for position. I had no idea how they did it. One day, I would send them pizza or something.

That made me think of Malachi. I dug out my cell phone. It rang four times before he answered, sounding out of breath and irritated.

"Blake," his voice was husky and I knew he was in the middle of a case or sex. I didn't really care either way, I needed to pick his brain.

"Hey, I'm in need of some info," I told him.

"Can it wait?" He asked.

"Maybe, but more teen boys will die."

"Will they really die or is it just a possibility?"

"Mostly, it's a possibility. Did I interrupt?"

"Well," there was a strange grunting noise and I heard Malachi yell at someone. He was on a case, by the sound of the noise, he had just broken someone's nose. "Ok, we're good. What do you need?"

"Suspect handcuffed?" I asked.

"Yes."

"Good, then I can have your full attention for a moment. So, I'm in Columbia. Do you remember the Sarah Anderson case?" Malachi was four years older than me and had a better memory.

"Girl, killed by jaguar, stuffed in grain silo, feet found much earlier by the river, I believe your father was one of the detectives," Malachi answered.

"That's the case. I was young when it happened. Do you remember a string of child disappearances before Sarah Anderson?"

"Yes," Malachi paused. It wasn't for effect, it was him accessing his memory center. Malachi had a didactic memory. It meant he never forgot, anything, unless he wanted to forget. "Five girls went missing in the space of four months."

"That's all you've got?" I asked.

"I was like eight," Malachi answered. "One of the girls was in my class. Her name was Joan Ferris. They never found her. Joan Ferris was the second to go missing in February. The first was another girl, about the same age, went to a different school. In March, a third went missing, that one was a grade younger. In April, there was another, a grade younger than the third. In May, Sarah Anderson went missing, she was the youngest at six."

"The file says she was eight."

"The file is wrong," Malachi answered. "Her brother was a year older than me. We went to high school together. She was six when she went missing. There was something shady about the disappearance, the family, everything. Her brother was abandoned and the family returned to their native country after Sarah's body was found."

"What was shady about them?" I asked.

"I don't know. But they were from Argentina and Anderson isn't a real common name for that part of the world."

"Ugh," I put my head on the table. "Anderson with an 'o' isn't, but with an 'e,' kind of is."

"You know something about Argentina and Andersons that I don't?"

"Lots of Germans fled to South America after World War II."

"You think they were Nazis? That's farfetched, even for you."

"Well," I pursed my lips together. "Shady family from Argentina, Sarah was definitely not Hispanic. She's a red head with blue eyes. Sounds like German origins to me."

"Not everyone is a war criminal," Malachi informed me.

"I know, some are serial killers."

"I'm sure for you, that's logical. For me, it's a stretch. What does missing little girls have to do with dead teen boys?"

"We found feet. They had teeth marks in them, like fang marks. The feet belong to a teenaged boy."

"Eerily similar, but you don't change your pedophilic preferences from little girls to teen boys."

"That's true," I answered. "But what's the chances that it's a coincidence?"

"It's been twenty-five years. What has the killer been doing for twenty-five years?"

"Breeding jaguars illegally and raising a family," I suggested.

"Ok, that makes more sense than your fleeing Nazi theory. Hold on," there were loud noises on Malachi's end of the phone. "Ok, I'm back."

"Who are beating up?" I asked.

"Some jerk off that thinks he can take the VCU," Malachi answered.

"What'd he do to attract the attention of the VCU?"

"He killed thirty-two women with a sledgehammer. Serious overkill on all of them, their bodies were mangled and gruesome. Do you know the kind of damage a sledgehammer will do to a body?"

"I can imagine." Unfortunately, I really could imagine. Bloody, bashed heads filled my imagination. Brains and gore leaked from them along the concrete floor that my brain had put into the thought. Fragments of bone were lying several feet from the anonymous dead body.

"You probably can, stop thinking about it. Being eaten by a jaguar is pretty gruesome too."

"There are different kinds of gruesome," I told him. "Yours is gruesome in a different way than mine."

"Is that all?"

"For now," I answered.

"Good, I have a suspect to haul into the FBI office and try not to kill along the way."

"Good luck," I said and hung up.

"Well?" Gabriel asked.

"I do not know," I answered.

SEVEN

Malachi was right. Pedophiles didn't go from attacking little girls to attacking teenage boys. While one might argue that he wasn't a pedophile, there is an intimacy to watching someone being eaten. There was actually a whole fetish devoted to it. A serial killer in Germany had placed an advert once, asking for volunteers to be eaten. He'd gotten several responses and although it had theoretically been consensual cannibalism, the German government tried and convicted him on murder, desecration of a body, and cannibalism charges.

I didn't think watching a jaguar eat your victim qualified as cannibalism, but I'm sure there was a psychological term for it. We'd already caught one cannibal in the year and a half I'd been a Marshal, but only one. He'd been fond of neighborhood barbecues, even had a huge spit that he cooked the meat on. True cannibals were few and far between in the United States. Eating people just wasn't acceptable, even among serial killers.

Then there were the superstitions and folklore associated with it. I'd heard tales of Satanists, Voodoo Priests, zombies, and wendigos while on the hunt for the cannibal. I had never met a Satanist or a Voodoo Priest, but I was fairly certain that most of them did not practice cannibalism. As for zombies and wendigos, I wasn't willing to rule them out, but they lived more in the realm of chupacabras and werewolves, so they weren't exactly my prime suspects either.

Five girls, progressively getting younger, one with a fake birth certificate and Argentinian origins. My mind was definitely leaping to conclusions. As far as I knew, jaguars weren't real common in Argentina and neither were Nazi war criminals. History had proven that some Nazi war criminals had fled to South America, but it wasn't like other Germans weren't fleeing there as well. Furthermore, all sorts of people lived in South America, Germans were a small portion of the population and birth records weren't always easy to come by if the village was rural enough. Despite the two year difference, a smart child could pass as being older, but petite. I had.

I filed away the information about being from Argentina and the theory that her family were

Nazi war criminals trying to sneak into the United States. So, they had moved back to Argentina, without their son, after their daughter had been found dead. It was dodgy, but not the most confusing thing I'd ever heard. The son had probably been raised by relatives here, his parents wanting him to get an American education. They had probably gone back because the Land of Milk and Honey had turned out to be tainted with blood and death. If they had wanted their daughter eaten by a jaguar, they could have gone on vacation to the Amazon and gotten the deed done faster and easier with fewer questions.

So, we were back to the five girls who were progressively younger, until they reached six years old. Sarah Anderson was an outlier, not because of her birth and family history, but because her feet and body had been discovered while the others had not. One side of my mind told me I was grasping at straws, wanting the death of the girl who had rocked my father's world to mean something more. The other side told me I was on to something, if I could just focus long enough to grab it.

Unfortunately, my stomach had started to think about Shakespeare's Pizza. It growled loudly, forcing me to check a clock. It had been seven hours since I had eaten Sub Shop. A little pizza might re-energize me and make the connection that half my brain said was there. Or it might make me sleepy because I had no willpower when it came to good food.

"Dinner?" I asked. The guys turned to look at me. I wondered how long I had been quietly locked inside my own thoughts and what they had been discussing while I was there.

"Sure," Gabriel stood. "I could go for pizza. Tomorrow, we go knocking on the door of the animal sanctuary."

"Whatever," I stood and stretched. Everything felt stiff. The damage to my body required movement. I had definitely been sitting in one place, probably one position, for far too long.

We picked Xavier up at the University of Missouri Hospital and made our way downtown. It was bustling despite the cold weather and snow accumulations outside of the city. Shakespeare's was even busier. Families, college kids, adults out for a night on the town, were all inside, waiting at the tables for their orders. Getting a table for four was nearly impossible. A table of teens, obviously finished with their food and now just enjoying each other's company, occupied a table near the interior. I wanted the table. It would be warmer than one by the windows or in the upper room.

Shakespeare's doesn't really have an upstairs, but there is a small set of steps that lead up to a raised room that leads to the patio. Tables in this room are a little more crowded than on the main floor, a feat, considering there was hardly any extra space in the main dining room.

"Stop glaring at those kids," Gabriel told me.

"Sorry," I looked away, staring out the window. "They have a good table and they aren't eating. It's just habit."

"This place is packed," John said. "Maybe we should get it to go."

"Absolutely not," I answered. "The first time you have a Shakespeare's Pizza, it should be inside Shakespeare's, not take out. The atmosphere is almost as important as the pizza. We should get a Masterpiece and All-The-Meats."

"You won't eat a pizza that just has meat on it," Xavier said.

"That's why we need a Masterpiece, it has everything. I'll pick off the sausage and ham."

"What about the pepperoni?" Gabriel asked, knowing that I rarely ate pepperoni because it was a pork product.

"If you order nothing else on a pizza, you have to have pepperoni here. I've ordered the veggie and had them add pepperoni. It comes from The Hill in St. Louis and is probably the best pepperoni in the world. They get all their meats from The Hill. Maybe we should order that as well," I thought about it.

"Three pizzas?" John asked.

"Three large pizzas," I answered. "You won't regret it. You'll be eating the leftovers for days."

A table became available. I sent John and Xavier to grab it. Gabriel and I walked to the counter. I ordered three pizzas, three beers, and a Mt. Dew. Gabriel gave me a strange look.

"You'll thank me later," I said as I handed him a beer from a local brewery. I didn't drink beer or any alcohol really, but I had been told the beer was almost as good as the pizza.

"This place is packed," Xavier shouted over the din of everything that defined Columbia on a Friday night. "It's hard to talk."

"I'm fine with that," I answered. "We only talk about death and the occasional football game, but John's a Denver fan, so football's out." Two of us, meaning Xavier and myself, were Kansas City Chiefs fans. Gabriel was a Chicago Bears fan. We could tease Gabriel, but talking football with John had led to at least one Tasering incident. Surprisingly, I had not done the Tasering or been the recipient.

I slouched in the chair, lacing my fingers together behind my head. I didn't have the attachment to my hometown that a lot of people had. There was no sense of nostalgia when I visited, no yearning to be home, no desire to reconnect with the people that lived here or that I had once known. However, I did enjoy sitting back and just taking in the sounds, smells, and sights at Shakespeare's. It was a sensory symphony.

My name was announced over the loud speaker, telling me my order was ready. Gabriel and I stood up. For perhaps the first time, no one really turned to look at us. A few did, but we were used to getting stares and sometimes, glares, from a crowd. Xavier appeared at our heels and we carried the three large pizzas back to our table.

"Holy hell," Xavier set the one he was carrying down. "That thing is loaded."

"A pound of meat, a pound of veggies, a pound of cheese, and those are the weights after they are cooked. You get what you pay for here and most of the meat is super fresh because it was delivered from St. Louis," I took a slice that was so hot it burned my fingers and the cheese stretched to my plate, dragging toppings with it, as I set it down on my plate.

Xavier and Gabriel both risked burning their mouths as they took the first bite. John was more civilized. He got up, found the silverware and came back with a fork and butter knife. He attempted to cut it into bite sized pieces. A smile formed as I watched Gabriel and Xavier struggle to close their mouths around the piping hot pizza.

"Um excuse me," a woman stopped at our table. Her hair was in a ponytail, she looked like a student.

"Yes?" Gabriel swallowed hard without chewing much of his first bite.

"Are you here about the missing boys?" She chewed on her fingernail.

"No, we got stuck here in the storm," Gabriel told her.

"Oh, well," she seemed to be unwilling to leave the table. "Could you look into it? We've had several boys go missing over the last year."

"Is there any reason to think they are anything other than missing?" Xavier asked.

"They've been finding feet," the color drained from her face. "My brother went missing a few months ago, he wouldn't have run away like the police say and he was on his way to the park."

"Which park?" I asked.

"Cosmo," she frowned. "He was headed to the skate park there. I was supposed to meet him, but I got held up at work."

"Where do you work?" Gabriel asked.

"Here," she answered. "I'm a student, I live on campus, but my family lives in town too."

"How late were you?" I asked.

"Twenty minutes, maybe thirty, not much. His skateboard was at the park, but he wasn't and no one could remember him being there. But his skateboard was there. He loved that thing."

"How old was he?" Xavier asked.

"Thirteen," she answered.

"We kind of need the police to invite us," Gabriel lied. "However, we'll see if we can get any information for you." He passed his card to her. She took it and walked away.

"You lied to her," John said.

"Sometimes, it's necessary," Gabriel answered. "Most people don't want to know we are in town working. It makes the serial killers real. Besides, the grief stricken tend to break down when they find out we are investigating a case. They lose hope and automatically think their loved one is dead."

"Aren't they?" John asked.

"If they were taken by the killer?" I looked at him. "Yes. But if he isn't a victim of the serial, then who knows. It is better for the family to maintain hope."

EIGHT

The evening was quiet. Xavier had gathered
DNA from the feet and from articles given to the
police by the missing boys. The samples had been
sent to our forensics lab. We'd have DNA in a few
days. Until then, we had feet in socks.

The socks were a name brand available at
just about any store. Since there were at least three
dozen places in town that sold them, John had
hacked into the stores' sales database and was
checking for large purchases of the socks.

Honestly, feet tied into socks wasn't much to
go on. It might be related to the death of Sarah
Anderson twenty-five years ago or it might not. We
were sitting on our hands, my least favorite part of
the job. My favorite cases were the ones where we
went in, figured out the bad guy in less than a day
and busted down doors. I wasn't an investigator, I
wasn't a detective. I thought like a killer, nothing
more.

As I stared at the ceiling of my bedroom, I tried to think like this killer. Why boys? Why feed them to a predator? Was the predator just the means of disposal or was there something more to it? This brought another problem to the forefront.

A pet required work and attachment. I was too lazy to have a pet and too emotional detached to attempt to bond with an animal. However, bonding with an animal was probably easier than bonding with a human, animals were more logical. Even their unconditional devotion made sense to me, it kept them from relying upon their wits and instincts, from being tossed into the cold to live the life of a wild animal. Creature comforts applied to animals, at least in my mind.

This theory applied best to dogs. Cats were a little more hit and miss. True predators I couldn't fit into it, no matter what way I turned the piece. A true predator was just as likely to kill you as lick you. That I also understood.

If we were back to a sexual aspects of the killings, there was no way it was related to the Sarah Anderson killing and the link was coincidence. If it wasn't sexual, I had no idea why the killer was abducting teenaged boys to feed to a predator. It seemed like a lot of work to look after something so large and wild, even one born in captivity. Sure, people did it all the time, but those people were not normally serial killers. Serial killers had pets, but they tended to be loving, loyal pets, meaning mostly dogs and the occasional house cat. The animals tended to be protective. Exotic pets might be protective, but they also had a feral streak.

This circular logic engulfed me. It kept me from sleeping, not that this was a hard task, I wasn't great at sleeping in general, but when my mind had a puzzle, it was much worse. This was a puzzle that I was pretty sure my hyper-logical brain was overcomplicating.

Then a piece grabbed my attention. Was the foot alive or dead when it was bitten? That could make a serious difference. Sarah Anderson had been killed by the jaguar. Her body had been dismembered after death. The feet were being taken post-mortem. But were they being killed by the predator or simply disposed of using the predator? If the first was true, it explained the bite mark on the foot. If the second was true, it didn't. Why take a foot after a predator has chewed on it?

I called Xavier. He groaned instead of telling me hello.

"About the bite," I started.

"No, I don't know, the removing of the flesh and bone was done postmortem. I don't know about the bite."

"But if you are going to put the feet on display, would it make sense to cut it off after the animal had feasted upon it if that isn't the manner of death?"

"No," Xavier sighed. "Why?"

"Well, Sarah Anderson was killed by a jaguar and then dismembered. I think we are looking for the same killer again."

"Sarah was a girl. These are all boys."

"I know, I haven't figured that out yet. But I believe cause of death is traumatic injury from animal attack."

"Great," Xavier hung up on me.

I texted the thought to Gabriel. He responded with an "Ok." Obviously, everyone but me was sleeping. I checked the clock. I'd been in my head for several hours, it was almost two in the morning. No wonder Xavier had hung up on me.

We were set to go to the animal sanctuary in the morning. It was technically morning, but I was fairly certain that the guys wouldn't like me waking them up to go out there now. I crawled under the covers and turned on the TV. There was a documentary on, the star of the show was a lion. I watched it and learned a little more about lions than I needed. It ended and was replaced by something on mermaids. My need to know information about mermaids was even less than my need of knowledge about lions. I changed the channel and found a movie. I set a sleep timer on the off chance I feel asleep before the movie ended and grabbed my Kindle.

One of the nice things about eBooks, was that I didn't need a book store to be open to grab a book on just about anything. I grabbed one about jaguars. It had lots of pictures and very little new information. I bought a second book. This one proved a little more useful, but again, it was mostly pictures. When I finished both, I had gained the skills to identify a jaguar, in all of its patterns and colors, but most of the information I had already known.

My clock told me it was now five thirty in the morning. Going to the animal sanctuary was now acceptable. They might not like it, but it wouldn't be the first time. I called Gabriel. He answered with a groan and informed me he was getting up.

I climbed from bed, turned off the TV and got dressed. I could sleep later. Right now, I wanted to see what all was hidden in the animal sanctuary.

I was in the hall, waiting, when the guys finally stumbled from their rooms. A Mountain Dew was already in my hands and I had drank about half of it in the last twenty minutes. Xavier gave me a look of pure irritation, so I smiled at him.

Gabriel handed him a cup of coffee. Xavier perked up and stopped glaring at me. John was the last out of his room. He shoved a ball cap over his messy hair that had US Marshals embroidered on it. We all had a wardrobe full of Marshals logoed clothing, but rarely wore any of it.

"I slept like shit," he announced.

"I slept fine, until Ace called me," Xavier said.

"Me too, until she texted me," Gabriel added.

"I didn't sleep," I turned and began walking down the hallway.

"We know," Gabriel and Xavier said in unison.

"Tonight, I'm giving her a pill," Xavier told Gabriel.

"That might not be a terrible idea," Gabriel tried to whisper.

"I can hear you," I rounded the corner and hit the button on the elevator. "I would take one, if we weren't on a case. But I'm not allowed."

"You keep texting me at three in the morning and I'll make an exception," Gabriel shouted down the hall at me.

"Good," I smiled as the doors opened. I had to hold it for the others.

Being in my hometown, meant Gabriel was letting me drive all the time. He made a phone call.

The person on the other end was pissed. Gabriel kept trying to turn down the volume and I could still hear the person yelling at him.

"Did you just tip off the sanctuary?" I asked.

"No, but I did piss off animal control. It appears they have business hours and six in the morning isn't part of their regular work day," Gabriel snarked.

"Ah, yeah, in Columbia, if you have an animal problem before eight a.m. or after five p.m., you better hope like hell the police department will respond, because animal control won't. They don't even have an emergency number. Some things never change."

"You've dealt with them before, I take it?" Xavier asked.

"Yeah, Nyleena and I were leaving a concert one night and hit a dog. We got out to check on it, the dog went on the attack. I called animal control and they informed me I had to call the police. The police agreed to send out an officer," I told him.

"I hear a 'but' in this story," Gabriel said.

"Well, the cop took too long to respond and I had to kill the dog because he had nearly ripped off Nyleena's arm. She still has scars from the attack and surgery. Thing was rabid. Not a good day to be her or me. We both had to get rabies shots." I remembered the series of painful injections like yesterday. Maybe that's why I didn't own a pet. "Then the dog owner sued my mom and Nyleena because it turned out to be a pure bred whatchamacallit worth some money. Nyleena counter sued, my mom counter sued. The entire thing was a giant mess."

"How'd you kill it?" John asked.

"I broke its neck," I said flatly, turning off of Highway 63 onto Oakland Gravel Road.

"Good grief, how big of a dog was it?" John pressed.

"Small," I answered.

"Was it a Chihuahua?" Xavier giggled the madman's giggle.

"No, it was a cocker spaniel."

"A rabid cocker spaniel?" Xavier giggled even harder.

"Vicious little beast," I turned again onto a gravel road.

"Do you know where you're going?" Gabriel asked.

"Yep," I answered turning one last time and stopping at a large fence. "We're here. They have expanded. You might keep your Tasers at the ready. When my cousin lived near here, one of the large predators got out of its enclosure and went on a rampage."

"Did it hurt anyone?" John asked.

"No, just a Rottweiler, a horse, and a Great Dane."

"What the hell was it?" Xavier asked.

"Something meaner than a Rottweiler and bigger than a Great Dane," I shrugged and got out of the SUV.

It was cold. The sun was starting to brighten the sky, but it hadn't risen above the horizon yet. January in Missouri can be brutal. This year wasn't an exception. Until this week, the temperature had been hovering around thirty-five during the day. I had no idea what it was now or what the wind-chill was, I just knew that my body was already starting to ache from the cold. I considered climbing back into the SUV and waiting for animal control, but that could be hours knowing them. Better to get it done and over with. If the sanctuary said they didn't have a jaguar, I believed them and we needed to explore other options.

Gabriel cut the lock on the gate and opened the door. Something stirred from an enclosure next to it. The enclosure was covered, keeping whatever was inside hidden from view. Surely, they wouldn't put a large cat next to the gate, would they?

NINE

I pulled out my Taser. The others followed suit. Technically, I was the point man for our unit, so I took the lead. Gabriel held a flashlight behind me, I kept one hand free while holding the Taser in the other.

The creature made a grunting, growling noise. John yelped. The crackle of electricity made me turn around. Tawny fur writhed in pain, making even stranger noises. I jerked the Taser out of John's hands. The animal was still stunned and made small grunting bleats. I yanked the Taser prongs out of it.

"You can have this back when you can learn to use it properly," I scolded my coworker. The camel was pissed, but unable to stand yet. I searched through the pockets of my coat and pulled out a whistle. I handed it to John and tucked his Taser into that pocket. "If you get into trouble, blow the whistle."

"Why do you carry a whistle?" Xavier asked.

"Some self-defense class I took taught me to carry a whistle. I've never used it," I added the last quickly.

"What if I'm being attacked?" John gaped at the whistle.

"Hope we get there before you get eaten," I started moving again. The incident had brought attention to us. The animals were all making noises, moving around in their enclosures. Some I could see, some I could hear, some I could just tell where there, in the dark. Camels weren't my favorite animals, I thought they were nasty, but they didn't deserve to be Tasered just because they were roughly the same color as a lion and a US Marshal was jumpy in the semi-dark.

A low, chuffing noise caught my attention. I stopped, tilting my head to hear it better. My ears had trouble finding the sound, but it reverberated through my body. Few animals made sounds like those, most were auditory, without the bass needed to create pressure waves of sound that could be felt inside. As far as I knew, it was exclusive to big cats. Some memory told me that the noise was coming from a tiger. However, where there was one cat, there were probably more.

"I've heard that before," Gabriel whispered. "As a kid, my dad took us to India, we were staying in this small hut beside a game preserve and for a couple of nights in a row, I heard that noise. The locals told us it was mating season."

"I believe it's a tiger," I told him.

"I'd like to know why you went to India," Xavier said.

"We'll discuss it later," Gabriel said.

I started towards the sound. Gabriel's light found the enclosure. It wasn't a vibrant orange, but a dark, dingy orange with long black stripes to break up the color. The fur looked soft. Large yellow eyes with flecks of gold in them stared back at us. I'd seen tigers at the zoo, but I'd never been this close to one. The hair on the back of my neck stood up. Logically, I knew we were fine. The tiger was in a cage. However, the eyes sent a twinge of anxiety racing through me. It could easily overpower us. The massive teeth would tear us apart.

"What are we looking for?" Xavier asked.

"I don't know," I admitted. I had hoped to find an animal covered in blood that could be tested. The tiger was pristine. I realized most of the animals would probably be in the same condition. Cats tended to be clean animals, they wouldn't have three day old blood on them.

To our left, there was a growl. Another cat, the sound more physical than audible, it caused me to whip around to look at it. My gaze fell on another tiger. This one larger. I began to back away slowly.

"What are you doing?" Gabriel whispered.

"The way the cages are set up, we are surrounded," I pointed at a third cage holding a tiger. "One gets out, we might not have time to react, because we will be distracted by the others. They will go nuts."

We went back to the SUV and waited for the sun to rise. It did nothing to warm the frozen landscape, but at least we could see. During the hour wait, no one had spoken. Each of us contemplating our encounter with the tigers. I had been up close and personal with a wild predator of the exotic type once before. The standoff had ended when the predator had wandered off.

With the sun up, it was easier to see into the enclosures. Most were at least partially covered with thick tarps. Shelters could be seen within them. A few eyes peered out at us as we skulked around. The majority couldn't be bothered by our presence and kept inside where it was warm and cozy.

One enclosure caught my attention. It was easily the largest one there. A tree inside had a few ropes hanging from it and there toys strewn about the ground. The occupant or occupants were invisible, hidden within the depths of the enormous shed like building.

It didn't take a genius to figure out that the licensed gorilla lived on the other side of the metal. The others waited beside me. They were quiet, although I was sure they were questioning why we were standing outside a gorilla cage.

While part of me was standing there with the intent of seeing the creature that dwelled on the other side, another part had become trapped in thought. Not of gorillas, but of chimpanzees, chimps were notoriously aggressive and had large teeth. It was far more likely for a chimp to go on a rampage than a gorilla. There was always the possibility that the fang marks didn't come from a predatory cat, but from something more apish.

It was easier to obtain a chimpanzee than it was a jaguar. A chimp would have the strength to bite through bone. It would also be able to rip a teenaged boy limb from limb, which might be why we weren't finding anything other than the feet.

There was movement from the shed. A hatch opened and the first appearance of the large beast came into the morning sun. His face was black with large canine teeth that hung over his lower lip. His head was wide, one ear had been injured at some point and had healed into a grotesque curl that folded in on itself. However, the eyes were bright.

He stared at us. I looked at the ground, trying not to stare at him.

The large male came the rest of the way out of his home. It wasn't a gorilla. The ape was orange with large cheek pads. He swaggered over to the edge of his enclosure and I felt the men with me step backwards. I was close enough to feel his breath upon me.

I glanced at him from the corner of my eye. He seemed non-threatening. He also seemed as curious about me as I was him. Of course, I knew better than to trust his curiosity. He could become aggressive if I moved wrong.

"Ace," Xavier whispered my name. I took a step backwards, then another. A hand shot from between the bars, reaching for me. The fingers brushed my coat, but failed to grab hold. I continued to back away slowly, eyes averted, until I was well and truly safe from the orangutan on the other side.

"Communing with nature?" Gabriel whispered once I was back with the group.

"It's hard to explain," I told him. The licenses hadn't included an orangutan. "Was there any mention of the great ape?"

"Not that I recall," John answered.

"Why?" Xavier asked.

"Not now," I turned and looked at the rest of the sanctuary. All of these animals were safe, I wasn't going to ding them on having an orangutan. Especially since I was pretty sure I knew the gentle giant. If I was right, he was about ten years older than me, more than halfway through his life cycle. If he was happy at the sanctuary, I was fine with leaving him there. "Can we get them a license before animal control shows?"

"Yes," Gabriel answered.

"Good, let's get a license. Do you need a name?"

"John?" Gabriel looked at our geek.

"No, I'll be in the SUV, faking paperwork should you need me to dummy up any more official documents," he sulked back to the SUV. I thought he should be happy to be out of the cold. The SUV was running and warm.

The orangutan hooted at us. I waved at him. He waved back and climbed his tree.

"You know him," Gabriel said.

"I think so," I answered. "Now to search for the dangerous animals."

"You will explain, later," Gabriel informed me.

I frowned. I could explain later, but I felt no desire to do so. Getting the information out of me might be difficult, I had history with the ape behind the bars. I wondered if he was cold. Maybe I would be a good pet owner.

We checked the rest of the cages and found no other unregistered animals. John found us as we finished, license in hand. Gabriel took it from him and called the sanctuary owners. Their panic was evident over the phone as Gabriel tried to reassure them.

About ten minutes later, animal control showed. Ten minutes after that, the sanctuary owners arrived. There was quite a mess and I huddled in the car for warmth while the people in charge worked it out.

A woman knocked on the window. She was older, around the same age as my mom. The sun had wrinkled and tanned her face. Her arms were thick, strong for her age, conditioned by caring for the animals. She wore a flannel coat over jeans and a lined shirt.

"May I help you?" I rolled down the window.

"I just wanted to thank you, Ms. Clachan. We've been trying for years to get the orangutan a license, but there was always so much red tape, it never went through."

"It's Cain now, not Clachan and you're welcome. I suspect he is well cared for and in good health," I didn't make it a question.

"In the best possible health," she said. "You are welcome to come see him any time you're in town. He remembers you."

"Thank you," I answered.

"Since you're here, you could take a few minutes now to go see him," she pressed.

"Mrs. Rivers, I'm not sure how happy a reunion it would be," I answered.

"I understand he grabbed for you earlier. He doesn't do that unless it's someone he knows," Mrs. Rivers told me.

"Knows, perhaps, wants to be around," I frowned at her.

"Orangutans do not hold grudges like people, Aislinn Clachan. It would do you both some good to see each other."

"Fine, but I'm keeping my Taser." I opened the door and re-entered the cold.

SECRETS

Patterson was livid. He paced inside his motel room, trying not to feel like a caged animal. However, that was exactly what he felt like. He'd given the note to the hotel clerk, but for some reason, Aislinn hadn't followed up on his tip. There'd been no sign of activity at either of his sisters' homes.

They were the last of the older generation; Nina, Gertrude, and himself. The vanguards of a dying age. He had thought long and hard for the past week about it. Nina was dying of cancer. Gertrude was fit as a fiddle, albeit insane. He was also in prime shape. The difference was that only Gertrude knew about him.

And she was being her usual self; bitchy, whiny, and controlling. The entire family was locked in a strangle-hold because of her. Terrified of Joseph, his son, who had been raised by the lunatic after his disappearing act, because the man was clearly as insane as Gertrude.

This made him smile. He judged Gertrude and Joseph insane, but not himself. He thought it was because he controlled himself better. His rage was kept in check most of the time, despite having every reason on the planet to kill his bitch sister who was the keeper of skeletons.

He firmly believed there were things the younger generations didn't need to know. Things that would scare them, like his father's habit of burying farmhands instead of paying them. Or the fact that his mother had been a prostitute during The Great Depression, with the consent of her killer husband. Nor did they need to know that the farmhands weren't all buried in one piece. The Great Depression had been hard on the family, it had been cheaper to kill the livestock than take care of them, but this meant that food was often scarce and the farmhands had helped supplement their diets.

They didn't need to know that after The Great Depression ended, his brother Virgil had been killed by their father. His father consider Virgil's death a mercy killing. Virgil had gotten too accustomed to eating the flesh of his fellow humans. They didn't need to know that Bernard, Fritz, and he had joined the military to get away from their parents and their habits.

The final secret, was that Nina had gotten pregnant at the outbreak of war, by a man joining the service. The family had locked her away and when she gave birth, they let her back out, but never without an escort. As for the child, he was positive his father had killed it, too ashamed to let anyone know that Nina had given birth out of wedlock. Luckily for the soldier who got her pregnant, he died overseas. Their father had given strict orders to all the boys that when he returned, they were to kill him.

The secret of the Clachans wasn't that they created serial killers, it was that they hadn't created more than a handful. Gertrude had raised her son to be one. Nina had never tried to have another child, fearing for its safety. Most of the rest had been devoted parents, lavishing their children in order to break the cycle of abuse. Patterson had tried and failed. When his failure had become obvious the day of Lila's death, he left, hoping to keep them from growing up to be the monster that he was.

Nyleena had, fighting against those that terrorized the country. Eric had not, but a man could only be pushed so far. Aislinn was still a question mark. His letters to her were meant to scare her, push her away from the lifestyle and madness that claimed so many lives. He hadn't counted on her being cut from the same insane material as him.

After realizing that it wouldn't work, he'd considered stopping. But it was the only contact he could have with any of his grandchildren and it served a purpose, because Gertrude thought he was trying to drive the girl crazy. There was more to it than that though, he could relive his kills to her, like a grandfather telling his granddaughter a bedtime story, and it helped suppress the urge to kill. Not all the time, but most of it. He enjoyed the act of taking a life, watching their blood weep from them as their eyes glazed over, but his kills were directed at people that had wronged him and his family. Or people like August.

He wrote a second note to Aislinn and dropped it off at the hotel. It was exactly the same as the first. It was time to go follow Gertrude.

Patterson sat in his car and watched the people come and go from the store. Her car had pulled in over an hour ago and she had yet to come out. As he waited, he thought of Nina. His beautiful younger sister with no family of her own, supported by the family trust because everyone thought of her as a leper. Ruled by Gertrude's madness and iron-fist. Poor abused Nina, always suffering for the sake of someone else. It had been her that had found the body of Lila, sparing his children from the task. It had been her that had arranged for the children to be taken in by anyone but Gertrude. Unfortunately, Joseph had been a problem child and he'd been caught molesting a cousin. He would have been shipped off to reform school, but Nina stepped in and made sure that Joseph went to live with another relative. It had been Gertrude, but Nina had done her best.

She was the closest thing to a saint the Clachan family would ever have. For this, Patterson believed she had suffered long enough. If Gertrude was captured by Aislinn and the Marshals, he'd kill Nina so that she wouldn't have to deal with the fall out.

Joseph was also on the list of those that Patterson considered a waste. His own son was a child predator. He might not have been caught as an adult, but that didn't mean those urges had gone away. Patterson understood all too well that the urges never went away.

In his youth, during war, Patterson had been impulsive in his kills. German soldiers were his favorite targets, inflicting horrific wounds upon them and watching them die. However, when German soldiers were in short supply, the general population was good enough. Once home, the urges hadn't gone away, but he'd suppressed them, reliving moments from the small tokens he'd taken as trophies.

His murderous rages had been contained, every couple of years, he'd take a victim, but he'd always been very careful not to expose his family to it. Until that day with Lila. He switched his preferred victims that day, he'd been symbolically killing his father over and over. He was smart enough to know that. After the incident with Lila, he'd started symbolically killing Gertrude. After the death of his son and granddaughter, he'd just started killing for revenge. He didn't care about the reason, he cared about the kill.

Gertrude came out of the store. Patterson jumped out of his car, determined to get the whereabouts of her deranged son. For an old, fat woman, she moved fast and he looked suspicious chasing after her. He slunk back to his car and got behind the wheel.

As they pulled out into traffic, Patterson got too far behind. He could see her car, but wasn't close enough to make the light. She drove further away. He slammed his hand against the steering wheel. The sting wasn't enough to distract him from his irritation. This was the second time he'd lost her. She hadn't gone straight home either time. The light turned green and Patterson made the same turn she did. By the third light, her car was completely gone.

He continued travelling east, but the city gave way to more rural areas. He drove down the road all the way to Fulton. When he reached Fulton, he turned around and drove back down WW, hoping to see her car. He didn't.

There was a Casey's Convenience Store at the entrance to a suburb. He turned into their parking lot and got out. He stretched and went inside, grabbing a bottle of tea and a slice of pizza. He'd had an epiphany while driving down the rural highway.

Food and drink in hand, he got back on the road and headed east again. This time, he flipped on his blinker and turned onto a property that was deserted. He'd been here once before. He scanned the area. The house was abandoned. It appeared to be in the process of falling to pieces. This wasn't uncommon on farms in the area, one house became abandoned as the family upgraded. However, he didn't see another house, only a field with the mangled stalks of last year's harvest. Someone was obviously farming the land.

He knocked on the front door and got no answer. He tried the knob, but it held fast. Patterson walked around to the back door. It was also locked, but the knob jiggled in his hand. With a little effort, the lock gave and Patterson entered the house. It had been a while since he had been inside.

Everything had been cleaned up and cleaned out. A few pieces of rotting furniture and the detritus of animals was all that remained. He stared at the kitchen floor. He'd nicked several of Tennyson Unger's veins in this room before holding him down with his boot and breaking his legs, ensuring he couldn't walk. Then he'd left him for the mongrel dog that Tennyson had loved to abuse.

Patterson stepped out of the kitchen. A quick search of the house revealed that no one was living there or had lived there in a long time. He imagined the Blake family had sold it as quickly as possible after Unger's death. They hadn't been a close family.

Outside, he surveyed the tree line. There were a few buildings set behind them. Tractor tires had used the road in the years since Tennyson's death, leaving deep ruts. There wasn't a house back there and there weren't any cars. The barn and shed had been there when Unger had died. A newer metal building had been erected, but he could see a large garage door set on the side of it from where he was. Whoever had bought the land was using it as best they could. One day, they'd probably tear down the house.

Another wasted day.

TEN

Animal control left with some snide comments. That left Earl Rivers, Janet Rivers, my fellow Marshals, and myself within the confines of the sanctuary. It also left Henri the Orangutan and a whole past I had pushed to the back corners of my memory, never intending them to see the light of day again.

"I don't think this is a good idea," John said as Janet led me around to the gate of the enclosure.

"Aislinn and Henri have history, they'll be fine together," Earl spit tobacco juice onto a thin layer of snow as if to emphasize his point.

"What kind of history?" Xavier asked.

"She and her dad are the reason Henri is still alive," Earl answered. I frowned at him. "The bum ear and the scar on his back are his only physical scars. But he's got emotional scars that run deep."

Obviously, Earl didn't care that I was frowning at him.

Henri came close to the gate. He didn't grab for me this time. He just stuck his hand through the bars, palm up, fingers slightly curved. I'd seen the gesture once before, he'd been dying at the time after going head to head with a mountain lion. Since he was here, he hadn't died, but it had been nothing short of a miracle. I didn't know where my father had taken him after those couple of days, but now I was preparing for a reunion with the ape that had once been a patient in my house.

"Go on," Janet told me. "Remember, they are gentle giants, he'll be interested in you. Might sniff around and touch you some, just don't panic and you'll be fine."

I repeated the phrase "don't panic" in my head. It reminded me of a book, Hitchhiker's Guide to the Galaxy. It had also said "don't panic." I wondered if that was possible at the moment as I felt my heart rate increase.

Henri shuffled towards me slowly. His movements seemed deliberately exaggerated and at half speed. I wondered if he could tell I was nervous.

A large, rough hand gently brushed my face as the orangutan reached for my hair. I held my breath. He was gentle, barely touching the strands as they ran through his fingers.

"Talk to him, girl," Earl called to me.

"Hi, Henri," I said quietly.

Henri made a face at me. He didn't bare his teeth or make a kissy face, both were things I associated with ape aggression. This was more like a wrinkling of his nose and eyes. He took hold of my hand with his. The rough pads on his palms were cold.

"Are you cold? Do you need to go inside?" I pointed to the shelter. Henri cooed at me. This was why I wouldn't be a good pet owner. I didn't know what he wanted and he couldn't tell me.

Henri suddenly stood. He was taller than me by several inches. His wide arms engulfed me and he picked me up off the ground. With my arms pinned to my side, there was little I could do. I didn't fight, which was my first instinct. Henri held me firmly, but not so hard as to hurt.

"Calm down," Earl said, probably not to me. "Henri's been socialized with humans. They call it identity confusion. He's giving her a hug."

As if to confirm this, Henri set me on the ground, feet first. He let go and just stared at me for a moment. I didn't frown or smile nor did I make eye contact. He blew a raspberry at me. This made me smile despite trying to be on my best behavior.

He did it a second time and I giggled. Finally, I put my arms around Henri and hugged the orangutan from my past and let the memory come back to me.

My father had been off duty. I had been nine at the time. We'd been horseback riding at the farm of one of my cousins. Dad and I had both noticed a lot of cars at the neighbor's house and he'd been curious. Our cousin informed us that there were illegal activities taking place, an animal fight. My dad had thought it was a dog fight.

He had taken me with him to go investigate. We'd snuck around to the barn. Inside wasn't a dog fighting ring, but a large cage. Inside the cage was Henri and a mountain lion. My dad called for backup, but there wasn't much time.

My father had fired a few shots into the air. People had scattered. I think he planned to shoot the mountain lion, but he didn't need to. With the people running, he opened the cage and the mountain lion sprang to freedom. He'd landed a few feet away from me. We'd stared at each for a couple of seconds before he lost interest and ran off.

My dad was holding the hand of the dying orangutan. I rushed into the cage and found the ape was bleeding from his ear and most of his back had been exposed by a swipe of claws. Our cousin rushed over with a gun of his own because he'd heard the shots fired. Together, he and my dad had removed the orangutan from the cage.

Our cousin was a large animal vet. He wasn't sure the ape would live, but I insisted we had to try. My dad made the decision that the only way the ape had a chance was to not be found by the local police. He'd be put down for being "aggressive."

They had whisked the orangutan to the cousin's house. The cousin and I worked on the orangutan while my father lied to the police and said he'd found two mountain lions in the cage. Both of whom were released by the property owner when my dad arrived. He'd fired at them in self-defense, but wasn't sure he'd hit either of them.

I don't know what happened to the owner or why no one ever found out my dad had rescued an orangutan. I just know that for a week, the orangutan stayed at our cousin's house and we visited every day. When he got better, he came to stay with us for a while. However, it was hard to hide an orangutan in our neighborhood. I came home from school one day and the orangutan that I had named Henri, in honor of French physicist Henri Becquerel, was gone. Dad told me he had gone to live in a place that could house him better than our small family home.

We had both cried that night. It was the only time I had seen my father cry. Seeing him breakdown into tears as he explained why we couldn't keep Henri had been torture. He appeared broken by the decision to remove the animal. I wasn't sure if it was because he wanted to keep Henri or because I did.

Seeing the orangutan now made me sad. Not an emotion I experience very often. I was sad that one of the few connections I had made with my father had outlived him. Henri was alive and well and my father was dead.

I wasn't a spiritual person and I didn't imagine the ghost of my father was looking over the animal and myself. The best I could come up with was the knowledge that my father had cared about the animal and I had cared about the animal. It was a tenuous connection, but a connection was a connection.

We left the sanctuary. Xavier and Gabriel kept giving me looks. I knew they wanted to rehash my past, but I was not going to give up the ghost easily. Maybe one day, I would, but for now, conversations about my father were off limits unless it related to the case. It wasn't just that my father had died when I was young, it was that the memories of him were sacred.

The trip had taken my mind off the dismembered feet and given me an idea. A great ape was capable of doing immense damage. To them, the human body was a fragile, frail thing and a sexually mature chimpanzee was capable of going into a rage without provocation.

It was this thought that I relayed to the guys. They looked at me like I was crazy for a few minutes. We had arrived at the Columbia Police Department before any of them said anything.

"So, you now think it could be a chimp?" Gabriel asked.

"I think it's a possibility, just one of many," I said.

"You were convinced it was a jaguar yesterday," John pointed out.

"Yes, well, I have reconsidered my position. It could be a number of predators. Even the expert was not certain it was a cat, just mostly certain. It is possible that the fangs of a large cat could be similar to the canines of a chimp."

"We found a head," Detective Russell said as we entered the secure part of the station.

ELEVEN

It doesn't matter how many times you look at a severed head, there is something surreal about it. This head had been floating in the Missouri River for a while. Large chunks of the recognizable pieces were missing, like the nose, eyes, and lips. Strips of flesh still clung to the forehead, jaw, and cheek bones. The scalp still had hair hanging from it. It dripped dirty water on to the table.

Xavier was examining the head with those strange magnifying goggles that made him look like a bug. John looked a little green. Gabriel was chatting quietly with the detective. I was trying not to peel the skin off the head.

This sounded morbid, but I was anxious to see the condition of the skull. I wanted to know if it had been crushed. Xavier was more concerned with identification.

"Teen boy, Caucasian, time of death unknown," Xavier was rambling information into a microphone hooked to a tape recorder. "Would you go get food or read up on cannibals or anything that gets you out of my way?"

"Me?" I asked.

"No one else reads books about cannibals," Gabriel confirmed.

"Ok, I'll grab lunch and see if I can find a new book on cannibals. I think I've read them all though," I answered.

"You can eat while reading about cannibals?" John appeared to turn a little greener.

"If it wasn't a biohazard, I could eat in this room while Xavier boiled the head," I told him.

"Boils the head?" John frowned.

"That's the best way to remove all the tissue," I walked out to the sounds of John running for the trashcan. I couldn't eat with that noise. My stomach was good with gore, not so good with vomit. However, I felt a little better knowing that I had pushed John over the edge. It was petty, but sometimes petty was the friendliest thing I could muster.

I did not buy a book on cannibals. I bought a book on chimpanzees. I also bought lunch in the cafeteria of the University of Missouri Hospital. As I sat down, a few people moved away from me. I told myself it was the smell of antiseptic, but I knew that I also smelled a little bit like decay. It was impossible not to pick up some of that smell. The odor would attach to my clothes, my hair, my very skin and only a hot shower with some good soap would get rid of it.

The book brought back information I had forgotten and filled my head with more. There was a lot I didn't know about chimpanzees. For example, I didn't know that female chimps learned faster than males or that chimps laughed. I did know that they were a hell of a lot stronger than humans, despite their smaller stature and that they used tools.

I finished the book on chimpanzees and bought a second book, this one on bonobos. As I finished my lunch, I finished the second book. Bonobos were a lot less violent than chimps and much more sexually explorative. A bonobo was more likely to sexually assault a person than kill them. If a person was killed by a bonobo, it was probably an accident due to their high sex drive.

Armed with this new information and a full stomach, I headed back to the morgue. John and the detective were sitting in the hallway. The detective smiled at me. I smiled back.

"I think they are waiting on you," Detective Russell said to me.

"Thanks," I walked into the room.

"How was lunch?" Gabriel asked.

"Good, I read up on great apes and ate a turkey sandwich. I was told you were waiting on me."

"We're about to start x-raying the skull, we figured you would want to be here for it," Xavier told me.

"You thought right," I said. "I bought you a sandwich. Wait, why were x-rays not taken before you began examining it?"

"They were," Xavier pointed to a piece of film. I picked it up and held it to the light. It only sort of looked like a human head. There were too many bones and debris, something was definitely wrong with it. As I stared a little longer, a fish began to take shape.

"Is that a fish?" I asked.

"Small flathead catfish to be exact," Xavier answered. "We think it crawled in through the neck where it had been detached from the torso and took up residence in the skull. I took out the fish while you were eating, which is why John is no longer in the room. The fish is over there."

It was indeed a small catfish, maybe six inches in length. Xavier had put it in a jar full of fluid. It didn't seem like a six inch catfish would fit inside a human skull. Also, to make room for a catfish, the brain would have to be gone.

"Where'd the brain go?" I asked.

"The beauty of being submerged in water with tiny scavengers. Tiny water creatures, probably fishlings, swam up the nose and in through the eyes and ate the brain as it decayed. After it was gone and other small scavengers ate at the neck region, that catfish swam inside the head and got stuck," Xavier said.

"Not a very smart catfish," I shrugged. The intelligence or lack thereof in catfish was not something I knew enough about to debate. However, it didn't seem like a very smart move.

"Now, if you wouldn't mind," Xavier pointed to some gloves. I put on a pair of the nitrile gloves, they were purple and about a size too big. "I'd like to take x-rays and then I'm going to boil the head. Gabriel said he'd take a rain check on the head boiling, but I figured you could assist."

"Sure," I shrugged. "However, it's that time. You need to eat. X-rays and head boiling will have to wait." I pulled a very squashed sandwich out of my hip pocket. Gabriel laughed. Xavier shook his head.

"You should invest in a bag," Xavier took the sandwich. "Not a purse, but like a tote bag to carry around your Kindle and for food runs. I get tired of squashed sandwiches."

"At least it wasn't a salad," Gabriel laughed again. "Let's get him an unsquashed sandwich and take a break."

"Uh," I frowned. "Can we do the x-rays really quick?"

"I guess," Gabriel leaned against the table. "It will give you something to do while the rest of us eat."

"Thanks," I said, ignoring the dig. Xavier took X-rays. The nice thing about the digital age was that it took no time for the film to develop. I grabbed the six print-outs and we left the morgue.

Once inside the cafeteria, John sat quietly sipping some water. He refused to look at the plates of the others. I believed it was his first autopsy and boiling heads wasn't setting too well with his stomach. Neither was Xavier's chicken salad sandwich or Gabriel's cheeseburger. Some people just couldn't eat after being in a morgue.

The new x-ray was in my hand, being held up to the shoddy lighting in the cafeteria. It was hard to make out any real details. To improve the lighting, I was shining a flashlight through the back, but it was still a poor substitute for a light booth or whatever they called them.

The skull seemed to have lots of fractures. Spider web cracks that radiated from central points on different sides of the head. I picked up another film and found a black spot in the ghostly white image. A few inches away was another black spot. The spider webs were more apparent in this shot.

I put the film and my head down on the table. We could ignore chimpanzees, lions, tigers, and bears. The black spots were missing pieces of the skull. Few things could do that; alligators, crocodiles, and jaguars. I was finding the more I thought about it, the more I realized there were a lot of things capable of attacking and killing a human being. Especially a teenaged boy. Even a large anaconda or Burmese python might be able to do some serious damage to a skull. I'd heard of them killing people before, full grown adults, but only children seemed to be at risk for being eaten.

"What's the bite force of an anaconda or Burmese python?" I asked.

"It's not a snake," Xavier said. I stared at him. We all still had secrets, but the way he put it made me wonder if he'd seen snake attacks before.

"Crocodile or alligator?" I turned to the other predators that had instantly leapt to mind.

"That's possible," Xavier agreed. "Ok, Miss Morbid, let's go boil the head."

"Hey," I stopped him. "What's that?" I pointed to a spot on the film with my flashlight.

"A spot," Xavier told me.

"Is that the technical term?"

"Yes, it is." Xavier stood and cleared his tray. "Now, if you would like to join me for some skull boiling, we'll see what that spot is."

"Right behind you," I stood.

"I'm going to sit this out," Gabriel stood. "I'm sure I have other things I need to do."

"Like what?" I asked.

"Important things," Gabriel answered, "like keep my lunch down."

TWELVE

The skull was clean. The room smelled like ammonia and boiled meat. Combined it created an unpleasant odor, add to it the knowledge that the meat smell was coming from decaying flesh and well, my stomach certainly wasn't growling.

Xavier had his magnifying goggles back on. I had my own set. We were rubbing shoulders, literally, as we looked at the skull. Xavier kept talking into a microphone. I didn't have a microphone to talk into, so I said nothing and just looked intently.

There were four definitive punctures. They were evenly spaced and between them were small marks that Xavier had confirmed were from the other teeth scraping the bone. Cracks spider webbed out from the puncture marks, except along the cranium sutures, where the skull was slightly misshapen. The cranium sutures were where the two halves of the skull fused together. This one had a jagged break where the sutures had broken. Small chips of bone were missing from there as well.

This was the weakest part of the skull. The break and missing chips were caused by excessive pressure being placed upon the sides of the skull, forcing the bone to give. I compared it to a picture from my file that had once belonged to my father. It was similar, but it wasn't exact.

"Uh, Houston, we have a serious problem," Xavier suddenly stood up and stepped back from the table.

"Ok," I stepped back as well, suddenly concerned about biohazards. Xavier didn't step back from bodies very often.

"We need an odontologist," Xavier told me.

"Why?" I looked at him.

"That spot," Xavier pointed. "I'm pretty sure it's teeth marks."

"It's been mauled by an animal."

"No Ace, I think they are human teeth marks. I think someone bit down on the brow hard enough that their teeth left an impression on the top of the eye socket and the forehead."

"Who bites an eye?" I asked.

"Someone fighting or," Xavier didn't say it.

"Or someone feeding." I made a face. "That isn't exactly a fleshy area."

"True and I saw no evidence of cooked flesh," Xavier said. "Maybe it was a fight."

"I've bitten some odd places when fighting for my life." I reassured him.

"Like?" Xavier raised an eyebrow.

"The fleshy part under the arm. It's very tender." I stopped. "Of course, I didn't do it hard enough to leave teeth marks on bone. I've taken off ears."

"With your teeth?"

"No, actually, since my teeth are mostly fake, I try not to bite. The ones I have might not hold up under the pressure. The fake ones might come out of my mouth."

"Ok, so we won't jump to conclusions, one bite mark does not make a cannibal."

"Especially since there has been an animal feeding on the body, a powerful animal. That might be why we have a head and feet but nothing that goes between them." Even though the words were coming out of my mouth, I wasn't buying them. Some years earlier, a man had walked into a fast food restaurant in a major city with a machete. He'd cut off the head of a patron and held everyone hostage while he chewed on his victim's face. Two hours into the hostage situation, police had managed to shoot him.

No one understood why he did it. He had seemed like a normal, well-adjusted guy who'd just celebrated his twenty-sixth birthday and the birth of his first child. There were no marital problems, no history of mental illness, nothing to indicate such an urge was building inside him. The news had reported it and a Native American shaman had spoken on record about the man being possessed by a wendigo. Since the subject had been killed by police, there hadn't been an answer to why he did it. Possession by a wendigo didn't seem that far out of the realm of possibilities to me.

We were used to senseless violence. Desensitized by the mayhem that we saw so often. However, the thought of a person chewing on the face of another person unsettled me. It wasn't the act of cannibalism. Those sorts of things I was used to, I'd once seen a body dressed like a headless hog and run across an open fire on a spit. The spit had been complete with long handled turner, cold beer, picnic tables, and all the neighbors. The victim had been missing their head, arms, legs, nipples, and genitals. All the identifiers to mark it as human and not swine.

It was the idea that our victim might have been chewed on raw or worse, while still alive. Cannibalism wasn't just taboo, it spoke of more primitive times, when Aztecs made sacrifices to their gods by drinking the blood or consuming the flesh of their fellow man. However, they cooked them first. Alive was different, it didn't speak of primal urges and early history. It spoke of wildness. It was more feral than primitive.

But, I too, was jumping to conclusions. Large predators didn't share their food well. Whatever had crushed our victim's skull, wouldn't have willingly shared the violence of the kill or the spoils of victory. Perhaps the bite to the face was done during the initial abduction. It was a tender spot, like the fleshy part of the underarm. Or in the process of shoving the victim into the cage, there had been a struggle and the bite mark had happened then. Or perhaps Xavier was wrong and it wasn't a bite mark, but something entirely different.

This last suggestion seemed the least likely. Xavier had seen things that most of us couldn't imagine. He and Lucas had spent time in jungles and deserts where the rules had no longer applied. I hadn't heard all their stories, just enough to know the two men had aged quickly due to the things they had experienced. I glanced sideways at him. Unlike Lucas, I never wondered if the dark haired man who always needed a shave and a shower, could read my mind. I did worry that one day, I would cross a line and hurt his feelings.

This desire to not hurt his feelings was not a natural instinct for me. During the time we had worked together, I had come to appreciate Xavier. Until I had joined the SCTU, I could count on one hand the number of people that were important to me. Now, I had to use two and Xavier was definitely one of them.

"Do we call Gabriel or the odontologist first?" Xavier asked.

"Do you know an odontologist?"

"No," Xavier answered.

"Then I suggest we call Gabriel. He's the one that usually arranges for us to have an expert."

"Ok," Xavier drew out his phone and called Gabriel.

I went back to examining the skull as well as the pictures that we had taken beforehand with the flesh still on it. The face had decayed. The features were relatively indistinguishable. There was a hole where the nose had been eaten away. The eyes had been missing. The eyelids had been missing. Scraps of flesh clung to the forehead, but not enough to show a bite mark. The lips and ears were gone. The teeth had begun to come out of the decaying gums, leaving only a handful on the top and bottom jaws.

I gave up on the pictures and went back to the skull. I didn't know what I was looking for, anything that jumped out at me. My gaze wandered back up to the top of the skull, where the sutures had split. It revealed nothing more, keeping the secret of what had cracked it hidden. We needed an animal expert. We needed an odontologist. We needed DNA results. We needed bodies. Bodies yielded clues, but the skull only gave us tantalizing tidbits of information that may or may not help.

I left the room, stripping off my gown, mask, goggles, and gloves along the way. We needed a zoologist. We were in the right place. The University of Missouri had once been renowned for its School of Journalism, but in recent years, science had taken the spot of the best program, particularly biological sciences.

The chief medical examiner had a very nice office located on the same floor as the morgue. The walls were a light gray, the ceiling slightly darker with lots of dark walnut wood furniture. It didn't have any chrome, silver, or stainless steel accents. All the accents were marigold yellow. I instantly disliked it. Yellow was my least favorite color. I abhorred it. It was irrational to abhor the color yellow, but I did.

"What can I help you with Dr. Cain?" The medical examiner asked as I walked into the office.

The door had been open, so I'd rapped my knuckles against it as I entered.

"We need a zoologist," I told him. "Or someone that can identify the animal that crushed our victim's skull. I figure the University is a good place to look for one of those."

"And you need my help finding one?" He asked.

"That would be awesome. If you know one, that would streamline the process, otherwise, Gabriel will find one." I sat down in one of the chairs. "But that is not why I'm here."

"Then why are you here?"

"I do not know," I answered. "It just seemed like the right place for me to be at the moment. How long have you been the chief medical examiner?"

"Seventeen years," he answered.

"Oh," I answered. "Did you work here when the jaguar attack came in twenty-five years ago?"

"No, I was still in school twenty-five years ago."

"Ever see a jaguar crush a skull?"

"No," the doctor gave me a queer look.

"In the time you've worked here, have you ever seen someone come in with a crushed skull?"

"Car crashes, boating accidents, skaters losing battles with pavement, being beaten to death, I've seen my fair share of them."

"I believe Dr. Reece has as well, but I feel like we could use a second opinion." It wasn't like me to question Xavier's judgment or my own. The ghost of my father could be felt.

"If you wanted a second opinion, you could have just asked," Dr. Burnett told me.

"I'm sure I could have, but I did not know that was what I wanted until about five seconds ago."

THIRTEEN

"I have seen injuries similar to this," Dr. Burnett was looking at the skull through another pair of the goggles. "Let me get the files."

He left the room. Xavier was leaning against a counter. He'd been silent the entire time that Dr. Burnett had been in the room.

"It's not like you to question me," Xavier said.

"I'm not questioning you," I admitted. "I'm questioning me. This case seems to be stirring up a few ghosts."

"Why?"

"Because it was my dad's case? Because I'm connected to it in ways that I can't remember yet? Because I want it to be a jaguar so that I can close the case on one of my hometown's open serial cases?"

"It's not like you to not remember things that are important," Xavier pursed his lips together.

"Why are you blocking this particular set of memories?"

"Age is the biggest part, I was young."

Dr. Burnett came back into the room with a stack of files. He sat them on the counter next to Xavier. Xavier became interested in the doctor's movements.

"This wound pattern is similar to a set of attacks we had about ten years ago." Dr. Burnett pointed to the files. "There were seven total, all seven died. Cause of death was a mastiff, the animal crushed their skulls with its powerful jaws. However, there was something not right about the case. The kids all came from the same neighborhood, disappeared for a day and then their bodies were found. We could never find a human element to the attacks though. It seemed the animal hunted alone, grabbed the children and skulked off with them. Eventually, someone found the animal and it was put down, after that, the attacks stopped."

"Why did you think a human was involved?" Xavier asked.

"Because a mastiff wouldn't have grabbed the kids by the skulls and carried them off, it would have gone for the throat. None of the throats were ripped out. I believe a person kidnapped the children and gave them to the mastiff." Dr. Burnett opened a file and handed it to Xavier.

"And you were positive it was a mastiff?"

"Yes and no," Dr. Burnett frowned. "A mastiff can do it and they've been known to do it, but it isn't their preferred method of killing. Also, while we found the bodies, they had been chewed up pretty bad, but the bones were mostly intact. It didn't seem very doggish to me, but the forensic expert was pretty sure it was the only thing in the area that could do that kind of damage."

"But," I mimicked Dr. Burnett's frown. "Other large, exotic predators could have probably done it. Who found and put down the dog?"

"A hunter, said he was attacked by it. When they did the necropsy, they found some human flesh still in the stomach, however, it had been three days since the last kill. Why did the dog still have that particular food in its stomach?"

"The hunter?" Xavier asked.

"A local fireman named Ben Forge. They cleared him of all wrong doing. An upshot detective handled the case, moved on to bigger and better things afterwards."

"Like what?" I asked.

"Took a job in Detroit as a detective, returned here a year later, paralyzed from a bullet in the back. A year after that, he ended up on a slab here after a home invasion." Dr. Burnett said. "I wasn't a fan of his work. He was a shoddy detective, just looking to move up the ranks. I guess I shouldn't speak ill of the dead."

"Too late," I chirped. "Ok, so is it possible it wasn't a mastiff?"

"It was my suspicion that even if the mastiff was responsible, it was only partly responsible. The animal didn't just attack them, eat, and run off. These children all came from the same neighborhood and they were found over two miles from the site of their disappearance. A dog might kill and drag the body away to eat at its leisure, but there was no evidence that the dog had attacked the children where they disappeared. I felt they were lured away, by a human, then given to the animal responsible."

"Much like now," Xavier looked at me. "And before."

"True, but the bodies were being found within twenty-four hours of going missing. It was a quick succession of victims. That was the other thing, they were being found very quickly, the deaths were happening very close together in time as well as area, and all the bodies were found in a creek. Dogs don't drag their victims to creeks."

"Did the creek have water in it?" I asked.

"Yes," Dr. Burnett looked at the skull. "It had rained a lot that year. The creek was actually at flood stage."

Twenty-five years ago, a handful of little girls went missing. One was found to have been mauled and eaten by a jaguar. Ten years ago, another handful of little girls go missing, this time mauled and eaten by a mastiff. Now, the feet of teenaged boys were being found on utility wires. One had predator teeth marks on it. All of them associated with water.

There were two fundamental questions behind my thoughts. Why did the victimology change? And what did the killer do during his periods of inactivity? I was convinced it was the same killer, I just wasn't sure I could answer either of those questions, yet.

"Any other serial killers in the interim?" Xavier asked.

"We've had three in the last twenty years," Dr. Burnett told him. If he'd gone back a few more years, the total would have been higher. "All caught, none of them with this sort of behavior. We've had a rapist who liked to strangle his victims with a wire coat hanger, a woman who liked to poison her family and friends with strychnine, and a guy who liked to mutilate his female victims by removing their female organs."

"A regular Jack the Ripper," Xavier quipped. "Any other animal related deaths?"

"Sure," Dr. Burnett said. "Dog attacks are pretty infrequent, but they happen. We've had a mountain lion that killed a child near Eagle Bluffs. Then there was a boa constrictor that got loose in an apartment building and ate an infant. And there was a strange case that involved a raccoon."

"I heard about that one," I looked up at him. "A large raccoon got into a house and killed a little girl. The raccoon turned out to be rabid and definitely closer to the end of his life than the beginning."

"Rabid raccoons?" Xavier raised an eyebrow.

"Much like plague, rabies happens," I answered.

"Plague?" Dr. Burnett looked at me. "We've had a case of bubonic plague in the last five years. A woman came back from vacation and got sick. By the time they figured it out, she was in decline and the antibiotics didn't work."

"When was that?" I asked.

"You are not to get distracted by plague," Xavier told me.

"I'm just curious," I snipped at him.

"Three years ago. Strange thing really. The autopsy didn't reveal any bites from animals or insects and the form of bubonic plague was very antibiotic resistant. The CDC came out and investigated it. Then last fall, they asked for any additional information we had on the case. There wasn't any, but they asked three times in as many weeks. I kept wondering if it was related to the California cases, but I didn't get an answer. She was about your age, Columbia native." Dr. Burnett told me. "Her name was Sue Brooks."

"I had class with a girl named Sue Brooks," I frowned. No need to mention the girl tormented me endlessly about being smart and then about killing someone. I was called "freak" by a lot of kids my own age when I was young. It was one of the nicer names.

"Stop," Xavier held up his hand. "We have a predator eating people. We do not have time to investigate three year old plague cases."

"I'm not suggesting we investigate," I told him.

"Not a good friend, was she?" Xavier gave the inappropriate high-pitched giggle. Dr. Burnett turned and gave him a horrified look.

"You get used to it," I answered. Xavier tried to recover. This made him giggle harder. "He has some issues."

"Brain damage by the sounds of it," Dr. Burnett began to examine Xavier from afar.

"Damage to the emotional center of the brain, trauma of some sort."

Xavier nodded and continued to giggle. The fit would pass in a few minutes as long as I didn't do or say anything to make it worse. Xavier didn't like to talk about taking a bullet to the head, but some very good doctors could figure it out.

I tuned it out. My mind was now being overwhelmed with information again. Had the Sue Brooks who'd died of plague been the same girl that had teased me? Was this somehow related to the dead prairie dog I'd gotten on my birthday? Was it related to the cases of plague in California? Was it related to my newest stalker? And what the hell was my mind failing to remember about the cases from before? There was still a fragment of something in there, something I couldn't grasp, but seemed important.

None of the animal related deaths aside from the streak ten years earlier seemed related to the case. I filed them away for use later, if need be. For now, I tried to concentrate on the girls that had died ten years ago.

"It strikes me as strange that a dog would only take female victims," I announced.

"Me too," Dr. Burnett confirmed. "Especially since there was a day when a six year old girl was taken but her four year old brother wasn't. However, they were both in the yard at the time."

"Was the boy questioned?" I asked.

"He said a demon took the little girl." Dr. Burnett answered.

"And he knew what a demon was?" I frowned.

"Apparently, his father was a preacher and his son was very familiar with the concept of demons," the disapproval in Dr. Burnett's voice was evident. Xavier's giggle fit was subsiding. Dr. Burnett turned his attention back to him. "How long ago was the injury?"

"A while," Xavier averted his eyes, refusing to meet the other man's interested gaze.

"Is it getting worse?"

"Not really," Xavier said. "I have a neurologist for it."

"Does it affect your work?"

"Not in the least, just my mood."

"Doctor, none of us are exactly even keeled," I defended Xavier by deflecting the doctor's attention away. "Most of us are damaged either emotionally or physically."

"So, I've noticed," Dr. Burnett motioned towards my hands. There were still burn scars on them, but they were fading. "I'm guessing you have full-blown psychopathy or you have congenital analgesia. One doesn't get those sorts of scars by feeling pain."

"I'm a sociopath," I corrected.

"By choice," Xavier added. "She's a sociopath by choice. She has the physical characteristics of antisocial personality disorder with psychopathic tendencies. She does feel pain, but not like you or me."

I opened my mouth to protest, but stopped. I was a sociopath that much I knew. However, I'd seen Malachi demonstrate his pain tolerance. Mine was just as high. I felt pain, I could just ignore it. Malachi had once told me he lived only because he could feel pain. At the time, I had thought he was being a masochist, but as I lived closer to the edge of all things pain-related, I realized that wasn't his meaning at all. He was alive because he could feel pain and ignore it. It was an indicator of his life force, so to speak. Being in pain reminded me that I was still alive and could fight for my life if need be. It could be ignored as necessary to keep my lungs working, my heart pumping, and my body moving.

"I've never met a sociopath who is actually a psychopath," Dr. Burnett thought about this a moment longer. "It is probably the rarest condition on earth."

"I believe she is the only one," Xavier answered. I said nothing.

FOURTEEN

Knowing I was a sociopath by choice, wasn't really life altering. Some part of me had always known it. I had all the physical benefits of a psychopath, but the mental benefits of a sociopath. Something in the nurturing aspect of my childhood had overridden the genetic component, something that I imagined had a lot to do with Nyleena, my mother, and my time in the hands of a pedophiliac serial killer. Besides, Lucas and Xavier had both been hinting at it for over a year now.

We'd been back to the hotel to shower and get dressed for dinner. Dressing for dinner didn't mean we were going anywhere fancy, it meant that Xavier and I smelled and couldn't go into even a fast food restaurant without washing and changing our clothing. I was in my usual jeans and T-Shirt. My T-Shirt said "It's Hard To Think When The Voices In Your Head Won't Shut Up." I was wearing it because Xavier had bought it for me as a

Christmas gift. The shirts I bought tended to have funny science or history things on them or they were band T-Shirts. I would never have bought this one for myself.

The highway had been open for a day or so now, but we weren't leaving anytime soon. We'd just hit the long haul, so to speak. We had lots of speculation and nothing solid, except a skull and some feet. Neither were willing to reveal the identity of their killer or the manner of death.

The little dive bar was busy. We'd eaten Shakespeare's and Sub Shop, the two Columbia staples, and were moving onto different local fare. Tonight, we sat in a crowded Booches'. Technically, this was a Columbia staple, especially if you loved burgers. However, it wasn't one of my favorite places. This was not because I didn't love burgers, I did, but because there was some strange sordid history. I didn't know the story, just that my father had detested the place. Somehow, that had rubbed off on me.

Sitting it in nearly ten years after my first experience, not much had changed. It was still a billiard hall and bar with slider style burgers and wax paper for plates. I had ordered one burger and a bag of chips. Booches doesn't serve fries.

Conversation at the table was limited. Everyone was weary and worn-out. John had spent the day making lists of missing teenaged boys within seven counties of Columbia as well as St. Louis, Kansas City, and Springfield. Gabriel had spent the day trying to rush the DNA lab.

Neither seemed to have enjoyed much success. There were lots of missing teenaged boys in Missouri. Worse, John was pretty sure he'd found a serial killer in St. Louis. He'd passed the information along to the VCU. With conversation at the table wanting, my attention was easily attracted to other places.

We had sat at a table near the middle of the room. All of us were paranoid, but we couldn't all sit with our backs to the wall. Our compromise was to sit at a square table in the middle of the room. This allowed us to watch the entire room, each responsible for the space behind the person across them. Xavier sat across from me, Gabriel had specifically positioned him there because I still wasn't sure I trusted John. This was not because of anything John had done or not done, he seemed good at his job. This was because I rarely trusted anyone.

My senses were in overdrive, the result of a strange day. The table to our right held three girls, all of them roughly in their early twenties. The table to our left, was a couple of students well on their way to having a hangover in the morning from draft beer and cheap burgers.

The girls caught my attention first. One was discussing her evening. She'd been in a fight with another girl at a club. The gabby girl had been grabbed by another girl. An argument had ensued. The argument had been about a guy. The girl telling the story was sleeping with the other girl's boyfriend. A fist fight had followed. The speaker proclaimed to be the winner, despite the black eye she was sporting.

I found it confusing. It seemed like a lot of energy had been wasted fighting over this guy. I sat at a table with three of them, one was technically married, but separated, while the other two were single. Obviously, the old adage of there being lots of fish in the sea was, in fact, true. Not only that, but why fight for a guy who is cheating. The girl speaking wouldn't want to date him, she was proof that he was cheating. The girl that he was cheating on shouldn't want to be with him, he was sleeping with someone else. The entire thing was a cycle. One of the many aspects of human nature that I didn't understand.

Next, my attention was drawn to the table of college guys. Here were some fish for the girls next to me. However, it was their loud, drunken boasting that won them my consideration. One of them was talking loudly about a girl he'd met the other night at a club. Maybe some fish were slimier than others.

His shirt was black with a white skull, a red rose clenched between the bony jaws. Beneath the skull, it said "Love Kills." The boy had said his sister had been taken by a demon. Not a person, not a guy, not a dog, a demon and he was supposedly well versed with demon ideology.

The word wendigo whispered through my mind again, like a breeze causing a flame to flicker. The spectral cannibal of Native American legends was said to be fierce looking. A tall, thin, featureless body cloaked in darkness; a long face with the skin stretched taut over the skull revealing its human like teeth that constantly gnash together, creating a violent chattering noise. It fulfilled the qualifications of a demon. However, I didn't really believe in demons kidnapping little girls or teen boys, even demons like the wendigo.

The human teeth marks on the eye socket still bothered me. I could tell Xavier it could happen in a fight all I wanted, but I didn't believe it. The wendigo theory held more water. People just didn't bite people on the upper eye socket during a fight. They were more likely to go for a cheek or an ear, maybe the lip or nose, but not the eye. The bone around the eye was hard, biting against it was going to hurt the teeth.

"Hey," Xavier snapped his fingers in front of my face.

"Hey yourself," I answered.

"What were you thinking about?" He asked.

"The wendigo," I answered. Gabriel frowned at me. I shrugged back, not voicing anything else that was running through my head.

"What's a wendigo?" John asked.

"A myth," Gabriel answered. "Native Americans believe it is a spirit that can possess people." Gabriel had an interest in Native American belief systems.

"Oh," John said.

"It turns them into cannibals," I added. John sat one of his half eaten cheeseburgers down.

"Just once, I'd like to go through a meal with you and not hear anything about death or plague or cannibals," John said.

"Good luck," Xavier grinned and finished off his third slider. He'd ordered six.

"I don't know why you're smiling, you are just as bad. Also, you talk with food in your mouth all the time. When I'm not being grossed out by the conversation, I'm being grossed out because I can see everything you shove in your mouth." John ranted.

"Done?" Gabriel asked.

"No," John was fuming. "You let them do it."

"Should I monitor them like children? Should I be holding their hands when we cross streets or scolding them for putting their elbows on the table? Death is what we do. It's the glue that binds us together. Yes, we talk about other things, but when a case is in front of us, it's hard to talk about anything other than that. I admit the plague obsession is unusual, but better plague than listening to her chatter about some guy or listen to Xavier brag about his latest conquest." Gabriel proved he'd been paying attention to the conversations around us as well.

John remained silent for the rest of our time at the bar. Xavier and Gabriel finished their pitcher of beer. We paid the tab and left.

"It was good," Gabriel said as we got into the SUV.

"It was good," Xavier said. "I like these little hole in the wall local places and we rarely find them because we rarely know anyone from the town."

"Now, why were you thinking about wendigos during dinner?" Gabriel turned in his seat.

"Xavier thinks he found human teeth marks on the eye socket of the skull. I keep trying to tell myself that it was the result of a fight, but even I don't buy it. People just don't bite people's eyes. It isn't exactly the easiest place to get to, unless the person is on the ground and not fighting."

"Xavier?" Gabriel asked.

"Dr. Burnett has made arrangements for a forensic odontologist to come in tomorrow. I agree with Ace, it is an unusual injury to say the least. I think someone munched on our victim's head. The fact that they did it at some point before or after it had been crushed by a jaguar is strange."

"Jaguar slobber," I cringed. "I can't see a human doing it after a jaguar, but I can't imagine a scenario in which the human manages to munch on the face of the victim before the jaguar kills it."

"Not everyone is as germophobic as you," Xavier pointed out.

"True, but to chew on a face after a jaguar has been chewing on it? Those are special germs. I have no idea what sorts of diseases jaguars carry that can be passed to humans, but I'm sure there are a few."

"Wow, something Ace doesn't know," Gabriel smirked.

"Oh, I can guess," I answered. "Rabies and bubonic plague come to mind immediately."

"Oh boy," John groaned from the back seat.

CONFRONTATION

The mind was a terrible thing to waste. So was the body. At least, Patterson believed that. At eighty-six years old, he had the body of a fifty year old. Most people guessed him to be in his early sixties, but only because his face was heavily lined and he had developed a habit of walking with a fancy cane simply because he felt it was sophisticated.

Unfortunately, his mind was starting to fail him, meaningless meanderings through memories that were unrelated and useless pieces of information cluttered his thoughts. Without something directly in front of him to hold his attention, he found his waking thoughts to be scattered, jumbled, and random. He saw it as not only a weakness, but as a sign that regardless of how long his body lived, his mind was going to go before his heart.

As night fell upon the city, he was south of town, parked at the gates that led to his own personal hell. He wasn't here to check out the house. He was here to check out the property. He didn't think his sister was stupid enough to build a house for August back here, but stranger things had happened.

He slipped from his car and using the darkness, moved without detection towards the house he had once lived in. The property was clear of new buildings. However, his house caught his attention. There was a light on in the living room. That bothered him. In the fifty years since he had killed Lila, he expected the house to go to rot and ruin, not be lived in.

He moved closer. The outside was in good condition. The light in the living room illuminated a solitary figure. The dumpy silhouette moved around the room with purpose.

Patterson couldn't resist, he moved closer. His sister was inside with a broom. She was cleaning the house. Patterson didn't know whether to be enraged or horrified. Through the window, he could still see the blood stains on the floors, ceilings, and walls. He knocked on the door.

Gertrude opened it, wearing a robe over some sweat pants and a long dressing gown.

"I knew you'd be back," she smiled at her older brother.

"What are you doing?" He asked.

"Keeping the place tidy for you."

"You're insane."

"This coming from the man that tried to feed my son to a hog and then butchered his wife," Gertrude snorted. "That's rich."

"I didn't try," Patterson stuck out his chin. "I nearly succeeded in sending that abomination to Hell. If your stupid husband hadn't rushed to the rescue, he wouldn't be cutting up children to feed to animals. Where is he?"

"Oh and I guess you don't feel responsible for that?" Gertrude puffed up her chest.

"Where is he?" Patterson asked.

"To hell with you," Gertrude shoved past him. "You turned my son into a killer, you reap what you sow."

"He was a killer before the incident, you just couldn't see it like I could. Now where is he?"

"What? Worried he'll get your precious granddaughter?" Gertrude spat at him. "She's here you know, searching for him. She won't find him either."

"I should kill you," Patterson said.

"But you won't," Gertrude cackled at him. "Familicide was always your downfall. You just couldn't stomach killing Virgil or our parents. You even failed to kill August. You're weak."

"I'm not weak," Patterson's arm shot out and the fingers closed around Gertrude's throat.

"Remember if I die, August is supposed to mail a package to your precious grandchildren with your location, your multitude of fake identities, proof of your war crimes, a diary our mother kept, and pictures of your wife, mutilated on the floor of this house and Joe is supposed to kill both of them after you've been caught."

Patterson let go, he hadn't been holding her tight enough to do any damage anyway. It was a reaction. Gertrude cackled in his face again.

"Just wait, Gertrude," Patterson told her. "You can only avoid this for so long. I am going to kill you and I'm going to enjoy it. Until then, know that I will find August and I will feed him to his own fucking pets."

"Don't use empty threats against me, Patterson, it doesn't suit you. You're a man of action, not words. Stop trying to be rational. We could have put all this to rest if you had just killed Aislinn Clachan when she joined the Marshals."

Patterson threw his head back and gave a full laugh at that. His body shook with it. Finally, he wiped a tear away.

"If you think killing Aislinn is that easy, you obviously haven't paid attention to her. She's twice as tough as August or me. I couldn't kill her any more than I could fly to the sun with Icarus. Guess what, if she finds August, he's going to regret it. You think I'm a big, bad son of a bitch, she's worse. She's smarter, faster, stronger, and meaner than you can imagine. I've seen what she does up close and personal, she's the real deal." Patterson told his sister. "She's the perfect predator contained by a moral code created by Nyleena. The two are a formidable pair."

"So you've said. I don't see it."

"Because you're blind," Patterson told her. "I have a news flash for you, sister dearest, I'm the one that told my son to make sure Nyleena was a part of Aislinn's life. She has spent many years teaching Aislinn to be a good person, despite her mental state. I think this makes Aislinn even more dangerous."

"You're delusional."

"Am I?" Patterson looked down at her. He wasn't tall, but he had a good six inches on his fat sister. "The perfect predator taught to control herself. When she is able to unleash those violent desires, it makes her enjoy every second and inflict as much pain and horror as possible because she knows she is going to have a long wait before she gets to do it again. Aislinn is my pride and joy because she has the control that I never could manage. August is just a weak, deranged boy who likes to masturbate. If he had any backbone, he'd be doing the eating himself, not using pets to tear his victims to shreds."

Gertrude looked like she might slap him for a second. Anger clouded her face and her hands balled into fists. She wouldn't strike Patterson, she was afraid he'd strike back. He wouldn't kill her, but she knew he would beat the hell out of her and enjoy it. Instead, she turned and walked away.

"I will find him!" Patterson shouted at her back. "And if I don't, Aislinn will!"

Patterson took a breath after his sister had stormed back to her house through the tree line that separated the properties. The tree line that hid the corpses of dozens, if not hundreds, of dead farmhands, that had been butchered for food. The thought sickened him, just as it had all those years ago. Only Gertrude and Virgil had enjoyed the extra meats from of his father's killings. As he thought back to those days, his stomach gurgled. He ran to the side of the house, away from prying eyes, and threw up. It was a reflex that he'd had for decades now.

On days his mother had prepared human flesh, the house had carried a rich, fatty, pork smell.

Depending on how she cooked it depended on whether it tasted more like pork or beef. As a result, he'd become a vegetarian, eating only fish and on rare special occasions, fowl. His children had eaten lots of seafood, despite living in a landlocked state. He never discussed why they couldn't cook beef or pork in the house, just that it made him feel ill.

The night was not going well. He'd lost control. Gertrude knew he was in town and looking for her son. Aislinn still wasn't responding to his notes. She had never welcomed his help in the past, but she had never ignored it either. At his age, he didn't really have time to waste. He considered driving to St. Charles. He was fairly certain he had seen the sniper at the Adams County Fair. He was also fairly certain that the burly black man had not seen him. He'd followed him back to his house in St. Charles, Missouri. He could drive to St. Charles and kill the sniper that had nearly taken out Aislinn or he could stay here and deal with family issues.

Looking through the trees made the decision for him. He would stay. Nina might need his protection. Aislinn might need his help, although she had been ignoring him up to this point.

FIFTEEN

Being in my hometown had stirred up ghosts. Not physical ghosts, but memories that I hadn't thought about in ages. Alone in my room, with nothing to really think about except jaguars, cannibals, and Nazi war criminals living in Argentina, I found myself thinking about these ghosts instead.

One would assume that my lack of emotion would also mean a lack of emotional memories. This was not the case. I did have memories with emotional baggage attached.

After my encounter with Callow, my father would have locked me in a tower and thrown away the key, if he could have. Fortunately for me, that kind of stuff was only legal in fairy tales. Instead, I'd been watched like a hawk. When my parents or siblings weren't around to keep an eye on me, it was my great-uncle.

My great-uncle had been elderly even when I was young and spry. He walked with a stoop and carried a cane. I couldn't remember his face, but I could remember his pants being just a little too short and showing his ankles and black socks. His brown loafers were scuffed and well worn, one heel had broken down more than the other creating a fake limp that I wasn't sure he had ever noticed. He was bald, completely, not a single strand of hair was visible on his scalp. His shirts were always loud, Hawaiian print with bright colors and strange floral designs.

However, all of these details paled in comparison to the sensory memory attached to him. He smoked a pipe. Instead of the stale odor of tobacco, he smelled like cherries. After he died, I learned that his pipe was always filled with cherry tobacco. It was this scent now that filled not just my memory, but my nose. It was as if the old man was sitting in the room with me, enjoying a pipe and telling me stories.

For the first time, I realized I had never known his first name, just his nickname: Chub. The origin of his nickname was just as unknown as his first name to me. However, I had liked him. I had liked spending time with him. I spent hours sitting on the floor or on his couch, listening to him go on and on about life experiences.

My father and Uncle Chub had made some kind of arrangement after my kidnapping. The old man had sold his house and bought a house just a few doors down from us. He walked me to school every morning and home in the afternoons. If my parents and siblings were out, he waited with me for one of them to come home. He was the only person my father had ever allowed to smoke in the house.

Uncle Chub had died just a year before my father. I distinctly remember being more upset at his funeral, than I had been at my father's or my sister's. He had made a dent in my hard exterior where the others hadn't. It seemed strange that I couldn't remember his face considering how important he had been to me as a child. I didn't consider it odd that I couldn't remember what my father or sister looked like, they had been emotional blips in my life.

Surprisingly, the worst part of being a sociopath, was the lack of memory about people. I couldn't remember the last time I had actually thought about my sister. She hadn't been mean to me, there was no sibling rivalry between us. From what I could remember, we'd had a decent relationship. There were no major memories, she had never called the school and told them I was sick so that she could take me to a water park. We'd gone to a few movies together, but I couldn't remember what we had seen. She'd never skipped school to hang out with me when I was sick.

Those things had been done by Nyleena. I had gotten measles once, I was sicker than a dog. Nyleena had been in college at Stanford at the time. She'd ditched class for a week, flying home to help my mom take care of me. My memory of my bout with measles is limited, because of the illness, but I did remember rolling over in my bed one day and throwing up. Nyleena had been there, holding my hair and soothing me. My mom had rushed in a few seconds later with a cool rag to place on my forehead after I stopped tossing my cookies. I remember Nyleena being on Spring Break one year and calling my school to tell them I was sick. It was late May and very hot. She and Uncle Chub made arrangements to meet at my house before school. The old man had given me pocket money I hadn't needed and sent me off with my cousin. We'd gone to World's of Fun in Kansas City.

My father had been furious when we returned late that evening. My mother had just smiled and shook her head. It was Uncle Chub that eventually smoothed things over and got the three of us out of trouble. I believe my mother might have been in on the spur of the moment day trip.

My sister had been named Isabelle. She and Eric had been closer in age and more emotionally connected than I had been with either of them. Even before Callow, I had been closer to Nyleena than my own siblings.

Perhaps it was because she was an only child and I wasn't a rowdy, mouthy child, but a reserved, mature child who was much older than my age would suggest. But she had taken me to movies and bookstores long before I had become a survivor. She had taken me to see Nine Inch Nails when I was only ten. She had spirited me off to New York to see a play on Broadway and take me to the Museum of Natural History when I was eleven.

Surprisingly, after the incident with World's of Fun, my father never complained again about Nyleena taking me anywhere. She was about the only person allowed to take me places other than my parents.

I never questioned it, any of it. I had never noticed the twelve year age difference between us, even when I was a child. As an adult, I usually felt like the older of the two of us. I didn't know why she had become my friend and not just my cousin. I didn't know why she stayed my friend with my sociopathic tendencies and magnet for dangerous people.

It was another mystery of the universe. I would unlock the secrets of black holes before I understood why Nyleena had been my companion since I was five years old. Since it was something I couldn't answer, I choose to ignore the reasoning behind our strange friendship, just letting it exist.

My thoughts were interrupted by another face. This one much younger than my own. The face of a three year old girl that had been plastered all over the news in the weeks before I was abducted. In the pictures, light blue eyes had sparkled from under thick black curls. She had been smiling and holding a kitten. A normal three year old by all accounts, except that she had gone missing and her uncle had been Mr. Callow. She was suspected to be his first victim. Her body had never been found. I didn't know why I remembered her face or the photograph of her that had been in the newspaper and on the TV news. My mind worked in mysterious ways, even for me. I racked my brain for her name and came up empty.

My father had come home from work one night, a day or so after her disappearance. He'd been angry. Not at us, his family, but at life in general. He'd been a God-fearing man; praying at meals and at night, tithing to the church, going to mass when his job allowed. It was the first time I ever remembered him swearing. He'd slammed the door to his home office and shouted "God Damn it!" at the top of his lungs. After that night, he no longer made us pray before meals or came into my room and prayed with me before bed. He swore more often and stopped going to church. That Christmas, he skipped Midnight Mass and then never returned to church again. Somehow, in the short months that Mr. Callow had been committing dreadful acts of violence against the children of the city, my father had lost his faith. He never found it.

While I believed my father was most likely a sociopath, I didn't believe he was like me. I believe he was more capable of feeling. I also believe that at some point, he just gave up. It's hard for a sociopath to feel, it requires effort. The only real emotion is anger. My father was an angry man for the rest of his life. I think after Callow and the other child murders he'd seen, he just stopped trying to be human and started letting the monster take control.

SIXTEEN

"We have body parts!" Xavier shouted through my door. I flopped over in the bed and stared at the ceiling. There were some phrases that required caffeine before being shouted. That was one of them. I hadn't slept well, even for me. My dreams haunted by images of my father. In my dreams, he had a face; a face that I knew was his, but couldn't exactly put together now that I was awake. When I got home, I might ask my mother for a few photos of him and sister. Not being able to remember their faces bothered me, but I wasn't sure why.

Xavier began knocking on the door. It was a formality. He had a key card to my room. Mostly he was giving me time to be prepared so that I didn't kill him when he rushed in.

Which he did about ten seconds or so after he started knocking on the door. His excitement was evident. I glared at him.

"Did you hear me?" He asked.

"Yes," I answered. "What time is it?"

"About seven," Xavier told me.

"In the morning?" I frowned, looking for soda or some sign of caffeine.

"Yes in the morning," Xavier followed my gaze. "There's soda in the car."

"Great, is there one in my room?" I asked.

"I don't know, did you stock any in your room?"

"Good question," I climbed from between the covers. Now that I was standing, I had a better view. There had been a few sodas last night, but I wasn't sure if any of them were left.

"If you drank less soda, you might sleep better," Xavier suggested.

"If I drank less soda, I might kill people," I found a bottle of Coca-Cola on the table. It had been opened, but I was pretty good at tightening the lids back so they didn't go flat. I opened it and downed what was left.

"How much soda do you drink?" Xavier frowned.

"I don't know, three most days, four if they are really long days." I answered. I preferred soda, but tried to curb the addiction by adding in bottles of water. Unfortunately, I couldn't convince myself to drink tap water, which was much cheaper. Also, the water had to be flavored. I'd found two brands of flavored water that I could drink. One wasn't all that great for me, but I loved it. The other was better for me and I liked it a lot less. "I'm usually too busy to drink more than that."

"Maybe you should drink Sprite or something in the evenings," Xavier suggested. I pulled an empty 7-Up bottle from the trash. "Well, what do I know then?"

"Exactly. So, do you want to tell me about the body parts?" I asked.

"They're body parts, what is there to tell?"

With that, I grabbed clothes and went to take a shower. The shower was very quick, just long enough to lather up soap and get my brain into functioning mode. I ran on pure instincts for the first hour I was awake, unless I showered.

As I pulled my hair up, still wet, into a messy bun that would require work later in the day, I caught a glimpse of my reflection. The face that stared back at me was a stranger. It always was. The scars, eyes, and hair were mine, but the rest of my features, weren't part of my memory. The skin was still tanned from summer. The eyes had dark circles around the bottoms of the lids. Three small scars were near the lips, created when my teeth went through it in my younger days.

I spent roughly thirty seconds staring at the reflection that stared back. A reflection that was me and yet, not me. There were glimpses of my mother in my face, but the dark hair and dark eyes were entirely those of my father. My mother had blue eyes and light brown hair. Genetics told me my father had to have had dark hair and brown eyes.

Hair up and clothing on, I left the bathroom and the stranger in the mirror. I had never asked Malachi about his feelings on his reflection. I wondered if he felt as disassociated from it as I did.

"You look pale," Xavier frowned.

"I always look pale," I answered.

"No, you look like you, overly tanned with bags under your eyes from not sleeping. Right now, you look pale, wan, like you've seen a ghost."

"I don't know what to tell you." I shrugged.

"And now your color is returning," Xavier frowned harder. "This has something to do with the reason you don't have mirrors in your house, doesn't it?"

"I have mirrors."

"You have one mirror, in the guest bathroom."

"It's a mirror."

"One day, Lucas and I will pry it out of you. You should just make it easy on yourself and tell us what you see in the mirror."

"I see," I thought about it. "I see what you see."

"For some reason, I doubt that very much," Xavier ushered me out of the room.

Xavier had said body parts and I had expected an arm, maybe a set of legs. I was staring at six waterlogged extra-large duffle bags. Each sat on its own table. From what I understood, their recovery from the Missouri River had been difficult and one person was being treated for exposure and hypothermia.

The Missouri River is dirty, smelly, and unpleasant on good days. On bad days, it was dirty, smelly, unpleasant, and body parts bobbed to the surface and got stuck in the ice that formed near the edges. However, how ice formed anywhere in the river amazed me. There was actually a limit on the number of fish you could eat from it because of pollution.

Of course, it was a favorite dumping site for serial killers in Kansas City as well as other cities along its winding route. I wasn't sure why the Missouri seemed to hide more bodies than the Mississippi, but it did.

Anything that spent any time in the water, smelled. It was a strange, dank, dirty, oppressive odor that smelled of fish, decay, and only the gods knew what else. The fact that the body parts were decomposing added to the aggressive odor that permeated the bags and filled my nostrils.

"Good grief," Gabriel exclaimed as he entered the room behind us. "I thought the cold slowed decomp."

"It does," I answered. "That distinct aroma is from the water in the river. There's a reason I would never swim in it as a child. Even then it reminded me more of sewage than water."

"It isn't that bad," Xavier said.

"Your nose must be dead," I answered.

"No, yours is just extra good." Xavier countered. "Ok, let's see what's in the bags."

Xavier opened the first bag. The arm he pulled out had definitely been in the water a while. The bag had protected it from the scavengers, but it had lost its color and sheen, making it appear waxy. There were marks all over it. Some were definitely human bite marks. I frowned.

By the time he emptied the bag, we had a head, torso, both arms, hands attached, both legs, sans feet, and an assembled body. However, saying we had a full body was incorrect. We had most of a full body. There were definitely some important pieces missing.

The first noticeable problem was that the torso had not only been cut above the waist, but it had been sliced open in front. All the organs were missing. The ribs and back had been cleaned, meaning the flesh and muscle was gone and bone was visible. The same was true of the thighs. The femurs were there, but only the ends had any tissue left.

Once you stopped noticing the very obvious missing chunks of the body, the smaller ones became apparent. Small and medium sized wounds covered the arms, legs, face, and torso. There seemed to be an equal number of human bites and bites from something larger.

Xavier and I exchanged looks. Neither of us said the "c" word out loud. Technically, people did bite others hard enough to take out chunks of flesh and spit it out. A famous boxer had done it with an ear during a match.

"What are the chances those were made postmortem?" Gabriel asked.

"Why bite someone that's dead?" I asked.

"I'll have to examine them," Xavier said.

"How long?" Gabriel asked.

"A couple of hours," Xavier answered.

"Quick estimate on how many bite marks are there?" Gabriel pressed.

"Human or other?" Xavier countered.

"Human," Gabriel was staring at the corpse like it was going to get up and strangle him.

"Over sixty," Xavier answered.

"That is a lot," I frowned. "Why bite someone over sixty times?" As soon as the question popped out of my mouth, I wished I could shove it back in. I knew the answer. A fetish biter might bite over sixty times, but not all of them would remove chunks of flesh. That was hard on the jaws, unless you were used to eating raw meats. The average person takes 90 bites a day for their total meal intake. I didn't know why I knew that, I just did. If the majority of your diet is raw meat, that's where the most bites are going to come from. A human could live on meat alone, as long as it wasn't rabbit. It wasn't recommended, but a healthy human could provide a cannibal with a pretty good diet.

"Hey," Xavier said, "this one didn't have a crushed skull." He pointed to the x-ray of the bag. His gloved fingers played over the decaying flesh.

"How'd he die?" Gabriel asked.

"I'm not Houdini, I can't just make answers appear from thin air, I'm going to have to examine him," Xavier snipped.

"Fine, call when the two of you find something," Gabriel left. John practically ran over him as they both exited.

"Cannibal," Xavier said to me.

"Eating is the only reason I can come up with for taking over sixty bites out of a single person."

"Me too. On the flip side, he didn't die of the bites. His throat was crushed."

"Is that supposed to make it better or worse?"

"Better," Xavier put on the goggles. "I can tell you now that some of these were post-mortem, but others, well, this kid was alive for them."

"Of the six cannibal cases we've dealt with, none have eaten people raw. They've all cooked them, like food."

"Yeah," Xavier poked a rod into one of the larger holes. "So, I'm looking at these other marks and they are definitely not human. Who eats raw meat with an animal?"

"Maybe the human fed the leftovers to the animal."

"I don't think so," Xavier looked at me. "This one, he was still alive when the creature bit him. Since some of the human bites took place after he died and some of the animal bites happened while he was alive..."

"They fed together," I cringed as I finished Xavier's sentence.

"Do you want to tell John over dinner or do you want me to do it?" Xavier gave a snort of laughter. Yes, we were still in the hazing phase with Poor John.

SEVENTEEN

"Because raw meat is so incredibly hard to chew, humans tend to cook it first," Xavier said, cutting into a steak that bled profusely. "Seasoning, tenderizing, and cooking, all make meat more palatable. Otherwise, the muscles in our jaws would be very powerful, like a tiger or crocodile. However, they aren't, so we've had to invent ways to eat meat."

It had been John's suggestion to go for steak, so I had obliged and taken him to George's Pizza and Steakhouse. Columbia, like most cities, had a no smoking policy in all public buildings, including bars and restaurants. However, George's was just outside city limits and much to everyone's chagrin, you could smoke before, during and after your meal. But they had good pizza and good steaks.

If I had been slightly less of a jerk, I would have taken them to G&D Pizza and Steakhouse. It was all owned by the same family, but you couldn't smoke in G&D. Of course, G&D would have been busier, as it was, there were only a handful of people, most of them men, hanging around the restaurant.

I was eating a pizza. Gabriel and John had ordered steak. John had since pushed his well-done hunk of sirloin away and was looking a little green. Gabriel kept at his, not letting Xavier's conversation bother him. Although, he had ordered his steak medium well, which was unusual for Gabriel.

"Also, given the number of bites," I continued. "The person has to be feeding. We counted ninety-two on one victim, not counting the predator bites. That is not a person with a fetish, that is a person enjoying a single meal. On average, a person takes one hundred bites a day. If you only eat one meal a day, then it would make sense that the person gorged at the single feeding."

"And it isn't like the person woke up one morning and decided that eating raw human flesh was a good idea," Xavier interrupted. "They've been at it for a long time. They must have massive jaw muscles. Humans have to develop those muscles to get to the point where taking that many bites of raw meat is even possible. Not to mention chewing the stuff."

"Is this a theory you're working with?" Gabriel asked.

"Everything's a theory until it isn't," I answered. "Of course, there are some problems with the theory. For example, we think the human and predator are feeding at the same time and I can't imagine why. Most large predators are not keen on sharing food, unless they're pack animals, but cats tend not to be pack animals and the skull crushing kind of leads away from dogs. A bear or crocodile might do it, but a crocodile wouldn't leave such neat bite marks. A domesticated bear might share, but honestly, I can't think of a single predator that I would want to share a meal with, especially not that close. That's like eating off the same plate."

"Another problem is the length of time it would take to build up jaws strong enough to take chunks of human flesh out, chew it, swallow it, and go back for more," Xavier jumped back into the conversation. "We agree that this would take conditioning. This person didn't start out eating people, they started out eating other things and moved up to people."

"How does this jive with the case from twenty-five years ago?" Gabriel asked.

"I'm not sure, according to the notes I've read, there were no human bite marks on the single body they found. Of course, if the river was the dump zone then too, there's no telling. The river hides most sins, at least for a while." I thought back to a rash of drownings that had happened in the Missouri River during the same time. Six people in three months, it didn't seem like a lot, but it had been to me. All the victims had been young, like I had been, and it seemed disproportionately high compared to the number of swimmers. However, the current was strong and swift, the bottom littered with debris, both natural and man-made, in hindsight, it seemed easier to go missing than survive a swim in the muddy Missouri.

"We have experts coming in tomorrow to give us more information about the human and animal bite marks," Xavier finished the conversation as he polished off the steak.

"Anything you'd like to add?" Gabriel looked at me.

"The pizza's good," I answered.

"I should have ordered a salad." John groaned.

"You get used to it, eventually." I smiled at him.

After dinner, we returned to the hotel. As I have said many times, I would rather be busting down doors and breaking skulls than investigating. Investigating required patience and finesse, I had neither. We'd made preliminary identifications on two of the victims dragged from the bottom of the river. However, we weren't handling the notifications, we weren't exactly "family friendly." Families thought we were cold, callous, and occasionally, crass. Once in a while, Gabriel would have the hellish task of dealing with families, but for the rest of us, families were off-limits. I was fine with this. I didn't understand my own family, understanding other families was impossible. I tended to find the faults and ugliness just beneath the surface of grief and poke at it until it reared its mean head. I'd done that in Alaska and found a serial killer, but I'd done it in Mobile, Alabama and nearly gotten shot by a woman who had been aiming at her husband after he had molested her daughter. A daughter that had run away because of the abuse and that I had taken all of about three minutes to figure out once inside the family. Monsters came in all shapes and sizes, I brought out the worst in them and they couldn't hide behind their masks for very long when I was in a room.

There was a soft, polite rap at my door. The knocker gave it twenty seconds and pushed it open. Gabriel looked tired. His face was pale, making the spattering of freckles more noticeable. His normally kind and sparkling eyes were dull.

"Stop being mean to John," he told me taking a seat at the table. I pulled out my headphones, despite having turned the music off the moment he knocked.

"That is a monumental task," I answered.

"Ok, consider it an order," Gabriel met my gaze and held it, daring me to look away.

"Fine, I'll consider it an order, it will still be a monumental task."

"Just because he's new and you haven't learned to trust him?"

"I still feel like he's an interloper. He isn't half as entertaining as Michael and he doesn't like me much."

"How incredibly perceptive of you," Gabriel smirked, keeping eye contact.

"I know I'm a pain in the behind."

"If I was in his shoes, I wouldn't like you very much either."

"Yes, yes," I waved dismissively, breaking eye contact. I could be defiant to the ends of the earth and he knew it. Giving up just a little bit, letting him be the dominant, kept the group working harmoniously and I preferred the harmony. I could get into a pissing contest with Gabriel, but it would upset the balance, things would slide into the rabbit hole that I still secretly feared.

"Good," Gabriel continued to sit.

"What's on your mind other than my being an ass?" I asked after several minutes of quiet. Gabriel and I had a rapport. It wasn't the same that

I had with Xavier or Lucas. Lucas watched out for me, feeling some need to play knight to my damsel. Xavier treated me like a co-conspirator, in an elaborate spy-ring or some such adventure. Gabriel was my equal. He understood he was alpha only because I wanted him to be. He respected what it meant to both of us and treated me accordingly.

"I've been thinking about what Xavier said, about building up the muscles in the jaws," Gabriel frowned. "How long would that take?"

"It would depend on a lot of factors. Someone with dentures could do it faster, because they wouldn't have sensitivity in their teeth. Starting out young would help, because the teeth that they broke while building up those muscles would be replaced by stronger, permanent teeth. If they started young enough, by the time their adult teeth started growing in, they'd be able to rip out good sized chunks from just about anything. Also, chewing on leather or some other material would help. Part of the reason dog toys are made of rawhide is to help them keep their jaw strength."

"Well, I have a crazy theory," Gabriel said. "What if the kidnappings and murders from twenty-five years ago are related to our current case? What if he was kidnapping children and feeding them to his pet jaguar, but found a child the jaguar didn't kill for whatever reason?"

"Jaguars don't live long in captivity. In twenty-five years, he could easily have gone through four if not five jaguars. How do you keep acquiring jaguars that don't kill a human interloper, but has no problem eating other people?"

"The human would have to be a pretty successful survivor," Gabriel sighed.

"Someone like Malachi," I pursed my lips together. "Under the right conditions, a human can become feral. It's normally with dogs, wolves, apes, pack animals, but a single female jaguar is more willing to allow another female to live in its territory. Especially, if the female is not the alpha, a condition that could happen if the person was a psychopath. A few fights for dominance, the human wins, the animal becomes the submissive. However, it would be nearly impossible to create a feral human."

"Nearly impossible." Gabriel repeated the phrase.

"It happens, but it happens in nature, not artificial environments. For every one feral child, there are dozens, if not hundreds, that are killed by whatever finds them. To create one in an artificial environment would require no human interaction. Meals, medicine, even watching them, results in some interaction. The child would grow up stunted, I can think of a famous case of this, in Germany, but the child wasn't feral."

"The famous case in Germany?" Gabriel pressed.

"A boy was locked in a room all his life, feed through a door, given sparse toys, he grew up to be timid of humans, but he recognized himself as such. He was eventually released from his prison and quickly integrated with society, until he was stabbed to death. We'll leave it at that because that's where facts give way to conspiracy theories. But a feral human wouldn't recognize themselves as such, they'd relate more to the animal that raised them. Of the few feral humans ever found, they did poorly in human society, because they are more animal than human. Proof that we are all just one step away from devolving."

EIGHTEEN

There are rarely places to sit in a morgue, this one was no exception. The overly bright room that reeked of antiseptic had two stools on rollers. I sat on a stainless steel table that had been covered with a clean sheet. There were other tables in the room, but they were all filled with decaying body parts. The smell of decay permeated the antiseptic, giving the room a terrible odor. My nose had peppermint balm under it, making my upper lip tingle and keeping me from getting a migraine from the mingled scents.

Xavier and the odontologist were working on bite marks. I was not, however, my presence seemed to be required, so I had stacks of folders in front of me. I'd spent the morning sorting them into piles by age and sex. They were all the missing persons reported in Boone County, Missouri over the last thirty years. I had to admit, there was a staggering number.

Mostly, I was looking for young children and teens, of both sexes. Everyone else went into a different pile. So far, I had over a hundred case files sorted into the "important" piles. The stack had gotten smaller, but it didn't feel like it had dwindled much.

Technically, this was a "John Job." He was the geek that searched files and did magical things on his computer to sort them by relevancy. However, someone had decided it needed a more hands on approach, so I had hard copies of the files to look at.

"I'm not sure I'll get a good impression from any of these bites," the odontologist said loudly. His voice held a pitch that said not only was he frustrated, but horrified.

"Why?" I asked, ready for a break, however brief.

"They aren't clean bite marks," Xavier answered for the odontologist.

"Ah, more like worry marks than bite marks," I sighed. "I could see that."

"If she could guess that from sitting on a table looking at God knows what, why am I here?" The odontologist asked.

"Because I can't make bite impressions," I answered. "Besides, I didn't know they were going to be worked out instead of just torn out, I've never eaten a person. But now that you've said it, it makes sense. Even strong jaws would require a little work to tear through skin, muscles, ligaments, nerves, and tendons. Neanderthal might have been able to accomplish it, but Homo sapien sapiens, probably can't."

"Who says the sapien twice?" Xavier asked.

"I do," I answered.

"Yeah, only you," Xavier shook his head.

"I am technically correct." I frowned at him. "Try on a thinner area, where teeth would scrape bone, like the face or arms."

"Teeth scrapes on bone do not give a good impression," the odontologist told me.

"Maybe not, but if teeth scrape bone there, you might be able to find a good impression nearby where teeth collided with bone. Like when you eat ribs." I offered the only example that came to mind. "You don't mean to bite the rib bone, but sometimes it happens."

"Oh, the scapula might have something," Xavier became animated. I left him and the odontologist to it and went back to looking at files.

I opened one and just stopped. The picture that stared back at me was of a smiling young girl missing one of her front teeth. She had a large bruise on her chin and a scrape near her hairline. Long brown hair was pulled up into a loose braid, strands had begun to break free and framed her face. Large brown eyes sparkled with a smile that was both genuine and happy. The file had been marked "Gennifer Evans," but the photo was of me. I had been a cute kid, but I didn't remember ever being that happy. I didn't know Gennifer Evans, she had gone missing after I had killed Callow and was a few years younger than me. I wasn't sure how my picture had ended up in her folder, but I removed it. I'd already found my case file, wedged carelessly into another, one that had never been found but was suspected of being a victim of Callow.

     "Whoa," Xavier said from over my shoulder. "Add a few scars, some frown lines, and a tan and that could be you."

     "That is me," I told him.

     "Really?" Xavier looked at me. "Huh, you're right. You had a lot fewer scars, but what's with the bruise?"

     "I fell off a bicycle, scraped my face and scalp, bruised my chin, and all two days before picture day. I went missing the following week. I have no idea how this picture even found its way into a file, let alone the wrong file. My parents wouldn't have had it when I escaped." I thought about it, then looked at the folder again. "If I had to make an educated guess, I would say my father did it, but I do not know why. I didn't know the girl whose file I found it in and my case file was in another folder."

"Why would your dad do that?" Xavier asked.

"There are many things I don't know about my father, his work life is one of them," I answered. This wasn't because my father was enigmatic, but because my father had gone off the deep end. I had once been his "little girl," but things had changed after Callow. Our relationship had gotten cold and distant after I returned home, now a killer at the tender age of eight. I had never dwelt on it before, but it had changed. There were no more bedtime stories, he didn't pray with me at night or encourage me to find faith and meaning. He hadn't taken me anywhere or allowed me out of his sight when he was home. While my mother was encouraging me to make friends, my father was banning them from the house for sleepovers or even birthday parties. The rotating poker game my father had loved had stopped rotating and become a permanent fixture in our house. He became overbearing and oppressive at times, monitoring my movements with every resource he could muster. He never called me his "little girl" again. Perhaps he hadn't been protecting me, but protecting the world from me.

"I got one!" The odontologist suddenly shouted. Xavier jumped. I turned to stare at the man like he had just manifested maggots from thin air. One thing about being a sociopath, I didn't have much of a startle reflex. I was more annoyed that he had interrupted my reverie.

"Great, what does it tell us?" Xavier asked.

"Well, if you can find a person, I can tell you if it's a match," the odontologist answered. "Otherwise, it's just a piece of evidence. One molar is chipped, but not badly. They could use braces." He gave me a sideways glance at this. I took out the dentures on top and frowned.

"Braces always seemed like a waste," I answered, putting the dentures back in. "I've lost a lot of teeth over the years. Straightening them would have been pointless."

"Are you always combative?" He asked me.

"Yes," I answered flatly.

"It isn't personal," Xavier stepped in. "She's like this with everyone until you get to know her really well, then it's worse." Xavier smiled at his own joke. I raised an eyebrow and said nothing.

"I see. Well, that's about all I can give you. An educated guess says that all the bite marks are from a single person. You can see evidence of the chipped tooth in a couple of different places, the size is roughly the same and the way they worked loose the flesh with their teeth is similar."

"Similar, not exact?" I asked.

"It will never be exact. If you gnaw on a hundred bones, each will be slightly different based on the size of the bone, the amount of tissue adhering to it, the effort you put into the bite, and honestly, your overall mood can impact it."

"Close enough?" I pressed.

"It's all very close, I'd give it a 97% chance that all the bites were made by the same person."

"I'll take 97%," Xavier jumped back into the conversation, steering it away from any doubts I might have. "Thank you for taking the time to help with this."

"You're welcome, I hope you catch him soon," the doctor nodded at me and shook hands with Xavier. I gave a small wave.

"Did you learn anything from the files?" Xavier came back over to me.

"Maybe," I answered cryptically. "There are a lot of missing persons in the county. If we widened the search, I can't imagine how much larger the number would grow to be. I can tell you that over the years, there have been increases in missing persons all around the same age and gender. It goes on for a few months then it stops."

"How so?" Xavier asked.

"Well, we have the group of girls, progressively younger, from twenty-five years ago, then we have another cluster, this time boys, progressively younger about twenty years ago. In the interim, there are boys and girls that go missing and might or might not be related. Then we jump ahead and sixteen years ago, a group of girls went missing again, this time they were about twelve when they went missing and got progressively younger. So, it goes in spurts. Some could be attributed to other killers, but the progressively younger bothers me. Also, there's been a handful of feet found in the county with no bodies. Some have belonged to boys, some girls, some young children, some teenagers, one had a tattoo on it, and so I'm guessing that one was a little older. It's almost like he's experimenting to find the right age and sex."

"Meat ages different," Xavier said. "You don't want a steak from a cow that's got one foot in the grave."

"Crude, but accurate," I said. "I think the deviation is about finding the right age and gender that produces the best food."

"By the way," Xavier quickly snatched the photo of me. "You were adorable."

"That inspires me with terror," I climbed down from the table.

NINETEEN

Twenty-nine file folders were spread out on the spare bed in my hotel room. Twenty-nine folders that held significance to my father, but I didn't understand why, yet. Each had a notation somewhere within the folder. The abbreviation for August. However, only one of them had disappeared during that month and it wasn't the first missing persons' case.

August had been the month my brother had been born. My niece, Cassie, had an August birthday, but Cassie. I stopped. I couldn't remember whether Cassie was born before or after my father died. Honestly, I couldn't remember the exact month my father had died. My brother had climbed a tower a few years after his death, but a few years, could mean that Elle was pregnant with Cassie when my father died.

The trial had been long and drawn out. They'd filed multiple motions to change the venue because Boone County didn't have a proper jury pool. A crack addict killing a pair of cops with an AK-47 after killing two women, one of whom he had beaten to death, had been major news. After the venue was changed to Greene County, there was a fiasco with mental competency. He'd seen doctor after doctor after doctor. He'd been declared incapacitated, then fit, then incapacitated again, finally, a specialist had signed forms saying that being high wasn't enough to impair his judgment and make him think that killing was socially acceptable. After a year and a half, a mistrial was declared and another one set. A year after that, the bastard had walked on a technicality. Something about evidence tampering, I never got the full story. Two days later, my brother had climbed to the top of a building outside the Greene County jail and began picking off prisoners.

Now that trial had been quick. Six weeks to send my brother to the Fortress, two and a half years to let a cop killer go free. The world didn't make much sense.

I tried to remember how old I was when my father had been shot. I couldn't pinpoint an exact date, meaning I wasn't sure how old I was. I called Malachi.

"What's up?" His voice was gruff, I had interrupted something, again.

"How old was I when my dad died?" I asked.

"Thirteen," Malachi answered and hung up. Thirteen explained why I felt I had immediately gone to college after it had all ended. I texted a "thank you" to Malachi.

So, I had been thirteen when my father had died. Cassie was fourteen years younger than me or maybe she was only thirteen years younger than me. I thought about last summer, I had thought she was fourteen, I had been twenty-eight. However, time wasn't exactly my friend. If people didn't tell me how old I was, I would forget. She hadn't been driving a car, but that didn't mean she wasn't old enough to drive a car. I hadn't gotten my license at sixteen, I'd just started college and there were enough changes going on in my life without worrying about driving. I'd gotten it on summer vacation after my freshman year.

It was issues like these that I kept secret. Nyleena was aware that I couldn't hold onto the passage of time. But she was alone in that respect. She reminded me every year how old I would turn on my birthday and sent me reminders of other birthdays and the ages of the birthday celebrators.

Figuring out what August had represented to my father was maddening. I stared at the notations, trying to will it to give up its secret. The twenty-nine cases held their tongues. The first group of girls was in it, the second group, all boys, was in it, but there were others. The others were missing persons of different ages and genders that were sporadic.

I tore my gaze from the pictures and names and stared at the ceiling. Eliminating the eleven that were clustered left me with eighteen. I double checked, two disappearances a year were marked with the Aug. reference. One in January, one in July, every year that my father had been making cryptic notations on the files. I pulled the other case files back out and began searching for missing persons in January and July each year. There was a cluster. I'd found the pattern. I could pull out missing persons for each year for the two months. Only problem was they were completely different victims from those in the clusters. In my father's files, every January it was a homeless person that went missing, gender and age, meant nothing. In July, it was a male, but the ages were going up. Two years ago, it had been a 22 year old male, the year before that, the male had been 21. They all had similar features; blonde hair, blue eyes, athletic build. I didn't know what that meant, but it had to mean something.

My options were limited, it was late, well after midnight. My team would all be in bed, sleeping. Some more peacefully than others, to be sure, but they didn't need late night calls from me. I called Malachi again.

"I'm busy," he growled into the phone.

"Are you with someone special?" I asked.

"If by special, you mean staking out the house of a serial killer, then yes," he answered.

"Oh, weren't you just on a case?" I thought for a moment. "What sort of serial killer?"

"The sort that kills people, Aislinn. And yes, there were two in this town, now there's one and I'm watching his house. So what do you want?"

"You're very grouchy."

"I'm fairly certain he has a victim inside right this second and I can't break down the door and rescue her."

"Why?"

"Because he is a politician."

"So?"

"Despite the fact that the Marshals have carte blanche to do as they please, the FBI still has some protocols it has to follow and until I hear a scream or some other sign of distress, my hands are tied."

"You don't have some random scream from a woman on an audio recording that you can play and claim you heard a scream?"

"That would be illegal."

"Are you close enough that I could come break down the door for you?"

"I appreciate your futile attempts to help, but is there a reason you called me, again?"

"Yes, I have a cannibal with very little victim preference and he's been at it for a long, long time. And everyone I know but you is asleep."

"We are just as picky about our food as we are our sexual partners," Malachi answered.

"Really? Does that mean you aren't picky about food? Because I'm pretty sure I've seen you send your food back when it wasn't right, multiple times."

"Did you just call me a man-whore?"

"I thought I was being subtle by implying you were pickier about food than what girl warmed your bed at night."

"Like a freight train, Aislinn Cain." My name rolled off Malachi's tongue as if coated in chocolate.

"Ok, Dr. Seuss."

"It did rhyme, didn't it?" Malachi paused as if lost in thought. "Fine, perhaps some people are pickier about food than bed partners and some are pickier about bed partners than food. However, if I was eating someone, I'd want to make damn sure they didn't have a disease before I started cutting off bits to throw in a crock-pot."

"That is an interesting point, thanks," I hung up again. My imagination had conjured an image of a hand sticking out of a crock-pot cooker, but it was the disease thing that struck a chord. Eating people raw was definitely not for the faint of heart or for germophobes.

One of these things was certainly not like the other. Homeless people were easy victims for the right sort of predator, but they were also the most likely to carry diseases.

Unfortunately, my thoughts quickly turned and instead of having great thoughts like Holmes in *The Speckled Band,* it became a myriad of mixed meanderings more in the style of *The Island of Dr. Moreau.* I wasn't sure how the pieces fit together, but my imagination was conjuring blonde haired jaguar men. I didn't know exactly why I thought the blonde haired men were being used for breeding purposes, but the thought had taken hold. That left the children and the homeless people left unexplained. I was willing to overlook the fact that men, blonde haired or not, could not breed with jaguars to create a super-race of half breeds ready to take over the world.

Eating homeless people might boost the immune system. Eating kids might be like a treat. Eating the blondes might be more black-widowish. That would mean our cannibal was a woman. I didn't know of any female cannibals in modern history. Those were my last disturbing thoughts before sleep began to call my name.

Surprisingly, I didn't dream of cannibals or even serial killers. I dreamed of Nyleena. Not a normal, holy crap, she's been hurt, dream either. I dreamed that we were on a road trip, in August and she kept running over mailboxes while talking on her phone, despite my screams from the passenger's seat. She just ignored me and kept running over the mailboxes. I wondered if I was a ghost.

"Come on sleepy head, the animal specialist is meeting with us in an hour," Xavier's voice woke me up. I opened my eyes and found my room completely empty. I sat up, rubbed my eyes, and then looked again. There was still no Xavier. I got up and checked the bathroom. No Xavier in there either. I checked my phone, not so much as a text message.

The clock told me it was almost dawn. I tore off the patch I wore, put on a robe and slippers, and grabbed my emergency pack of cigarettes. Outside, the air was frigid. My nose instantly got cold. My toes started to tingle despite the slippers. I lit the cigarette wondering if I really wanted it that bad.

As I stood there, I remembered the zoologist had come the day before. He'd confirmed the bites were that of a large cat, most likely a jaguar. So,

why had I dreamed about him waking me up?
Another question to which I didn't have the answer.

Gabriel came running outside. His face was
flushed with color. He handed me a stack of
clothing, including shoes.

"You can dress in the car," Xavier said,
coming out behind him.

We had a lead.

FAMILY

Patterson stood outside the door of his sister's condo. He hesitated. He wasn't sure whether he wanted to knock or not. Nina was not going to be happy to see him. She might call the police or she might shoot him. Or she might welcome him in and give him a cup of tea. Her moods were more regulated than Gertrude's, but she was still prone to unpredictability.

"I'm tired of you lurking," Nina opened the door as she spoke. Patterson looked surprised. "They called me and told me I had a visitor almost ten minutes ago. Since no one really comes to see me, especially older gentlemen, I knew it had to be you. Shut the door behind you."

"Nina," Patterson followed her inside, shutting the door behind him.

"I take it that Gertrude has finally tired of me and you're here to finish the job." Nina smiled. "Just can't wait another couple of months, I'm too much of a drain on the resources of the family trust. Old bitch."

"I'm not here to hurt you Nina," Patterson motioned to a chair. Nina sat down. Patterson sat across from her on the couch. "I just heard about your cancer. I'm sorry."

"Patterson, we both know that sympathy is beyond you, drop the act." Nina sipped a cup of coffee that smelled strongly of alcohol. "What do you want?"

"I'm here to find August." Patterson said. "He's alive, Nina and he's still killing."

"You're alive," Nina left off the last part. It hung unspoken between them in the air.

"Did you know?" Patterson asked.

"I've suspected for the last year or so, but I don't have proof." Nina sighed. "Do you want coffee or tea?"

"Coffee would be fine," Patterson answered. "Why have you suspected?"

"When the feet started turning up again, I got suspicious." Nina answered from her tiny kitchen. She was living in a small condo in an assisted living facility. It was actually a hospice for those that could still get around, but neither wanted to dwell on that. "So, you're here to kill August."

"That was my original plan," Patterson admitted. "I know it isn't a job that anyone wants to talk about, but as long as he's alive, Gertrude will do what she can to protect him and he'll keep killing."

"So, this is about justice?" Nina brought him a cup of coffee. It also smelled of alcohol. Patterson sipped it, feeling the creamy Bailey's swirl through his mouth with the bitter black liquid.

"No, it's about revenge, plain and simple." Patterson hesitated. "And Aislinn's on the case now."

"Protecting her from finding out the secrets of our past or from the deranged desires of August?"

"Both."

"She doesn't need you to hold her hand, Patterson," Nina scolded him. "She has grown into quite the woman. She has all your strengths and a different set of weaknesses, but I don't see her weaknesses as real weaknesses."

"I think they make her stronger than I ever could have been." Patterson hung his head. "I look back and think if I had been as strong as Aislinn, we wouldn't have these secrets."

"Maybe, but maybe we'd just have a whole different set of secrets. It has never been your fault that our parents were crazy. Or that we couldn't escape them."

"I should have done more for you."

"No, Patterson, you shouldn't. If you had, I would have ended up like Lila and you'd have one more death to regret."

"You think I feel regret?"

"I see it on your face. Even with your mental condition, I see the pain on your face every time her name is mentioned. I know that's why you have latched onto to Nyleena and Aislinn. They remind you of her."

"They do remind me of her. And you." Patterson looked at Nina. "How sick are you?"

"Very. Nothing they can do but give me painkillers to help me be comfortable. I think the girls should know. I think they should be informed of exactly what we've been hiding, exactly why you killed Lila. Aislinn is bound to figure some of it out if she catches August. She's so smart, Patterson, I wish you could really appreciate how smart she is and with Nyleena, they are going to start putting the pieces together. You can't hide anything from those two girls."

"I do appreciate it Nina. When they work together, they are unstoppable."

"They remind me of us," Nina said. "When we were young, I mean. Before the world went to hell in a hand basket. I could guide you, help you navigate the crazy world you lived in, knowing that I was the only thing keeping you from sliding over the edge. Then you meet Lila and she was so good for you. She knew exactly what you felt and yet, loved you anyway. She was the best thing to ever happen to you. I've considered killing Gertrude for that. And she didn't treat me like I was Lizzie Borden. She was good for both of us."

"If I could have done something to clear you of that, I would have," Patterson told his youngest sister. Gertrude and she were twins, but Gertrude was seventeen minutes older. When their parents had been found, there were lots of rumors about it being staged and the suspicion had fell on Nina. They could never prove it, but most still suspected her.

"I could have told someone," Nina looked at him. "I have a favor to ask of you Patterson."

"Anything," Patterson answered.

"After I've had a talk with the girls, because the two of them are strong enough to handle it and understand it, I want you to kill me. It's only going to get worse. Nothing messy, nothing painful, just two shots to the head to make sure that I die quickly and painlessly."

"I can't," Patterson told her.

"Please Patterson, I'm begging. I've tried and I just don't have the courage to kill myself. But you could surprise me and put me out of my misery."

"Ok, Nina, I'll do it, if you do me a favor. Help Aislinn to catch August."

"I've told Malachi that you're The Butcher."

"I know." Patterson said. "I bought a bunch of spy gear last year. That's how I found out about August being alive. Gertrude's been tapping your phones for years, I decided to return the favor."

"You aren't mad?"

"I was at first, but I know why you did it. There are still some people on my list, but I'm getting old, too old to continue this. Once Gertrude and August are stopped and hopefully, silenced, then I won't mind ending it."

"These secrets are killing us."

"Yes, they are. They should die with us."

"I disagree. I think Nyleena and Aislinn need to know why you were a killer. I think they need to know why we were as damaged as we were."

"They'll think less of us."

"The others might, but not the girls. If their opinions change, it will be for the better, not the worst. You underestimate them."

"I trust you. If you believe they should know, then you should tell them."

"Thank you, Patterson. Now, I just need to figure out how to tell them. Both have offered to get me out of this nuthouse and move me to KC to be closer to them and Aislinn's mother. Maybe I'll take them up on it. Trapped in a car with me for two hours, I can tell them everything. You can kill me after we arrive."

"You want me to follow you?"

"You already follow Aislinn." Nina frowned at him. "It won't be hard. I'm not sure about killing me in front of the girls though."

"I'll think on the best method. They live in secure housing, I won't be able to break in while you sleep."

"Plus, the moment the girls find out you're The Butcher and about my cancer, they are going to stick to me like glue."

"This won't be easy," Patterson finally looked up and made eye contact with Nina. "And I don't just mean the girls. Killing you will be hard for me Nina."

"I know, but you'll do it, won't you? To spare me more pain?"

"I will," Patterson stood up. "If I can. Blake's a good hunter."

"He is," Nina nodded. "But that's not why I told him."

"Then why did you tell him?"

"Because Aislinn and Nyleena needed to know. Malachi will tell them. You've hid this long, maybe it's time to come out of the shadows."

"I'll go to The Fortress. I'm an old man who still has a list."

"I can buy you time with Malachi."

"How?" Patterson asked.

"I'll tell him about Unger and August."

"You believe that's enough?"

"Yeah, I do. He isn't as controlled as Aislinn and he hated his grandfather. The thought of having an uncle just like him will not make him very happy. He'll drag his feet and you can slip away from him, for now. He or Aislinn will eventually catch you though."

"I know," Patterson looked at her for another few minutes. "However, I also believe they will be humane about it."

TWENTY

It wasn't a lead. It was a guy in full tactical gear with a home-made flame-thrower in one hand and a Glock in the other. He'd shot an officer and torched a K-9 unit. The officer was still in the "no-go zone," an imaginary line that separated everyone from the armed assailant. The dog had managed to limp back and was being taken to a vet.

The assailant was wearing a pumped up version of standard police tactical gear, complete with Kevlar suit and reinforcement plates. As a matter of fact, I had a very similar suit. It contained plates in the chest, back and abdomen areas. The legs and arms had a few extra layers of woven material. The helmet was shock absorbent and made of a polymer and coated with Kevlar. The face-shield was Plexiglas and fairly shatterproof. There was even a collar to protect the neck. I found it unwieldy and never wore it.

"What's he on?" Xavier asked someone wearing a commander's hat.

"PCP, Meth, Steroids," the guy answered.

"I don't like guessing games," Xavier snarked.

"No, I mean he's on all of them." The commander shouted over the scream of the flame thrower suddenly coming to life.

"Good grief," I groaned.

"How do you know he's on all of that?" Xavier asked.

"See the house next door that's on fire?" The commander asked. "That's his brother's house and his brother told us. The brother also thinks he killed his wife and kids before coming outside and trying to torch the neighborhood. Our problem is that our bullets aren't working and we can't risk a shot with a high caliber weapon because it could cause the tank to explode and we don't know what's in it."

"What do you think?" Gabriel turned to me.

"If you guys can create enough of a distraction," I shrugged and started taking off most of my weaponry.

"Enough of a distraction?" The commander asked.

"I'm a girl, I'm less of a threat," I answered.

"In theory," Xavier added.

"Fine, I'm less of a threat in theory." I revised my statement.

"What exactly are you planning to do?" The commander asked.

"Get close." I pulled off my jacket.

"Cain, if possible, try not to kill him," Gabriel told me.

"You got it, Kemosabe," I gave him a salute and put on a Kevlar vest that said US Marshals on the front and back in bright yellow letters. "Try not to let him roast me. I do not want another skin graft."

"Take a helmet," John handed me one of our tactical helmets from the SUV. "Just in case he aims for your head."

I fastened the chin strap and nodded at him. I had a plan. It was a good plan, as long as it worked. There would be no sneaking up on the guy, his back was too close to the house for that. However, I could rush him from behind, in theory, if I snuck through the house, but it would require people to keep his attention and eyes forward.

"No gun?" The commander asked.

"She won't need one," Gabriel answered. "Go down and around. We'll give you noise when you get to the back if you need to break in. Got your com on?"

I had to remove the helmet to get the communicator on. I stuck the black earpiece into my ear. Static crackled in my head as it turned on. Gabriel spoke and the sound echoed through my ear. I wasn't a fan of the communicator, but it was a necessary evil. I slipped the helmet back into place.

Using the cars for cover, I ran in a crouch. This is not as easy as it seems in the movies. The urge to stand is almost instant and overwhelming. I ran six houses down the block. I found a brown house with green shutters and ducked beside it. As I slipped into the backyard, I realized almost every yard had a fence. I could climb a chain link fence easy, but scaling the front of a privacy fence over six feet tall was going to be problematic. However, there was only one of those, as far as I could see at the moment.

All the yards had kids play equipment in them. As I moved from the first yard to the second, I noticed a dog house in the third.

"Dog, maybe," I whispered.

"Do you have anything other than the knives?" Gabriel asked.

"I forgot to pack the Milkbones in my Kevlar vest."

"Let me know." The line went dead.

I scaled the next set of fences and landed in the yard with the doghouse. I refused to breathe, waiting to see if I was going to be attacked. A beagle, not yet full grown, came out of the house and gave a howl. Curtains on the back window moved. I waved, the curtains closed. Probably not a bad idea to stay inside. As I went to next fence I stopped. The beagle was following me. I sighed and picked him up. He licked me. Peoples lives were at stake, but I had to put the beagle in the house. It would suck if he got barbecued.

I knocked on the back door very quietly. A man opened it, his face was ashen and his eyes too wide. I handed him the dog.

"Keep him inside for a while. Should be over soon," I told him. "Now, lock the door, don't open it again until the police give the all clear. Also, you might hide in an interior room."

I turned back to the fence. This was the privacy fence. I had no idea what was on the other side. I jumped and missed the top of it on the first try. I tried again and felt it slip through my fingers. I backed up and ran at the fence. This time, I caught hold and hoisted myself up. As I reached the top, I realized I could have just climbed onto the doghouse and climbed over. While silently berating myself for all the hard work for no reason, my gaze scanned the backyard. There was another doghouse. It was bigger than the first. I was betting the privacy fence was because this dog wasn't a cute little beagle.

I pushed away from the top of the fence, fully expecting something large to rush at me. Barking from inside the house caused me to whip my head that direction. This dog was larger, a Neapolitan Mastiff barked and clawed at a glass door. The thing was drooling. I suppressed a gag and moved on. Going up the inside of a privacy fence is much easier. There are support boards.

The next yard was filled with smoke. The house was hazy. Nothing moved. I moved to the next. This house was on fire. I'd reached the brother's. The house was burning pretty good. Thick smoke rolled off the walls. A flicker of yellow-orange light danced through the blackened air. There was no fence between the two houses.

"At the brother's," I whispered. "Back of the house is in worse shape than the front. Looks like he might have started it back here."

"Gotcha," Gabriel answered.

At the back door, I stopped for a moment. In theory, the house would have dead people in it. The sliding door opened easily at my touch.

"Inside, checking for survivors," I spoke quickly and quietly. A trail of blood ran along the carpet from the living room to a room with the door closed. It was a small trail. I followed it, knelt down and knocked very softly. "Hello?" I whispered.

Movement from the other side of the door.

"US Marshals," I whispered. The door opened.

An attractive fortyish-something woman opened the door. Her arm was covered in blood. It dripped from her fingers onto the carpet. I looked past her into the room. A girl sat in the corner, blood had pooled under her, but she was alive. Her older sister didn't seem to be injured, she held hands with the younger girl.

"Are you all injured?" I asked.

"Yes," the woman broke down. "He just went nuts."

"Ok," I told her. "I'm going to get help in here, but we have to disarm him first. Stay in here, lock the door if possible. Apply more pressure to your wounds. Is there anyone else in the house?"

"No," the older girl answered. I guessed she was about sixteen.

"I'll be back in a few minutes," I told her, pulling the door closed. I heard the lock click. "We have three survivors in the house, one seems to be bleeding heavily. Get paramedics ready. Heading towards the front door." I whispered into the com.

From outside, I could hear shouting. Nothing coherent. Mostly, it was just jargon and rambling. Gabriel and Xavier would be moving around behind the cars. They'd be instructing other officers to do the same. More people began shouting. Gunfire erupted, I used the moment to pull open the front door. In less than a heartbeat, I was out the door and onto the front step. Time slowed. I swung, jamming the knife into the knee of the jackass with the flamethrower and twisted the blade. I felt the kneecap separate from the bone. Tendons popped and ruptured from the pressure of the blade.

I jerked it out, twisting as I did. The guy turned, his knee giving out as he did so. My helmet jumped, my head instantly hurt and my com went dead. I stabbed him again, this time in the other leg. My method worked a second time and the other knee went out. He tumbled forward, firing his gun. The torch of the flamethrower fell to the ground out of his reach.

Jumping to my feet, I kicked it further away and then fell on the assailant. One hand found the tank, the other began cutting the straps from his back. Once the tank was loose, I tossed it aside. The gun was still firing, but it was hitting the bricks on the house, showering us with dust and debris. Something bounced off the Plexiglas of my face shield. I stabbed downwards and caught his wrist. The bones crunched under the force. The hand flexed and the firing stopped. The blade broke off as he twisted under me.

"Coming past," Xavier shouted as he ran past me. A weight at my back helped to hold the struggling gunman.

"Are you ok?" Gabriel asked.

"I think he shot me in the head," I told him.

"He did, that's why I asked."

"I have a headache," I shrugged.

"You've earned a day of rest."

"I never know what to do on a day of rest."

"Rest," John answered.

"Yeah, right," I looked at the handle of my knife. It was still in my hands. Other people were joining us. I climbed off and removed the helmet. The top was dented. I checked, no blood ran down my face or matted my hair.

A paramedic ran up to me. I waved him away. Xavier came out of the house. He looked at me.

"I bet you have a hell of a headache," he said.

"Yep," I answered. "But I'm not seriously injured." The helmet actually worked. I might have to wear it more often.

"I hate to rain on your parade, but you are injured," Xavier pointed at my leg. Blood was oozing through my jeans.

"Damn, Trevor just bought these," I answered.

"Is it a scratch?" Gabriel asked.

"I don't know, it doesn't hurt." I told him.

"Let me see," Xavier bent down. "Nope, she's been shot."

"Well, double damn, I guess I have to go to the hospital. I'll tell you about what I learned on the way."

TWENTY-ONE

Despite my protests, they gave me a morphine shot. My leg instantly broke out in hives and they pushed Benadryl into the IV. Within seconds, my brain got foggy. The morphine was rough, the Benadryl was downright coma-inducing.

"Ace?" Gabriel moved in very close to me.

"What?" I asked, feeling my tongue slur the word as it exited my mouth.

"You going to be ok?" He asked.

"I really want a nap," I told him.

"Holy hell," was the last thing I heard and I don't think it was Gabriel that said it.

I expected to wake up on a slab in the morgue or at the very least, a hospital bed. I woke up in neither place. I was in my hotel room. The window was open and it was freezing inside. Gabriel sat at the window sill, smoking a cigarette.

"Think you can get up and join me?" He asked.

"This is a non-smoking hotel," I answered groggily.

"Yep, that's why we are smoking in your room," Gabriel grinned at me. "See, then I can say 'well, it's Aislinn Cain and she's a little out of control sometimes, especially when she's medicated,' when the board calls me to complain about the bill to clean the room."

"And when we get thrown out?" I asked, climbing from bed. My legs felt like rubber.

"We'll change hotels," Gabriel shrugged. "You going to make it?"

"Uh," I thought about it. Was I going to make it? I wasn't sure. I couldn't remember the last thing I had done. "I don't know. Can you tell me how I got here?"

"You walked."

"To my room?" I asked.

"Yes. What do you remember?"

"I don't know. How long was I out?"

"Out? More like zombified," Gabriel said. "You were awake, but I'm not sure you were conscious. I've never seen anything like it. Well, that's not true. You slept for six hours and woke up violently. You punched the nurse and started ripping out IVs. We thought security was going to have to Taser you. Then you just sort of collapsed and started babbling about the month of August.

You did that for about two hours. Then we came back here, you ate and crawled into bed. Now, you're awake again and I'm not sure how awake."

"I'm awake. What did they give me?"

"Morphine and Benadryl," Gabriel told me.

"Next time, tell them to restrain me. This is why I don't like anesthesia. I've been known to wake up violently from it, but with no memory of the events. That nurse isn't the first to be punched and it is doubtful that she will be the last. Morphine wipes my memory, which makes me even more dangerous. Benadryl just knocks me out, like a good punch from Muhammad Ali."

"Did you just crack a boxing joke?" Gabriel blinked at me.

"I like boxing," I defended the joke. "I wasn't alive to see the Rumble in the Jungle live, but I've seen the replays thousands of times. I was watching the fight where Holyfield lost part of his ear."

"I didn't know you liked boxing," Gabriel seemed to think about that for a while.

"I still watch the Friday Night Fights when I can," I lit a cigarette. "You are setting a bad example."

"I figure you've been shot in the head, shot in the leg, doped up on morphine and knocked out by Benadryl, you deserve a cigarette." Gabriel looked at me for a moment. "And you vomited a Philly Steak Sandwich up on John. We think it was the morphine, because after that, you crawled into bed and went back to sleep."

"Poor John," I answered. "Is there caffeine around here somewhere?"

Gabriel pointed to the table. A one-liter of Mountain Dew was sitting there, sweating, despite the cold temperature. I unsealed it and took a long drink. Gabriel then pointed to a bottle of water.

"Xavier says you have to drink it. It has electrolytes in it."

"It's water," I told him.

"It's an enriched water beverage."

"Ah, it was expensive water," I sighed. "Did I tell you about the markings in the files?"

"Yes and I have been going through the files since the maid finished cleaning up your room. I can't figure out what they mean either. John is running it through the database. How long did you keep it a secret?"

"I discovered it last night," I told him.

"The night before last," Gabriel corrected. "Last night you were at the hospital and today, you've been mostly out of it."

"Ok, but I must have told you before I went under the Benadryl/morphine cocktail from Hell, so," I answered.

"Good point," Gabriel looked at me and flicked his cigarette out the window. "Is it possible your father knew who was doing the killings back then?"

"No," I stopped and thought. "I don't think so. I mean, my father was a cop first."

"But?" Gabriel asked.

"But, I don't know, but something."

"How well did you know your father?"

"Oh, as much as I could, considering I think he was a sociopath and I'm a sociopath and," I didn't finish the thought.

"And?" Gabriel pressed. "Tell me what you think."

"I used to think my father was protecting me from the world after my encounter with Callow. In the past couple of days, I've been thinking that maybe it was the other way around. He became distant, but was always on my case, about everything. I think he saw the monster in me and decided to lock it up."

"How do you feel about that?" Gabriel asked.

"If I feel anything about it, it's irritation. I wasn't a danger to myself and others, within reason, of course."

"Of course," Gabriel chirped. "So, why did you second guess yourself about the whole 'my father was a cop first' thing?"

"My father rescued an orangutan and put it in a sanctuary, illegally. That wasn't the first time and it probably wasn't the last time that he broke the law."

"You know this, for a fact?"

"Yes," I admitted. "My father was pretty good at roughing up suspects, even the ones that turned out to be innocent."

"He was a cop dealing with a world that was changing faster than the laws," Gabriel shrugged it off.

"Yes, he was. But," I tossed my cigarette out the window and pulled it closed. "His brother once got into a fight, beat the guy real bad, my father made it go away by visiting the victim in the hospital."

"I didn't know you had aunts and uncles," Gabriel sounded surprised.

"Really? Nyleena is my cousin."

"She could be a second or third cousin," Gabriel pointed out.

"Oh, I hadn't thought of that. No, she's my first cousin, on my father's side. It wasn't her dad that beat the hell out of some poor bastard for calling him a name, her dad is the mellowest of the siblings. This isn't saying much, since two are dead, one's in jail, and the other is abusive, but he is the mellowest."

"Which one is her dad?" Gabriel asked.

"He's the other one that's dead," I answered. "Killed by a coworker who dropped a scaffold on him as he prepared for a day at work. It was ruled intentional."

"How many people in your family have died of old age?" Gabriel gave me a look that I couldn't identify.

"Not many," I answered. "Perhaps my grandfather, a few great-aunts and uncles, maybe some cousins, but most have been unnatural deaths. Not all were intentional deaths though, one of my cousins died in a car accident, another fell off a house, one overdosed on heroin, a great uncle died of a bee sting in his nineties, and another was accidentally killed when her garage door malfunctioned and it fell on her, cutting her in half."

"That's depressing."

"Those who live, live a long time," I told him. "I had a great uncle that babysat me some when I was younger, he lived to be old, like really old. Older than my great uncle that died of a bee sting. And while his death wasn't exactly natural, it really wasn't unnatural either, he died of complications from heart surgery."

"Wow," Gabriel looked at me. "So, back to your father."

"I don't know what to tell you about my father. Before Callow he was a father, he took me to baseball games, attended parent/teacher conferences, and enjoyed holidays. After Callow, he was withdrawn, sullen, and brooding. I believe he was a sociopath, but not like me. I think he had more feelings and I think he had demons, just like most people."

"If the scientists and doctors are right and your condition is inherited, it would make sense that he was a sociopath. His sense of right and wrong might have been different than yours or his father's because of the influences around all of you. You learned from your mom and Nyleena. I don't know who taught your father or grandfather."

"Yes, it would, which is why I don't know if the notation was about connecting all the cases or giving a clue about the killer. If it was Malachi, I'd take him down, but I don't know what my father would do. I think it would depend more on the person."

"What if it was Nyleena?" Gabriel asked.

"That would be harder," I admitted. "I would turn a blind eye to it."

"Did your dad have an equivalent?"

"Yes."

"Who?"

"My mom." I answered.

"Anyone else?"

"Not that I know of," I told him.

"I don't believe your mom is a serial killer."

"My mom is afraid of most animals. She was attacked by a dog when she was younger. Has some scars from it, both physically and emotionally. And she'll gag if you feed a dog from a table or from a human fork or let them lick a plate clean. There's no way she'd willingly tear chunks of flesh from a person with a jaguar at her side."

"I was going to say that I didn't believe she was a serial killer because she's a good person; kind, gentle, loving, and she cares a lot about other people. I don't think it's a facade. I think she is honestly a good person, which makes her children sort of odd."

"My sister cared a lot about people, she's dead." I looked at him. "My brother cared so much about my family that he took a sniper rifle up to a roof and started killing people."

"Given the circumstances, maybe that wasn't a great argument."

"Maybe not."

"I can't think of a better one at the moment."

"How about because she's my mom. If the woman was serial killer material, she would have snapped a long time ago. She's way beyond that one stressor point."

"That's a better argument, logically. But I still think it's because she has a big heart. She's adopted all of us."

"So, she takes in strays," I shrugged.

"You care, you just don't realize how deeply you care. Remember, you cried when Xavier died via clerical error and you cried at Michael's funeral."

"I still think caring might be overrated."

"I would be upset if you died. Is that overrated?"

"No, I would expect you to cry if I died."

"Why?"

"Because it's me. Who else is going to stab guys in the knees to make sure that you get visits to see your children via your jack-ass brother-in-law?"

"How do you know that's why I keep him around?"

"Because he serves no other purpose in the universe."

"Good point." Gabriel smiled.

"Oh fruck," I said.

"What?" Gabriel jumped up.

"What if August isn't a month, but a person?"

TWENTY-TWO

Certain events leave more of an impression than others, particularly on children. Housing an orangutan for a time had been one of the more impressive moments. Coming face to face with a mountain lion also ranked up there. The fact that my father's cousin, August, had been the one harboring both animals during an illegal animal fight, was not.

However, August's death had been rather spectacular and fitting. He'd been mauled by a leopard. The leopard had then dragged his carcass into the roof rafters to rot. At the time, I had considered it poetic justice. Nearly ten years later, my opinion on the matter hadn't really changed.

Needless to say, the funeral had been a closed casket ceremony. I had attended with my mother and Nyleena, as was dictated by my duty to family. Secretly, I was pretty sure that most of those in attendance hadn't wanted to be there. Sure he was a Clachan by birth, but in a family whose hierarchy was dominated by matrons and money, August had been a bit of a black sheep.

The farm had been inherited. Any money that had come with it had most likely been turned into nose candy for August's addiction. Anything left was used to start his illegal importing business. The animal fights were just an added bonus to line August's pockets.

The farm had remained in the family. Twin cousins bought it. It was a nice addition to the land already owned by their parents across the road. As a matter of fact, travelling south between Columbia and Sapp, Missouri, better known as Hoop-Up, one could find a disturbingly large number of Clachan family farms. Something in our ancestry made the idea of giving up land revolting.

There was one big problem with the notation meaning August the person and not August the month. August the person was dead. He'd been suffocated by the jaws of the powerful predator clamped to his throat. At some point, the cat had taken a good sized bite out of his face. Then he'd dragged him to the roof rafters in the barn, where he'd been gnawed on for a couple of days before someone thought to check on the lonely, middle aged man.

Obviously, August wasn't our serial killer. He had no children to pass the murderous gene and technique onto and as far as anyone knew, aside from family, he didn't have friends. That lead me to believe the notation, while referring to August, was more likely to be about who bought the jaguar. In a city the size of Columbia, illegal animal importers weren't exactly numbering in the hundreds. There was a good chance it wasn't even in the double digits.

This would require a fishing expedition of sorts. I needed to talk to my family about it. However, I wasn't sure my family would be forth coming with information. They were a closed, close-knit group who guarded family secrets like crown jewels. There was a reason my father hadn't personally arrested August. Instead, he'd hidden in the shadows, awaiting back-up as the animals were set free. All the spectators had gotten away because my father was a Clachan first and a cop second.

Not me. As far as most of my family was concerned, I was barely a Clachan. My great-aunt had once tutted at me and told me I had too many of my mother's genes. I didn't know what that meant at the time, but sitting around the table, looking at my team mates, I understood. I had balked at the strategic course of life laid out by the family matrons. It had been their plans that I go to school, return to my hometown and settle down. Nyleena had broken the mold too, refusing to marry after law school and moving to Kansas City. We were more outcasts than even August.

"You look pensive," Xavier said.

"No one uses the word pensive," I told him, fiddling with a pen. "So, I think my family might know who is illegally importing animals. It used to be my cousin, August, but he's dead. It would make sense that someone else in the family took it over. That's sort of the way things work."

"Then you're frowning because we need to interrogate your family?" Gabriel asked.

"No, not in the least. I'm frowning because my family is a little like a cult," I told him and paused, thinking about it. "No, they are a lot like a cult. Don't you think it's weird that Nyleena and I don't talk about them?" I corrected myself.

"You, no," Xavier answered.

"I can tell you how to go about it, but I can't sit in on the interviews," I told them.

"Ok," Gabriel frowned.

"You'll get nothing out of the older generation, especially the women. You'd have better luck going after the younger ones. Of those, I'd say go hard at the men. The Clachan women are really good at hiding the family's dirty laundry. It's sort of a tradition. Even when a woman marries into the clan, they are given instructions for a harmonious family life by the matrons. My mother didn't fit the typical Clachan wife, but she was pretty good at it."

"Hiding the dirty laundry?" John asked, suddenly curious.

"Well," I shrugged. "My grandfather up and disappeared after my grandmother was murdered. I'd say there is about an eighty percent chance that my grandfather murdered her. But no one knows where he is or if he's still alive even. Of course, nobody says he did it. They don't even whisper about it. I was told exactly what I needed to know by a great-aunt and nothing more. My mom eventually elaborated after she moved to Kansas City."

"Why can't you sit in?" Xavier pressed.

"I'll throttle someone. The crones made my life miserable when I was a child. They won't be happy to see me now."

"Why do you think that?" Xavier prodded.

"When I was ten, my great-aunt told me she had picked me out a husband and that she only hoped I didn't get uglier as I got older because I wasn't much of a prize. I thought she was crazy, but then this boy started hanging around me. Turned out, she had really picked me out a husband. My father put a stop to it, but that just pissed her off. For a year, my father was not welcome at any of the family gatherings and he stopped making me go after that. As you will soon see, most of my family members are nutty."

"Should we be concerned?" Gabriel asked.

"Probably not," I said. "But you should know, that everything lives in a huge grey area with the Clachan clan. Nyleena, my dad, me, we are the exceptions because we don't like grey areas."

"Great," John groaned.

"Just remember that while they seem cooperative, they are going to be quietly hostile and consider you an interloper. They will do their best to be evasive and misdirecting without actually breaking a law. I'll watch and give you information while you talk to them. Also, I think Xavier and John should do the interviews. Don't take this the wrong way, but you're too much of a good ol' boy for it, Gabriel. Xavier will make them uncomfortable. John will get under their skin because of his appearance of superiority. If one does request to speak with a supervisor, treat them with contempt. I know it sounds counter-intuitive, but if you want to watch my family get their hackles up, put them in a room with Malachi. His contempt for them is not disguised and it pisses them off to no end."

"You want us to treat your family badly?" Xavier raised an eyebrow.

"If Lucas was here, I'd use his size. Unfortunately, he's not, so I'm hoping your issues will make them uncomfortable enough to start flopping their jaws. If that doesn't work, then I'm relying on John's 'good guy' status will do the trick."

"What if they don't think Xavier is off?" John asked.

"They will," I answered staring at my colleague. Xavier looks like a professor that just woke up from a multiple week bender. His hair is dark and disheveled, his clothes are always wrinkled, he has an odd smell and there is intelligence in the face and eyes along with something else. I don't know what this something else is, but I can see it. My family would as well. "I think you should start with the younger ones. Round them all up before the matrons have the ability to intervene."

"What are you going to do while we haul all your cousins in for questioning?" John asked.

"Read a book." I told him.

"You're going," Gabriel said. "We might need you."

"I'm not," I defied him.

"Sure you are," Xavier handed me a helmet with a hood that covered my face.

"They are going to know it's me. A face mask isn't going to stop that."

"Do you like your family?" Gabriel asked.

"I like Nyleena."

"Then does it matter that they know you are helping with the investigation?" Gabriel continued.

"The matrons are evil."

"I didn't think you believed in evil?" Gabriel said.

"You haven't met the great-aunts yet. They'll make you believe in evil. An hour or two with them and you'll find you believe in all sorts of things."

"Like the evil eye?" Xavier stifled a giggle.

"No," I answered. "But other things."

TWENTY-THREE

Somehow the Clachan family knew we were coming. Since we had only told a handful of people, I was pretty sure I knew who had warned them. Several of my aunts, great-aunts, uncles, great-uncles, and cousins were already gathered at the farmhouse of my cousin, Josh. His brother, Kyle, had built a house on the same property after the twins bought it from whoever had owned it after August's death.

I had agreed to the full tactical suit, including face mask. The bulky body armor hid my figure and all the scars that might have identified me. The mask was generic, leaving a small hole around my nose and eye slots large enough for me to see through, but not show my eyebrows.

My hand was on my Taser. The urge to use it was strong. I didn't particularly care for most of my father's family. The feeling was mutual.

They had gathered outside the house. Cars filled the driveway, forcing us to park on the two-lane highway that ran between southern Columbia and Hoop-Up. Lawn chairs proliferated the yard, making it look like a family reunion. Coolers were set around in different places and two large barbecue grills were both emitting heat. Considering it was the dead of winter and everyone was in coats and warm clothing, it was hard to buy the whole set-up.

"This is a private gathering," my great-aunt, Gertrude, stood up and walked over to meet our group.

"And you can return to your private gathering, after we've talked to a few of you regarding a matter of importance," Gabriel was showing his badge and identification to the old woman. The fact that all our clothing was labelled US Marshals wasn't enough. Even the badge wouldn't hold much sway over the family.

"Do you have a warrant?" She asked.

"We don't need one," Gabriel informed her. "We are the Serial Crimes Tracking Unit and we are here to discuss a serial killer. You can talk to us willingly or we can arrest all of you for hindering the hunt for a serial killer."

"That's a stupid law that violates my rights," my cousin, Kyle, said from a place near one of the grills.

"It doesn't violate your rights," Detective Russell stepped up. "Under this law, if you are suspected of having information regarding a serial killer, your rights are suspended. As of now, the only right you have, is the right to have an attorney present during the inquiry."

"You can't arrest all of us," Kyle boasted. I narrowed my eyes, hoping the stare would burn through him or make him spontaneously combust. I was fairly certain that we could arrest all of them. It might require Tasers, but I was good with that.

"Stand fast," Gabriel said, this was directed at me and I knew it. I stayed completely still. "We can and will arrest all of you. At this time, we only want to talk to five of you. If you press the issue, we will arrest all of you, using force, if necessary."

"We have the right to defend ourselves against unlawful arrest," my uncle, Joe stood up. I hadn't realized he was out of jail. I wondered when that had happened.

"Joe," Detective Russell shook his head. "It's just a couple of questions, you do not want to take on the Marshals over this."

Detective Russell was a good guy. The sort that was very law and order, but was quick with a smile and he made people feel comfortable. He'd been brought along because he knew most of the Clachan family. He'd even almost married one, but he'd gotten out of it, relatively unscathed, before it was too late.

"What sorts of questions?" Gertrude narrowed her eyes.

"The sort that we ask," Gabriel answered, staring back at the old woman with an unwavering gaze.

"We aren't involved with serial killers," Gertrude snapped. I snorted. "Aislinn Clachan! This is your doing." The woman was suddenly storming towards me. I pulled the Taser without thinking.

"Don't," Gabriel's voice was barely audible. I didn't Taser my great-aunt, even when she got within inches of my face.

"How dare you bring your people here with these absurd questions?" My great aunt slapped me. Her hand hit my helmet with a thud that I barely felt. It hurt her a whole lot more than it hurt me. However, my reaction was immediate. I grabbed her, twisting her arm behind her back and spinning her around. I held her close, like a mother comforting a child, keeping her arm between us. She yelped.

"You just assaulted a federal officer," I whispered. "I don't care if you are older than dirt, when I let you go, if you make any attempt to step towards me again, I'll break you in half and arrest you. I might Taser you just to see if your heart is as cold and dead as I think it is. Do you understand?"

Gertrude said nothing, so I didn't let go. A few people stepped forward but stopped. The helmet was obviously pointless now. I removed my arm from over her shoulder, but kept the other pinned between us. With the free hand, I yanked off the helmet and face mask as if I were doing a magic trick.

Xavier took the gear from my hand. Detective Russell stared at me for a few moments, his mouth slightly ajar. I was pretty sure I was going to break Gertrude's arm if I kept her held this way for much longer, but I had no desire to release the witch that had tormented me as a child.

"I'll play nice, if you do," I let her go. "We want to speak to Kyle, Josh, Joe, Phil and Rich. Everyone else can stay here and enjoy your freezing barbecue. We'll return them by the end of the day."

My great-aunt glared at me. I glared back. She flinched first, turning away from me and walking towards the house.

"Why would you want to talk to those five?" My other great-aunt, Nina, asked.

"Just a few questions," Gabriel informed her.

"I'm going too," Nina announced.

"Why?" Gabriel asked her with a sneer. "You won't be allowed to listen in." I shook my head and leaned into him.

"Nina's a lawyer," I whispered to him.

"But she can't represent family." He whispered back.

"We aren't arresting them, so she can technically sit in on the interviews as their representation." I told him. "If we arrest them, she can make arrangements for them to have different counsel."

"Any other lawyers in your family I should know about?" Gabriel asked.

"Just Nyleena."

"Why didn't you mention you had another lawyer in the family earlier?" Gabriel asked.

"She does tax law," I told him. "Not criminal law. I didn't think about it." I didn't mention the fact that she had her law degree and had passed the bar long before I was even thought of being born, but had never practiced a single day in her life.

"Peachy," Gabriel looked back at the group. "Are you guys going to step forward or are we going to have to pick you out?" None of the five men mentioned had come forward, only Nina had made any moves towards the vehicles.

Kyle and Josh came first. They both set down spatulas. Joe, who was already standing, muttered something under his breath but started walking forward. We still needed Rich and Phil. I motioned for both of them to come on. They got up out of their chairs, Rich handed something to his wife.

"Search them before you put them in the SUVs." I told Xavier. "How many of you are currently armed?"

Several of them started pulling out guns. John's hand moved to his own weapon and he began to look nervous. I shook my head.

"If you have a weapon, take it out now, slowly, and put it down," Gabriel was also reaching for his gun. I shook my head again and let out a long sigh.

"Ok, this is how it's going to work, you can keep your guns and knives on you, unless you're supposed to go with us. However, if any of you even pull out a weapon and give us a weird look, I'm going to start shooting. I'll ask questions while I fill out paperwork." I told the Clachan clan. This seemed to make them all stop and think. Kyle took a gun out of the back of his pants. "Don't you know that's a stupid place to keep a gun?" I asked my younger cousin. "You could paralyze yourself."

"Why are we letting them keep their weapons?" John asked.

"Because," I answered. "If they were going to shoot us, they would have done it when we pulled up. Black SUVs with tinted windows and no lights or sirens. They could have claimed they were defending themselves against unknown suspicious persons. They didn't, because they knew we were coming. The weapons were meant to intimidate us into not taking any of them."

"That doesn't make sense," John told me.

"That's because you didn't grow up around these nutjobs," I told him. "In our world, it makes perfect sense."

TWENTY-FOUR

The five men were loaded into three different cars. Gabriel, Xavier, and John each rode in a car with them. Nina was loaded into the front seat of the SUV with me as the driver. I wasn't sure I wanted alone time with my great-aunt, but at least Nina wasn't Gertrude.

"How have you been?" The ancient Clachan matron asked me. Nina had never married. She had never had children. She'd been "too smart" for any of that nonsense. Being "too smart" was a crime amongst Clachan women. Only a handful had ever been given this stigma, but those that did were doomed to live a lonely existence, at least in the minds of other Clachans. It was a lot like living in the Dark Ages, when women were only good for breeding and household chores. My grandmother had been "too smart," it had "directly contributed to her murder." I knew because I'd been told exactly that on several occasions by my family. Of course, she'd married into the Clachan family and hadn't realized it had been tantamount to treason to be smart.

"I'm fine, Nina. I have a job, friends, hobbies, and money, everything a Clachan girl shouldn't have. I do not have a boyfriend, husband, or children," I told her.

"Good for you," Nina said. "Children are oppressive and dull, especially in this family."

"Still harboring some resentments, I see."

"Why shouldn't I harbor resentments?" Nina asked. "You do."

"I do," I agreed. "That's why I don't come to family gatherings."

"You escaped. I didn't." Nina shrugged and I caught the movement in the corner of my eye.

"You could have. Nyleena tried to get you to move when she took the job in Kansas City."

"I'm an eighty-three year old tax lawyer without a retirement fund. What would I do in Kansas City?"

"Anything," I told her. "My mom is still working, part-time."

"Your mom is a good egg." She smiled finally. "That was quite a show you put on there."

"It wasn't a show. I really would have started shooting. If my boss hadn't been there, I might have Tasered Gertrude just for fun." I grimaced. "Mean old bitch."

"Age hasn't made her any more pleasant." Nina agreed. "So, back to how I would live if I moved."

"Nyleena and I would help." I told her. As far as nutjobs went in my family, Nina was definitely one of them, but not in the sense that most of them were. My family had a fund that the elderly could draw from. Nina had never worked a day in her life. Her father had pretty much kept her hidden, like a troll, until he died when she was in her forties. At that time, she'd gone to college, gotten her degree in law, and started her own business. Her sister, Gertrude, had made sure it failed. Now, Nina lived off the family fund.

"You have enough to handle with your mom, Ella, all the children and yourself. I'd just be another dependent."

"Nyleena and I both think you have Stockholm's Syndrome."

"Could be." Nina agreed.

"So, why are coming along?" I asked her.

"I'm guessing you want to talk about August."

"Guess or know?" I asked.

"Know," Nina admitted. "We knew the moment you guys hit town that eventually you'd want to talk to us about August. It really wasn't a surprise when we got the call today saying you guys were paying us a visit."

"Anyone still involved in the illegal animal trade?" I asked my aged aunt.

"Not that I know of," Nina answered. "That doesn't mean they aren't, it just means I don't know about it. But I can probably help answer questions about August, as long as the others don't know about it. I helped your dad the first time."

"Helped my dad?" I asked.

"You think he was visiting Greg by chance that day and just happened to cross the street to find an animal fight in progress? He was a good cop, but he wasn't psychic."

"I didn't know that."

"You were young," Nina shrugged again. "However, Gertrude suspects that I tipped your dad off to August's activities, so I don't get told much anymore."

"I'd like to torture her until she gave up the information," I sighed.

"Be real, you'd just like to torture her," Nina laughed.

"That's true." I hated Gertrude with a passion. How her and Nina were sisters always amazed me. The two were as different as night and day. I wouldn't admit it, at least not to many people, but I liked Nina. As she put it, she was a good egg, even if she did have Stockholm's Syndrome. "If you're being kept out of the loop, what is Gertrude going to think about you coming along to sit in on interviews? Especially, if she thinks you've betrayed the family before?"

"She can think whatever she wants. It's not like she can do anything to me. All the killers in the family are dead, except two."

"Eric and myself or Eric and Joe?" I asked.

"I had forgotten about Eric," Nina sighed. "And you didn't cross my mind either. I take it the feet being found are somehow related to the jaguars August used to procure?"

"I was unaware that August used to procure jaguars." I answered. "Who were the two if it wasn't Eric or myself?" I returned to the cryptic comment.

"Every couple of years he'd get one. He'd house it for a day or two and then it would be gone. You're dad thought he was selling them to a serial killer, but we could never pinpoint when the jaguars where coming in or going out. Then your dad died and the killings had stopped, so it just sort of went into limbo. However, even after the killings stopped, August continued to get in a jaguar every couple of years." Nina completely dodged the real question.

"I don't think they ever stopped." I told her. "Between you, me and whatever bugs might be planted in this car, I think the killings continued. I think the killer switches his victim preference every so often and when he does, the ritual changes. With kids, he disposes of the feet, leaving them to be found by the public, but there are a lot of vagrants and oddly, young men with blonde hair that go missing in the area. These stop when the child killings start and then restart when the child killings stop."

"That's not the way a serial killer operates," Nina said.

"Not normally, no." I agreed. "What do you know of the case, I mean really know?"

"Besides what you just told me?" Nina asked.

"Yes."

"Ok kiddo, all my cards on the table, I already knew that. Your father suspected it. Your father suspected that August was getting jaguars for the killer and that if the killer wasn't a Clachan, he was a family friend. That's why he handed in his detective's shield. He didn't want to compromise the investigation by being involved if he turned out to be right. His goal was to shutdown August's business and therefore, make the killer start looking for another source. It didn't work. Every time

August got caught, he got a slap on the wrist because he was Gertrude's son. Then came the reformation and the bad tip."

"Want to elaborate?" I asked.

"I heard that August was getting in a polar bear. I passed the information along to your father. The police raided the barn and found nothing. August claimed he'd reformed, he even gave a bunch of money to animal charities to prove it. A few weeks later, Chub walked in to find August with a polar bear. He couldn't really do anything about it. He told your dad. They raided the house that night and found more nothing. August filed a harassment suit against the department and particularly, your father. It cost the city an arm and a leg, not to mention your dad's part in the lawsuit, which he ended up paying out of pocket. A few weeks later, Chub died. I know it was from surgery complications, but I just feel like somehow August was responsible. Of course, there's no proof of that."

"That seems to be a thing with the family."

"Oh honey, you have no idea. Clachans are responsible for about half of all Clachan deaths. If you weren't who you were, you wouldn't have lived this long."

"What's that supposed to mean?" I asked.

"Gertrude's had it out for you since your father banned her from arranging your marriage. Do you know why your dad stopped making you go to family gatherings?"

"Yeah, I'm a sociopath and a killer."

"No, it was so that you could escape the family. He realized after you killed Callow that the family would be all over your talents and exploit them if they could. So, he stopped letting you have contact with most of them. Chub, Nyleena, and I were the exceptions, because he trusted us not to manipulate you. He believes Gertrude tried to have you killed twice after the Callow incident."

"That's insane."

"You've met the woman," Nina said.

"And now, you're riding in a car with me, telling me all the family dirt. Don't you think Gertrude will have a problem with that?"

"Yes, but if she kills me, it isn't a great loss," Nina reached up and pulled off her hair. I hit the brakes on the SUV, causing much honking behind me. "I have cancer and it's terminal. There's a lot for me to tell you. I think when I leave the police station today, I might go visit Nyleena."

"How long do you have?" I asked.

"Six months, maybe." Nina answered. "Liver cancer. Go figure. I never drank until I got it, now I enjoy Bailey's in my coffee and a good single malt scotch before bed. No sense living clean and sober when your liver has already committed suicide." She seemed to fall into thought. I started the car moving again. "You know, maybe for the next six months or however long I live, I'll take you up on your offer. I could use a change of scenery and there's a lot for you to learn about the Clachans. No one else is ever going to tell you, so I should."

"Like what?" I asked.

"Like how your grandfather murdered your grandmother. He's still alive and he sends you letters."

"He sends me letters?" I frowned at her. "I've never received a letter from my grandfather."

"Yes you have, Aislinn. You just didn't know it." Nina turned as much as the seat belt would allow. "He uses the name The Butcher."

"My grandfather is my creepy ass, not-quite-sure he's a serial killer stalker?" I asked.

"That was complicated." Nina's face changed to match my own. "Your grandfather is The Butcher and he is a serial killer. Your grandmother wasn't his last victim either. I don't know how many or how often, but I know he still kills now and again," she thought for a moment. "He hasn't really aged much, either. He has wrinkles, but his hair hasn't faded or disappeared, and no one believes he's in his eighties. They all think he's in his sixties. He's spry and walks with a cane, a habit he picked up after the war. A fancy cane, custom made, he doesn't need it, just thinks it improves his image."

"Was he in the war?" I asked.

"Yes. The reason you and Malachi keep coming up blank in your search for his victims is because you're checking the wrong databases. If there was a way to check for crimes against Nazis and civilians in Europe during WWII, you'd probably find his victims. When he came back from the war, he kept the urges in check, right up until he killed your grandmother."

"You've known all along?" I asked, anger bubbling up.

"Sort of, I suspected he was alive and I suspected he was your stalker. I didn't know for sure until a few weeks ago, when I heard Gertrude having a phone conversation with someone. I couldn't identify the caller because I couldn't hear the other line, but when Lee asked who she was talking to, she said it was a 'friend.' Lee accepted that with a slight nod. I called the number back and was shocked to hear a voicemail that claimed to belong to Oliver Patterson, but in my brother's voice. I confronted Lee who broke down and told me everything. I called Malachi and tipped him off."

"Wow, so Malachi really did have a lead on The Butcher." I let that sink in for a minute.

"It's a lot to take in. But there's a lot more than just Patterson being alive." Patterson Oliver Clachan had been my grandfather's name.

"How much more?" I asked.

"Much, much, much more." Nina looked out the window. "We'll deal with it a little at a time though."

URGES

Nina was in custody, helping Aislinn. This made Patterson feel a little better. She was a big girl, capable of taking care of herself, both of them were. But knowledge was power with Aislinn, most of the time. He didn't dwell on the times that it was a distraction.

He had something else to do today besides chase after Gertrude and August. He had a certain young man to deal with. Years ago, the young man had just been a punk kid who had shot up a parking lot. Now, he'd grown into a nuisance. Like Patterson, he followed Aislinn's cases. Unlike Patterson, he was killing in the cities that Aislinn visited. He was trying to frame her for murder because of a stupid high school grudge.

It seemed that one night, while at a movie, the punk's girlfriend had assaulted Aislinn. Aislinn and Nyleena had defended themselves and the band of girls, including the girlfriend, had been arrested. The girlfriend had gone to juvenile detention for her actions. When she got out, the punk and the girlfriend had married. A year ago, the wife had died in a car accident that the punk thought was Aislinn's fault. It didn't seem to enter into his logic that Aislinn hadn't been anywhere near the accident or that the wife had been drinking when she slammed into a guard rail.

Rage just needed a focus and an outlet. Unfortunately for this guy, his rage had focused on Aislinn. Patterson parked in the driveway of the small, green and brick ranch house. It had taken him several months to track down George Killian. Patterson was prepared for the younger man to be strong, after all, death had turned him into a serial killer.

Patterson though had the edge. It wasn't just that he looked harmless, it was that he was born to be a killer and he knew it. George had been born to be something else. Bad lifestyle choices had turned him into a killer. He wasn't capable of the physical feats that Patterson was and he'd feel every wound inflicted.

His knuckles rapped firmly and quickly on the wooden door. George Killian was Aislinn's age with a face that looked younger than her's and a body that held fewer scars. His hair hadn't even begun to turn grey. Patterson had already checked to make sure that they didn't have children.

"What do you want?" George slurred. He'd been drinking in the morning hours of a Saturday or doing drugs. It was never a good sign.

"George Killian?" Patterson asked, despite already knowing the answer.

"Yeah, what do you want?"

"I want to talk to you about an incident. May I come in?"

"You're too old to be a cop. Go fuck yourself."

"I'm sorry you feel that way," Patterson lashed out with his cane, hitting George in the head. George roared in pain and sprung at the old man. Patterson stepped aside, letting George's momentum carry him off the edge of the porch. Something snapped as George hit the ground and he began yelping. Patterson sighed and rolled his eyes. He hated amateurs. If you were going to be a serial killer, you should put in the time and effort to be good at it. Patterson grabbed George by the shirt.

"Now, do you want to talk or do you want me to continue to inflict pain?" Patterson asked.

"We can talk," George said. "Help me stand, I think my ankle's broke."

"That is the least of your problems," Patterson rapped him on the head again with his cane. "I will not help you up. You might have broken your ankle, but you've had enough to drink today to stumble back into the house of your own accord."

George began to grumble. Patterson hit him harder this time, knocking him unconscious. He couldn't kill him in the yard, someone might drive by. He also wasn't sure he could get the larger man into the house. However, necessity was the mother of invention and Patterson's mind was already developing a system to get George in the house.

Sixteen minutes later, Patterson had George secured to a chair in the living room. Not a kitchen chair, but a large recliner. Kitchen chairs didn't make for good places to restrain victims, they were unreliable. They broke too easily. Computer chairs were better, but they moved. So, Patterson had developed a system of restraint in any size recliner.

He tossed a bucket of scalding hot water on George's face. George awoke, his mouth gagged, but he attempted to scream all the same. His skin was already red and small blisters were starting to form from the hot water.

Patterson had opted for the computer chair. He now rolled it over to him and took a seat in front of George. He waited for the man's muffled cries to die before continuing. This took a while. George's eyes kept rolling wildly and he struggled against the bonds. Finally, he stopped and stared at Patterson.

"I was hoping we could do this in a gentlemanly manner. It's a very simple matter that needs to be cleared up. For several months now, you have been following around my granddaughter and killing people trying to frame her. I came here today to ask you to stop and turn yourself in. Sadly, that ship has sailed because you decided to be uncivilized. Perhaps it was the booze in your system or just the attitude of your generation, I don't know. I'm not even sure I care. Since we couldn't talk about it like gentlemen, I'm going to kill you. It's going to be painful. I'm going to enjoy it. You are not, unless you are among one of those few people who are truly so masochistic that they can enjoy the suffering of their own torture. Judging by your screams from earlier, I believe that is not the case." Patterson thought for a moment. "However, I did have the opportunity to kill a man once that was. He was a Nazi, for all the right reasons or wrong, depending on your view point. He was truly sadistic, torturing and raping women was his only form of pleasure, until I found him. As I sliced open his stomach and began pulling out his intestines, he orgasmed because he was so excited by the site of the blood and the feelings of pain. As a matter of fact, he enjoyed it so much, that I didn't enjoy it and instead of butchering him like he deserved, after a few injuries, I slit his throat out of disgust. I'm hoping that doesn't happen here."

George made weak suckling noises through the gag. His eyes once again rolled uncontrollably for a moment. The chair suddenly became damp under him. Patterson smiled. He'd scared the piss out of him, literally. This was going to be fun.

Patterson pulled out a long, serrated knife used for hunting. He started at the navel, inserting the blade slowly, then pulling it out.

"Oh, I forgot something," Patterson said in a sing-song voice. He hit the handle on the recliner and the footrest flopped out. "That's much better." Patterson cut open George's shirt, watching the blood already pooling on the younger man's stomach.

He slipped the knife back into the same wound. George tried to scream again. Patterson giggled. He applied pressure, moving the blade upwards. George's screaming was becoming frantic. The intestines, free of the captive flesh, spilled out willingly. Patterson had expected it, seen it happen often. However, he also knew a person could live for a long time with their intestines lying exposed as long as they weren't damaged.

It was a slow process. He removed the organs carefully, ensuring he didn't cause damage when he took them out. He scattered them about the house, turning it into a ghoulish scene. Unfortunately, his victims died quickly once the initial cut was made. Between bleeding from the wound and having their organs harvested, it was a quick, but painful death.

Patterson showered, dressed in a different outfit, leaving his suit on the bathroom floor and left. They'd find the body, eventually.

TWENTY-FIVE

With the exception of Nina, my family was unhelpful. The men clammed up the instant August's name was mentioned. Gabriel sat beside me in a small room with a video monitor. I had yet to be in a police station that had the giant two-way mirrors that they always put into police stations for TV and movies. Usually, there were three or four people crammed into a room the size of a janitor's closet while the investigators and detainee were in a room about the size of a small bedroom.

The idea of torturing them for information had already crossed my mind, several times. I was sure it had gone through Gabriel's as well. The fact that I hadn't stormed in there should have won me serious karma points. They kept repeating that August was dead, like this was a fact that we didn't already know. All of them claimed they knew nothing about August's activities while he had been alive. Their second favorite phrase was "he was a quiet guy."

The August I remembered was not quiet. He'd been loud and obnoxious. He'd been creepy and weird. He'd even gone so far as to hit on my mother at a few family gatherings. If August was the quiet type, then I was perfectly stable and well-adjusted.

I put my face down on the table on the backs of my hands. The skin was rough from the burns I'd endured last summer. It rubbed against my face like a lion's tongue, threatening to tear away the healthy skin.

"Go make them talk," I told Gabriel.

"I don't think I'm scary enough to make them talk," Gabriel told me. "After watching them, they don't seem to intimidate easily."

This wasn't true. They were used to people who were nuts, but they never knew what to say or do when I was around. Some tried aggression, some submission, others just tried to ignore me completely, hoping I'd disappear like a morning mist. They could be herded like sheep, if the right shepherd could be found. Sadly, I wasn't the right shepherd. Lucas would have been good at getting them to talk. He'd outwit them while lending a sympathetic ear, coaxing out the answers. But we didn't have Lucas. We had Gabriel, Xavier, John,

and me. They certainly wouldn't respond to me.
They didn't seem to be responding much to John
and Xavier either. I wondered if I could make
Gabriel scarier. It was a long shot. Gabriel just
didn't seem scary.

On the monitor, Xavier and John both stood
up. They left the interrogation room. Gabriel left,
joining them wherever they had gone. I stayed and
stared at the screen.

My uncle, Joe Clachan, was in the room with
Nina. The two were arguing. I leaned in, as if it
would allow me to understand them better, and
listened. Nina smacked him in the back of the head,
then went and beat on the door of the interrogation
room.

With my comrades off doing whatever it was
that they did, I went to the room. I didn't go in, just
opening it enough for my head to enter. Nina
frowned at me.

"We can't tell you," she said.

"Well, everyone else seems to have gone out
for coffee at the moment. I'll let them know you
want to talk to them." I told her.

"What do you mean they went out for
coffee?" Joe demanded.

"They went to get coffee." I answered,
speaking very slowly.

"What, I'm not important enough or something?" Joe stood.

"You were uncooperative," I shrugged. "So, they went to get coffee and, as Kurt Russell famously said, maybe a Danish."

"What the hell is wrong with you people? You drag me down here, send in two guys that act like Scooby-Doo and Shaggy to interrogate me and then go out for coffee and a Danish? That seems unprofessional." Joe responded.

"Hey, if you want professional police officers, we are definitely not the team for you. If you want federal officers that get the job down and bust down doors, you call us. I don't know what to tell you." I looked at Nina. "Do you want coffee or something while you wait? You don't have to sit in here, you can come out. He has to stay though."

"I would like a cup of coffee," Nina said, following me out of the room. I walked with her down the hall. I had heard the information and I desperately needed Gabriel to go into the room and hear it from Joe. I was hoping they were at the coffee machine. My wish was granted. The three men stood around a coffee machine.

"You have got to go," I told Gabriel. "Joe has a bombshell piece of information to share and I'm not sure how long he'll be convinced to tell it."

"Ok," Gabriel looked at me skeptically.

"Go," I shooed him with my hands. Nina stood next to me. "Coffee-like substance?" I pointed to the pot.

"How old is that?" She asked.

"It isn't as old as the coffee on Snow Dogs," Xavier giggled. "What's the bombshell piece of information?"

"My cousin, August, is alive." I told him, practically dancing.

"How is that possible?"

"That is an excellent question," I looked at Nina.

"Don't ask me, I just found out myself." Nina answered attempting to pour the coffee into a mug. "Crazy people."

"Was that directed at us or someone else?" Xavier asked. Nina seemed to think about this for a few moments. Her wrinkled face pinched up.

"Our family, but I guess it would apply to you guys," she finally answered. "Want to hear a joke?"

"A real joke?" John asked.

"Yes, a real joke," Nina scolded him. She should have been a school teacher. The scold and look she shot him would have made high school students wither in their seats as they tried to think of excuses as to why they didn't do their homework.

"I'm always up for a joke. Ace doesn't tell many." Xavier leaned against the counter holding the coffee pot.

"Aislinn has never had much of a sense of humor. Her father didn't either. However, he's the one that told me this joke." Nina answered.

"I have a sense of humor," I defended myself.

"I didn't say you had no sense of humor. I said you didn't have much of one. There is a difference. You've always been too serious to really have a sense of humor. On to my joke, before Aislinn starts protesting," Nina said. "Which side of the cheetah has the most spots?"

I stared at my great aunt, racking my brain for an answer and coming up with nothing. I wasn't sure there was any way to know which side of a cheetah had the most spots. Genetics, gender, even food sources could have an impact on the way spots formed.

"I give up," Xavier said.

"The outside," Nina chuckled. Xavier and John both chuckled with her. I frowned. "Stop thinking about it, kiddo, it's a joke."

"I'm not thinking about it," I told her. This was true, I had stopped thinking about it the moment I heard the answer. I had overthought a joke and ruined it as a result. Maybe I didn't have a sense of humor.

"She's just realized that she doesn't have a sense of humor after all," Xavier said.

"That is exactly what I was thinking about," I admitted. "Is Gabriel talking to my uncle alone?" I asked pointedly.

"No, Detective Russell is with him," Xavier answered. "He came in and said he was going to give it a crack a few seconds before you did. You didn't see him in the hall?"

"No," I answered, rushing back to the room with Joe and Gabriel. I flung open the door. Detective Russell and Gabriel sat at the table. Joe sat with them. They all stared at me. "Sorry." I closed the door.

"Everything okay?" Xavier asked sauntering around the corner.

"Seems to be," I answered, leaning against the wall. I had expected to find Joe strangling my boss. I was glad he wasn't. "Could you have been any slower about getting here?"

"That is a small room. I didn't want to be in there with you if things were not okay," Xavier sipped his coffee. "This is terrible."

"So the old adage of police station coffee being bad is true?" I asked him.

"No, most police stations have good coffee. Maybe we got it from the wrong pot." Xavier told me. "Since your cousin is alive, do you think he is still in the illegal animal trade?"

"That is an excellent question," I said. "But a better question is how is he still alive. They found his body in the rafters."

"No, they found a body in the rafters." Xavier said. "If he was positively identified, they may not have done much to prove it was your cousin."

"Not even compared dental records?" I asked.

"His face was eaten, what dental records?"

"His face was bitten, there's a difference."

"There is a difference," Xavier agreed. "Your cousin's face was eaten. I saw the photos. The lower jawbone was detached from the skull and gnawed on."

"Then we're back to how he was positively identified." I looked at Xavier. "Think about the numerous victims we've seen that had only part of their face missing. It was hard to identify them without DNA."

"Anyone else in your family missing?" Xavier asked.

"My grandfather is missing. Oh and he's The Butcher." I told him. Xavier's mouth dropped open. "Yeah, surprise! Nina just found out, she tipped Malachi, so I'm guessing the lead that Malachi called about was legitimate."

"Is he a serial killer?"

"It would appear that way, but aside from my grandmother, all his victims were in Europe during World War II. It was a serial killer's paradise. Any mutilated corpses were just assumed to be Nazi barbarianism. My grandfather served on the front lines. He could easily have committed crimes that were attributed to Nazis. I guess he used to brag about them once he came back, at least to family members."

"How do you feel about your grandfather being a serial killer?" Xavier asked.

"Annoyed," I said. "That gives me a serial killer and a mass murderer in my family. I'm starting to buy the whole argument that most serial killers are created by genetics."

"With ten thousand serial killers a year in the US alone, most people are likely to know one or two."

"How many can claim that they have two in their immediate family?"

"The girl from Alaska has two, her father and brother. I've forgotten her name." Xavier said.

That was true. The young teenaged daughter of an Alaskan serial killer could claim two. That meant there were at least two of us in the world with immediate family members who liked to kill. All I could say was at least Eric hadn't skinned his victims alive. I didn't know that a bullet was more merciful, but it seemed less painful in the long run.

"Did you really just play my mass murderer is better than your serial killer in your head because your brother didn't skin his victims?" Xavier asked.

"What the hell?" I glared at him. "The mind reader has to take a few months off and you acquire his powers in the mean time? Get out of my head."

"Wow, you did. So, we should sort out how your cousin was identified and find somewhere for your aunt to go. I don't think going back to the Clachan Cult would be very healthy."

"I think she is going to Nyleena's." I told him. "She has terminal cancer."

"I know, I can see the symptoms," Xavier said. "Do you want to call Nyleena while I get all the case notes from your cousin's autopsy and investigation?"

"Sounds like a plan," I told him, pulling out my phone.

TWENTY-SIX

Arrangements were made for Nina to go stay with Nyleena. She said she needed nothing from the house except her medications. Xavier and Gabriel went to get those. We figured my family was still huddled together waiting for the return of the guys, so they wouldn't be an issue, but better safe than sorry. Xavier returned with medications and a suitcase. The suitcase contained clothing and some photos that had been hung on the wall of my great aunt's apartment. They were photos of Nyleena and her immediate family and my immediate family.

One caught my attention. It was Nyleena and I at the park, we were both smiling. I looked about twelve in the photo. In front of us was a dog. I had never had a dog and at that time, Nyleena had been away at college. The dog wasn't hers.

"Who's dog?" I asked Nina.

"Eric's," Nina answered. "Eric took the picture."

"I don't remember going to the park with Eric and Nyleena."

"Obviously, you did," Nina answered.

"I look happy. It seems like something I would remember."

"Look might be the keyword," Nina said. "You were always hard to read, even as a young child. You were good at looking happy, even when you weren't. It was a skill your father had as well."

"My father was a sociopath," I told her.

"I know." Nina answered. "So are you. What's your point?"

"Nature versus nurture," I shrugged.

"You were a sociopath long before that picture was taken. I remember when you were three, I told your father that you were going to be like him. But damn you were smart and logical, you were so logical you could think circles around most of the family. That's why your Uncle Chub, Nyleena and I were sort of put in charge of caring for you when you needed a babysitter. We were the only ones that you couldn't confuse with logic. That's why Nyleena latched onto you. At a young age, you were her intellectual equal. She liked that and very mature. I've never seen a child so independent and mature as you. Some of that seems to have slipped, probably because you have friends now."

"I think that was an insult," I told her.

"Just the opposite. You were always too logical, too mature. It's good that you have friends and have someone that can relate to you. It's made you grow. I see it in you. So does your mom."

"You talk to my mom?" My mom had been ostracized after my father's death.

"Twice a month," Nina said.

"My, my, you have been keeping secrets," I raised an eyebrow.

"We all keep secrets. They usually eat us alive. That's why I have cancer, too many secrets. But I'm done keeping them." She told me. I didn't tell my great aunt that secrets hadn't caused her cancer. She wouldn't have believed me anyway. "Now, go do your job. I'll be fine here waiting on Nyleena."

Gabriel, John, and Xavier were in a conference room. A single box sat on the table. The guys had folders in their hands. Xavier was frowning very hard at his. If he concentrated or frowned much harder, his face would break and the file would combust within his fingertips. He slid the file to me. I read a few pages.

August had been identified by DNA. It was therefore impossible that he could be up and walking around, like Joe said. It was even more impossible that he was still importing animals illegally and selling them to a serial killer. While my family probably could have hid August for ten years, it was very unlikely. I slid the folder back to Xavier. Joe had lied to us. This didn't really surprise me.

Xavier caught the folder as John motioned him over. Xavier stared over the other man's shoulder at a computer screen. They talked quickly with Xavier pointing to things on the screen.

"Is there a history of inbreeding in your family?" Xavier asked.

"No," I told him.

"Are you sure?" He pressed.

"Sure as I can be. I'm not monitoring the bedroom activities of all my relatives."

"Are you adopted?" Xavier continued.

"Not that I know of," I responded. "Should I call my mother and ask?"

"No, I'll do it," Xavier took out his phone and speed dialed my mother. It said something when your coworker had your mother on speed dial. Of course, my mother lived in Kansas City. No one else's mother lived that close and I was discovering that occasionally, the guys just needed a mommy. Lucas had a term for it, but I hadn't paid enough attention to remember it. Essentially, my mother was a surrogate for all of them because she was close.

Xavier went through the same questions with my mother that he did with me. There were several minutes of silence on his end. After those minutes, he hung up.

"Your mother is about to call you," he said as my phone began to ring.

"Do I want to hear this?" I asked her.

"Probably not," my mother said on the other end of the phone line. "You and Nyleena are not double cousins. She's your sister. She's adopted."

"What?" I asked, not because I wanted her to repeat herself, but because I needed a minute to think about it.

"Well, Nyleena's mom couldn't get pregnant and your dad and I were having good luck with it, so we let them adopt Nyleena. I want you to understand that we got pregnant with the intention of letting them adopt the baby."

"Does Nyleena know?" I asked.

"No and you are not to tell her, do you understand?" My mother's warning was understood even over the phone.

"My lips are sealed, but if I get cancer," I told her.

"Don't be silly. Be careful," my mom hung up on me.

"Are you ok?" Xavier asked.

"What's with that question?" I scowled.

"I'm going to take that as a no. Do you need a minute?" Xavier continued.

"Why would I need a minute? My cousin is really my sister, but only by genetics. She's my best friend by choice. It's a little bit of a shock, but it isn't life altering. Now, how the hell I'm going to keep my promise to my mother not to tell her, is another story. I can't keep a secret. It is practically impossible for me to keep a secret unless it benefits me in some way and this doesn't."

"When you put it that way, it makes you sound like a bad person and a bad friend." Gabriel informed me.

"I'm not a good person and I would seriously question anyone that said I was a good friend."

"You're not a good person in the normal sense of the word," Gabriel told me. "But that just means you're a good person in a different way. You are a great friend, I don't know many people who would actually kill or die for their friends. So, you can't keep a secret, that doesn't make you the worst friend on the planet, it just makes you a blabber mouth who shouldn't be told important secrets." Gabriel thought for a moment. "Especially if that secret involves your best friend or a family member. Nyleena is double screwed."

"Maybe Nina will tell her," I said.

"Really?" John looked at me.

"Then it won't be my fault she found out and I won't break the promise I just made to my mother. It's a win-win."

"Don't you think that it will bother Nyleena?" John asked.

"Baby swapping isn't that uncommon," Xavier told him. "Especially in the days before fertility treatments like in-vitro fertilization. It was common for a large family to let a cousin or sibling who couldn't have children to adopt infants, newborns, and even young children. I admit, it wasn't as common in the 1960's, but it still happened. Which brings me to my next question, was August adopted?"

"Not that I know of."

"How close of a cousin is he to you and Nyleena?" Xavier continued.

"First cousin, once removed. He was Gertrude's 'miracle baby,' she wasn't supposed to be able to get pregnant. Why?"

"Because if August really is your first cousin, once removed, he should share about six percent of his DNA with you and Nyleena." Xavier told me.

"Is that why you're poking around with Nyleena's DNA? How'd you even get her DNA?" I asked.

"Standard operating procedure for anyone involved with serial killer cases regularly. You, me, Gabriel, Nyleena, Malachi's reclusive uncle that's a judge, we all have our DNA on file in case it's needed to identify our bodies." Xavier informed me.

"Oh, well," I shrugged. "So how much DNA do August and I share?"

"Zero. There isn't even an accidental gene overlay. There is absolutely no chance that you and Nyleena are related to this body, not even seventh cousins twice removed."

"Then the old witch isn't my great-aunt?" I asked. That would mean Nina wasn't either. She and Gertrude were twins.

"That's my guess at this moment," Xavier said.

"How fast can you sequence Nina's DNA?" I asked.

"Why?"

"Well, Nina and Gertrude are twins. They used to be identical, but age has changed them, a lot. One aged a whole lot better than the other. If you sequence Nina's DNA, you'll have Gertrude's DNA."

"Nina's DNA would be on file with the hospital. I'll need her to sign a release, but it's already been sequenced for her cancer treatments," Xavier told me.

"Great, I'll go get her consent and get the release signed." I left the room.

TWENTY-SEVEN

We all stared at Nina's DNA sequence, even Nina. She and I shared several DNA markers. There was no doubt that she was my aunt. She assured us that August was indeed Gertrude's biological son. This left a huge question: who was the man found in the rafters and how had my family substituted a DNA sample from the unknown victim?

At least we knew August was indeed alive. We didn't know where at, but we had a pretty good idea of where to start. I was looking forward to handcuffing my great-aunt. If I was being entirely honest, I was really looking forward to kicking her door in and drawing my Taser on her too. I might not need the Taser, but it would feel good just to have it out and pointed at her.

Nyleena collected Nina while we suited up for the raid on the house of my other great-aunt. My tactical gear was weighed down by the arsenal I was convinced I needed. I was prepared for everything, including jaguar attacks, invasions by extraterrestrials, and crazed great-aunts.

"Don't get trigger happy," Gabriel said as we exited the SUV. I decided not to take it as a comment directed at me specifically. Detective Russell was in an unmarked car, following us. There was also a squad car with two uniformed officers behind him.

Gabriel stood to the side of the door as he knocked gruffly on it. He announced himself, adding that we were coming in and then waited a few seconds. There were noises inside, but they weren't getting closer to the door.

Normally, Lucas kicked in the door and I went in first, gun drawn, ready for any horrors that might present themselves. Lucas's absence was being felt more and more. Instead, I dropped into my normal position and Gabriel took position at the door. His foot landed squarely near the handle. The door groaned and creaked, but didn't give. I shook my head. His second kick did a better job and the door actually gave a little in the frame.

"Good thing they weren't planning on shooting you," Xavier commented. I agreed. The third kick freed the door of the jamb and it swung haphazardly on its hinges into the foyer.

The house was old. It had been in the family for a long time. Gertrude and her husband Lee had lived in it for as long as I could remember. Nina had once lived down the road in another old farm house that had been acquired by the Clachans and passed down through the generations. It was now occupied by a cousin of ours, since she didn't have any children.

Lee sat in the living room. My great-aunt was old. But Lee had probably ridden wooly mammoths to school. He sat in a recliner, his small body enveloped by the La-Z-Boy. An oxygen tank sat on the ground, the wires running up to his face. Liver spots darkened his aging, bald scalp. While he had technically married a Clachan, Gertrude had retained her maiden name and passed it down to August.

"Where is August?" Gabriel asked Lee.

"He's dead," Lee answered between puffs on the oxygen mask.

"He's not dead, we ran the DNA from the body found at the site. The sample and the body carried no alleles in common with Nina Clachan." Xavier told him. "This can only mean that the dead body and the sample did not come from August and that he is very much alive."

"He's dead I tell ya," Lee protested.

"Joe Clachan is telling a different story. He says Gertrude faked August's death. He also says that the jaguars were for August's private collection." Gabriel stepped towards the oxygen tank. "How long do you think you'll live in prison? A year? Six months? We can make sure that doesn't happen, Lee. You need to be smart about this. If you screw with us, I will personally make sure that you get a hefty prison sentence in one of the worst federal prisons available."

"Ok, you don't want to talk about August." I interrupted. "Where's Gertrude? Did she abandon you to the mercy of the SCTU?" This seemed to shake Lee just a little. His papery skin grew a shade lighter, making his veins more apparent and the liver spots darker. A small tremble ran through his hands. I watched the older man for another few moments. "Holy hell, she's on the premises and she's warning August that we're here. She knows. She knows all about it."

"Gertrude wouldn't help a killer," Lee protested.

"Oh please, she helped my grandfather and this is her only son. She'd go to the ends of the earth and back to help him," I scoffed, already heading for the back door.

Outside there was a large pasture. In times past, it had been used to graze cattle. A broken down hog pen sat to one side, still carrying the faint odor of the previous occupants, despite the cold air or lack of animal life. Closer to the house was a chicken coop, also vacant and in need of repairs.

Behind the pasture was woods. Thick, dense woods, where trees grew close enough to make midday dim and shadows dark and scary. I couldn't remember how wide the tract of trees was, only that as a child, there had been a pathway through them. My gaze searched for the path and found it, but only just. Weeds and hearty grasses were trying to reclaim it. The path led to another Clachan farm. It had been used to take livestock back and forth between the two family ranches.

I began to follow the path. The snow was almost completely melted, but the ground was still too hard to leave shoe imprints. Footfalls caught my attention and I whirled around, Taser drawn and pointed at Xavier.

"Gabriel and John are staying at the house. What's this?" He nodded towards the overgrown path.

"A smuggler's path," I sneered. "The family used to exchange livestock using this path. The ranch on the other side raised Red Angus. This one raised Murray Greys."

"You might as well be speaking Greek," Xavier told me.

"A steak from a Red Angus is worth a whole lot more than one from a Murray Grey. People would buy cattle from one ranch, thinking they were buying a Red Angus and paying top dollar for it, but when it came time for the butchering, they'd end up with a Murray Grey. Most people can't tell the difference once the meat is cut, so they got away with it for a long time. Then most people started buying their meat at a store and well, there wasn't much call for the swap. Most of the beef now is sold directly to butcher shops that do their own slaughtering and they know what the cow looks like when it comes into the slaughter house. They wouldn't be paying Red Angus prices for Murray Greys."

"I didn't realize you knew that much about cattle ranching."

"I didn't grow up on the farm, but it was hard to avoid it completely. If you ever want to buy a side of beef or a whole hog, I'm the person to take with you. Some breeds can be identified after the butchering by smell, appearance, even the size of the meat cuts."

"I will keep that in mind," Xavier nodded once. We'd walked a few hundred yards and were at the cusp of the woods. Xavier drew his gun. I swapped the Taser for a more lethal weapon and put one of the Berettas in my hands. "What's back here?"

"As far as I remember, nothing. It's a straight line to the other farm. I don't remember how wide the tree break is though. It could be a few hundred yards or it could be a mile."

"Side by side, sweep the trees as we move," Xavier told me. I did as he said, taking position at his shoulder. My eyes scanned the trees, alert for movement and color variations.

It was quiet in the trees. Being January meant very little wildlife was actively roaming the hidden recesses. A few birds took flight from trees as we moved, but otherwise, nothing seemed alive. My ears strained to hear noises to the point that my heartbeat was audible.

The trees were barren for the winter, their leaves strewn about the ground. The few evergreens looked sickly from the successive years of drought. Lifeless bushes and naked vines were the only other things growing in the semi-darkness. It hadn't been thinned in as long as I could remember. In my youth, it had seemed like a magical wilderness. Now, it looked like a sad, neglected tree break in need of some care.

Light appeared in front of us. We exited the woods as easily as we had entered them. It had been about half a mile. My feet were cold. My nose was starting to run. I shivered. We'd found nothing in the tree break.

However, we stared at a different house now. This one was older. The years had not been kind. I shivered again, but not from cold.

"What's wrong?" Xavier asked.

"If there was ever a haunted house, that's it," I pointed towards the clapboard hulk. Large windows stared back at us. Aside from being vacant for decades, it was intact. No one had vandalized it.

"I didn't think you believed in ghosts," Xavier told me.

"I don't," I answered. "But around the turn of the century, two women were mutilated inside that house. In the 1960's, my grandmother was butchered there. Her entrails were used to decorate the walls. They found her breasts nailed to a floor in the kitchen. Her uterus had been removed and put on the fireplace mantel. Her heart was found sitting on the railing of the front porch. Her head was in the basement, sitting on top of freshly canned green beans. Her kidneys were in a bathroom. Her liver on the bed in the master bedroom and her lungs on the roof, stuck to the gable, like a weathervane."

"Wow," Xavier cocked his head, as if looking at the house in a different way.

"Yeah, but it didn't stop there. Her limbs and torso were cut into pieces and scattered along the driveway. My grandfather really did butcher my grandmother, all of her internal bits were removed. Her external parts were all dismembered at the joints. He even removed her ears and her brain."

"What did your grandfather do for a living?" Xavier asked.

"After being discharged from the military, he was a rancher. He raised cattle and hogs. Oddly, I've been told that when the women got together to kill and clean fowl for dinners, it would make him feel faint. He'd have to excuse himself. There's a famous story about him fainting after one of his hogs got loose and killed the family dog."

"But you believe he could have butchered your grandmother?"

"He couldn't kill an animal, but humans were a different story," I looked at Xavier, unwilling to turn my back on the house of horrors. "My grandmother may have been butchered, but he got into a fight with a buyer once and hit him in the head with a hammer. That incident didn't seem to faze him. The man didn't die and my grandfather spent a week in jail and paid a fine."

"How do you know that?" Xavier asked.

"Because my family gossips amongst themselves, they just don't like outsiders to know their secrets." I shivered once more and turned away from the house.

"August could be there," Xavier pointed out.

"He's not," I answered. "No one is there. The entire family thinks it's haunted. The driveway was gated over after the police got stuck with their investigation into my grandparents. When I was a kid, a few locals snuck onto the property, but they didn't stay more than an hour. People didn't realize that the house had never been cleaned. The body parts were removed, but the blood is still in there. It gives a very clear picture of what happened. I've never seen it, but I've heard the stories. It's gruesome."

"We should check it, just in case." Xavier said.

"Knock yourself out. I'll stand on the porch," I turned back around and stomped towards the house.

TWENTY-EIGHT

Xavier didn't hesitate to enter. Once through the front door, his footsteps stopped after only a few feet. I stared at the forest that was beginning to grow in front of the house. It obscured my view of the road.

"You're right," Xavier came back out a few moments later. "Nobody would live there."

"Told you," I said.

"You've never been inside?" Xavier asked.

"No."

"You should step inside, just once. Maybe take some pictures."

"No."

"It might exercise some demons from your past."

"No."

"Ace," Xavier stopped. "Ace, whatever you've heard, the reality is worse. You'd have to see it to believe it."

This peeked my curiosity. My feet moved without input from my brain. The door gave a small squeak as it opened. Like Xavier, I took a few steps inside and stopped.

If you didn't work with dried blood or blood stains, you would have thought it was age damage. I knew better. Splatter was thrown up all the walls and slung across the ceiling. A large, dark stain had ruined the hardwood floor. At first, it seemed too large to be a blood stain, but as my eyes adjusted to the dim lighting and grim surroundings, I could make out where it had run across the floor in rivulets and where it had congealed in large quantities.

Pictures still hung on the walls. An old fashioned television set was placed on a piece of handcrafted furniture. The coffee table had a cup and four books on it. Blood had splashed across the exposed book covers. But there was no blood on the cup, a smear was visible under the saucer. The sofa was also clear of blood spatter. A few drops had been smeared across the screen of the TV. It didn't take a genius to figure it out. As her body had gotten cold, the killer had wiped off the screen and watched TV while drinking a cup of coffee.

Looking closer, there were faded shoe prints in the blood. They led to different areas of the house, then came back into the living room, disappearing in the large pooled stain. However, they didn't lead to the sofa. The killer had butchered her, spread her body parts throughout the house and yard, then cleaned up, sat on the sofa and had a cup of coffee while watching TV.

Clearly, it had been premeditated. In order for the sofa to remain free of blood, it would have to have been covered with something heavy, like a tarp. It made me think that the reason for the final dismemberments had simply been to get the body out of the house. Everything else had been carefully placed in different rooms, but her body had been littered along the driveway.

All of this was disturbing, but not as disturbing as the next observations. There was no dust. There were no cobwebs. A lamp near the front door, a long brownish stain ruining the lampshade, was plugged into an automatic timer. The timer was plugged into the wall. I hit the wall switch and the overhead light came on.

I exited the house of horrors. Xavier still stood on the porch, staring at the railing. The paint had cracked and peeled. Any blood remnants had been erased by exposure to the weather. Weeds were growing up over the driveway, claiming the land by hiding and scattering the gravel. A medium sized tree was growing in the middle of it.

Xavier moved, walking down the steps and pointed to the side of the house. Brand new water and electric meters were connected to the building. I moved closer to them. They were digital allowing them to be read from a distance using a gizmo that you held in your hand.

"Maybe someone is living here," I said.

"No, while there wasn't dust or many signs of aging, there also wasn't any sign of life. People leave traces. The traces left in that house are almost fifty years old."

"Except for the cleaning," I pointed out.

"Yes, but if you noticed, the floors were swept, but not mopped. Someone is cleaning it, but they are being careful in the cleanings. It reminds me of a shrine, not a house."

"A murder shrine?"

"It's not the first shrine we've found. It's just never been an entire house. And someone is paying the electric and water bills. They've even had new meters installed so that the county doesn't have to come down the driveway. If I had to guess, I'd say they walk to the edge of those woods and read the meter," Xavier pointed back towards Gertrude's house. "Is your great-aunt bat shit crazy?"

"Yep, but it's not her kill, why would she keep it pristinely gruesome?"

"Admiration?" Xavier suggested. "Or perhaps she's hiding more than one family member."

"It's hard to hide a person for fifty years. It would be overwhelming to hide two of them for ten years."

"But not impossible."

"No one is that good at multitasking."

"We'll agree to disagree, but when we find both of them, huddled together in some shack, keeping warm with a jaguar, I get to say I told you so." Xavier smiled. "What did you think of the house?"

"I think that my grandfather was one sick puppy. He bathed, made coffee, and watched TV after slaughtering my grandmother. To me, I think tossing the leftover body parts in the driveway was just his way of getting the body out of the house."

"Why would he need to get the body out of the house after butchering it?"

"How about the smell?" I offered.

"It would smell horrendous." Xavier started walking back through the woods. "Where else would you hide your not really dead son?"

"Me?" I asked.

"Well, not you personally, but your family."

"I don't know," I shrugged at him. "I think most of them are nutty. It could be that none of the family members wanted to be involved or it could be that someone is putting him up."

"Why would none of the family be involved and yet Joe know?"

"Because we aren't good at keeping secrets from other family members. The outside world, but not within the family. And while they have been known to run moonshine, cheat on cattle sales, and be jackasses, murder, especially serial murder, isn't acceptable."

"They draw the line at murder?" Xavier gestured towards the disappearing house.

"It brings too many questions. If my grandfather hadn't disappeared, someone would have turned him in just to make sure that the police weren't poking around too much. Unfortunately, he went on the run."

"So, no one turned him in?" Xavier asked.

"No, everyone turned him in. The entire family was cooperative to try to avoid scrutiny. They all said he was the murderer. They failed to mention his war crimes, but it didn't matter. They went through everyone's lives with a fine-toothed comb. A few people got in trouble for tax evasion, but most of them were squeaky clean."

"Why are they so concerned if there wasn't anything to be concerned about?"

"Not all skeletons are illegal."

We reached my great-aunt's house. Gabriel and John had Lee outside. He wasn't handcuffed, but he was shackled at the ankles. He wasn't going anywhere anyway, his oxygen tank wasn't portable without help. Lee himself hadn't been able to move the portable tank in years. Time had been bad to Lee. Most of his body had given up, only his heart and brain were in perfect working order.

"We didn't find August, but Gertrude Clachan is a little weird," Xavier told our leader.

"Ha!" Lee snorted. "Weird? The woman is pure fucking evil. You guys are Marshals, put me in witness protection and I'll tell you everything. Like August ain't my son, we couldn't have kids because I couldn't have kids, not because she couldn't. And I'll tell you why she keeps that house so damn clean, including replacing the sofa."

I turned my gaze towards Lee. The sofa was clean because she had replaced it, but she hadn't replaced anything else. It made me wonder how much of the scene was staged by my great-aunt and how much of it was real. I really wanted to know though.

"Once Gertrude's behind bars, you'd be safe," John told him.

"Um," I frowned. "Lee is a Clachan, on his mother's side."

"Family tree forgot it needed to fork?" Xavier asked.

"No," I glared at him. "Yes, he's a cousin, but he isn't a close cousin. He's like Gertrude's sixth cousin or something."

"Seventh," Lee corrected.

"Ok, seventh cousin," I told Xavier. John gave me a look that was pure disgust.

"Actually, seventh cousins are perfectly fine to marry and procreate. Anything after five are genetically diverse enough to have a good chance of not passing along strange diseases. In some states, it's fourth cousins." Xavier defended my family tree missing a few forks. He could poke fun at it, but John wasn't allowed to have an opinion, yet.

"I still don't know why you'd need a new identity if we arrest August and Gertrude," I told Lee.

"You think that's all I know about?" He smirked. "For instance, I know how your grandfather always knows where you are. I also know that he was the murder weapon, not the murderer in your grandmother's death and that he's killed a few others along the way that weren't during the war. He tried to kill you."

"We'll discuss it," Gabriel put Lee in the squad car and everyone turned to stare at me. I felt like a bug.

"They are all pretty serious about your grandfather being your stalker," Xavier said. "Do you really think he'd try to kill you?"

"Did you close your eyes when you were in the house?" I snipped at him. "If he has tried to kill me, he failed but got away. I can't think of any attacks that match that description. However, I am interested in how he knows where I am, all the time. And if Lee can tell us where August is, that would be helpful."

I was suddenly shoved to the ground. The force on my back was hard enough to be painful. Warmth spread underneath my shirt and the skin burned. There was shouting around me. I rolled over onto my back. The pain increased. After a few moments, it began to fade. Clouds drifted lazily overhead. The sky was a lead grey, but not overcast. I never really took the time to look at the sky. I always expected it to be there when I looked up. So far, it hadn't disappointed me.

My ears picked up the sound of a rifle bolt sliding followed by another shot. I wondered if it was Michael's sniper.

I stared at the sky and waited for another bullet to tear into me. I hoped it was a headshot, I was convinced they were the least painful.

TWENTY-NINE

The shots had stopped several minutes earlier. My uncle, Joe, was in custody, along with an old bolt action Colt rifle. The clouds were still floating by overhead. Xavier was shouting.

"Oh god," he groaned. "I'm going to roll you over, Ace."

"He missed," I told Xavier.

"Not according to the blood pooling under you."

"My vest gave."

"What do you mean your vest gave?" Gabriel asked, coming into my vision.

"My vest gave out. I'm not bleeding from a bullet wound, I'm bleeding because the ceramic plate in the back of my vest cracked. It's stabbing me. Only, that part of the vest isn't rated for stabbing. It isn't life threatening. It's just annoying."

Xavier began tearing at the snaps and straps that held my vest onto me. He jerked and tugged, causing me to shake and jiggle on the ground. It didn't look dignified but I refused to help him.

"If you aren't injured, why aren't you moving?" Xavier asked. His voice was high-pitched and frantic.

"Really?" I turned my head to look at him. He stopped jerking on me. "My uncle just shot me in the back. Most of the people who try to kill me do it face to face."

"So what, you're contemplating your uncle's cowardice for shooting you in the back?" Xavier asked.

"No, I am realizing that aside from Eric, my grandfather, and me, my family isn't exactly adept at the whole killing thing. They should stick to running moonshine and doing bait and switches with cattle."

"Are you delirious?" Gabriel asked.

"Not in the least," I sat up and pulled off the vest that Xavier had been desperate to remove. The ceramic plate fell out in four pieces. A fifth, much smaller piece, was visible through the Kevlar backing. Xavier was already poking and prodding at the wound through my jacket and shirt.

"Then what are you rambling about?" Gabriel asked.

"Her family used to sell people fancy cattle but when it came time to butcher them, they'd switch them out for less fancy cattle, pocketing the extra money. Before that, I believe they were bootleggers or something." Xavier answered for me.

"Do you have a lot of criminals in your family?" John asked.

"Relatively speaking, no," I answered. "However, I have a huge family. The people you've met have just been first cousins, aunts, uncles, great-aunts, and great-uncles. My great-grandparents had nine children. Gertrude, Nina and my grandfather had been the three youngest, a few years separating them. One of the older ones died while he was young, Nina never had children and Gertrude had August, but the rest bred prolifically. One of my grandfather's brother's raised sixteen children. If we were to do a per capita of Clachan family members and crime, we have a rather low criminality rate. It's about one in twenty or so."

"Of course, when they do go bad, they go really bad," my cousin Kyle walked up to us. "We could hear the shots down the road."

"Go away," I told him.

"If you arrest Joe and Gertrude, you'll find a lot of us will become cooperative. How bad did he shoot you?"

"While he did technically shoot me, he didn't injure me. My vest gave out. Too many bullets over time." I told him. "I'm guessing Lee is dead."

"Yes," Gabriel said.

"Hey Kyle, do you know where August is hidden?" I bluntly turned on my cousin as I found my feet and stood up.

"No, but I know he's alive." Kyle admitted. "Do you need a reason to arrest Gertrude?"

"It would be helpful," I told him.

"Check her basement," Kyle nodded once and started walking away. "Oh and once the witch is dead, we're burning down your grandparents house, if you don't mind?"

"Why are you telling me?" I asked.

"You own it," Kyle said. "It passed to you when Eric went to prison. We sort of need your permission."

"Burn it down," I told him. "If you want, I'll bring the marshmallows."

"I thought you guys didn't like each other?" John said.

"We don't," Kyle told him. "Doesn't mean we can't be respectful."

"I'm confused," John said.

"Why is it confusing? She's Aislinn Clachan, killer of killers, granddaughter of The Butcher, and while the rest of us were being reared like sheep, she was bucking the system because she's a psychopath who everyone's afraid of. Why do you think she was so vehemently disowned?"

"And I believe that they are all sheep," I agreed. "I've never been fond of sheep. That's why I like Nyleena, she had the courage to not be herded into a life she didn't want."

"Why was she disowned?" John asked, he still looked confused.

"Because my grandfather's siblings were in charge. In me, they saw the man that butchered his wife. They knew they couldn't control me, so they voted me off the island instead."

"Her father was funny like that too," Kyle said. "Gertrude tried to use him, but when he refused, he was considered an outcast as well."

"So, this entire dislike thing is based on something as simple as genetics?" Xavier asked.

"We're all Catholic, so they couldn't hate me for my religion. That only left genetics." I answered.

"Yeah," Kyle started walking away again.

"You're family is dysfunctional," Xavier told me.

"All families are dysfunctional," I responded, already heading for my great-aunt's basement, curious to see what secrets were hidden in the dark recesses. "You show me a normal family and I'll find out what they keep hidden from the public eye."

"My family isn't dysfunctional," John mumbled as we walked in a group.

"You're wife left you because you couldn't find her little girl's killer, so you joined the SCTU," I told him. "How is that not dysfunctional?"

"How'd you..." John's footfalls stopped with his voice.

"Ace is very perceptive as long as she doesn't have to turn those powers of perception on herself." Gabriel answered. "You don't have to tell her things, she just observes and draws conclusions. Scary conclusions because they are rarely wrong. Which reminds me, we're going to talk about the fact that I think you knew your grandfather was The Butcher when we finish this case."

"I didn't know," I told my boss. "I suspected, but I didn't know."

I flipped on the light switch for the basement. No horrid, overwhelming odors reached my nose. No blood stains immediately jumped out for my eyes to find. It looked like a basement, complete with support timbers and concrete flooring. A washer and dryer sat on one side, the other side seemed to be storage. The storage area was very well organized with labels on every plastic container. My mind catalogued the labels. In the third stack, about half way down, was a large, black container with a lid duct taped on. The label read "Furs."

Without regard for the other containers, I jerked the handle, pulling it free. The others collapsed like the ending of a Jenga game. They bounced across the floor, skittering in all directions. The one I held had cracked around the handle from the rough treatment.

"Gloves," Gabriel groaned.

"Oh for Pete's sake," I groaned back and began searching my pockets for a pair of gloves. I came up with leather ones, lined in wool. They were fitted for my small hands. I pulled them on, knowing that everyone would have preferred I used crime scene approved gloves.

"Wait, should she open it? It's a conflict of interest," John said.

"This entire case is a conflict of interest," Gabriel said. "However, as long as she is monitored and acts within the boundaries of the law, then it's fine."

"It's a very wide boundary," Xavier snickered.

Ignoring them, I tore off the duct tape. Several different animal pelts could be seen just from my position over the container. However, one caught my interest immediately. It was black with darker spots. I pulled it out. Gabriel whistled. Xavier's mouth fell open.

"Melanistic jaguar?" I asked.

"It has to be that or a leopard," Gabriel answered. "However, it looks like a jaguar to me."

I set it aside and stopped. My eyes saw the skin, but my brain refused to accept it. With trembling hands I pulled it out.

"Holy shit," Gabriel stepped forward. We both gently held the white and black striped fur. White tigers were endangered, owning their pelts was illegal.

"Uh guys," Xavier had moved forward. He was pointing inside the box. "It gets worse." As he spoke, he was pulling on leather gloves himself. This was unusual for Xavier, since nitrile gloves seemed to reproduce in his clothing. Very carefully he pulled out a large pelt. It was a very bright orange, since I was staring at animal skins, I'd describe it as tiger orange. Large black spots decorated the pelt, but the spots had orange in the very middle. It was beautiful. I had never seen anything like it.

Xavier held it like it was made of very fragile gold leaf. As he showed it to us, he kept checking to make sure that it wasn't touching the concrete floor or being stretched too much in any area. After a few seconds, he carefully rolled it up and tucked it back into the box.

"Well don't keep us in suspense," Gabriel scolded.

"I'm not an expert, but I believe that's the skin of pantheras pardus orientalis." Xavier said.

"It's a leopard," I answered before anyone asked.

"It's not just a leopard," Xavier frowned. Before he could finish, Detective Russell joined us.

"Can we arrest her on this?" Detective Russell asked, looking at the tiger skin Gabriel and I were holding.

"Yes, she's in violation of several laws," Xavier put the lid on the tote without adding the pelt we were holding. "And we need an expert to know exactly what laws and how many."

UNGER

Patterson found himself back at the Unger farm. It still looked deserted, but appearances could be deceiving and he had been deceived the first time here. After killing George Killian, he'd gone to pay Lee a visit. Lee had been willing to talk, to tell secrets, one so devious, it had nearly resulted in Patterson killing him.

However, Patterson had regained control before lashing out at the man. Besides, his real rage was not aimed at Lee, it was at Gertrude. He held a piece of paper in his hand that made him shake with the rage. It was an unnotarized birth certificate with the name Tennyson August Unger, Junior on it. His sister had actually considered naming her son after her rapist. If Patterson could kill Unger all over again, he would. It was also the reason he was back on the Unger farm. The registrar currently had the deed registered to Tennyson Unger, Junior.

Night had descended upon Patterson hours ago. He had been leaning against a tree on the far side of the property for several hours trying to decide what to do. Obviously, the Marshals knew that August was alive and suspected he was responsible. He was waiting for them to come bursting through the trees and take down August. Yet, they weren't coming. He'd left a message at the hotel for Aislinn.

He wanted to kill August, but he didn't want to get caught. He had other things to do. It disturbed him that even with Nina's help, Aislinn wasn't charging in to capture the bad guy and possibly, kill him. Why wasn't she responding to his messages? That nagged at him more than he had ever thought possible.

The answer was obvious. In his own way, Patterson had come to know Gabriel Henders, Xavier Reece, and Lucas McMichaels. He didn't know the new guy. He suspected the new guy was intercepting all of his communication attempts with Aislinn.

Patterson dug out his cell phone and dialed a number. The line rang and went to voicemail. He immediately redialed the number.

"Hello?" Lucas McMichaels' voice came over the line. He sounded wide awake.

"Hello, Marshal McMichaels," Patterson answered. "This is..."

"Patterson Clachan," Lucas answered. "Malachi told me a few days ago that you were The Butcher. We all know by now."

"Yes," Patterson said. "I suppose you do. However, that isn't why I'm calling. I believe there is a problem within the SCTU. A very serious problem that if not addressed will become monumental."

"The SCTU is fine," Lucas answered curtly, but didn't hang up.

"How often have you known Aislinn to ignore my communications when I have passed along tips to her?" Patterson asked. Lucas was silent, it spoke volumes. "Exactly. I have attempted four times to contact her and tell her that August isn't dead. Yet, she didn't find out until today. This means that my messages never reached her. In the past, the SCTU has encouraged her to communicate in an attempt to track and identify The Butcher. Now, I am suddenly not getting any responses. Have orders changed? If so, is the SCTU ready to take responsibility for another dead body at the hands of August Clachan? Because he has killed since I sent the first message to her."

"When was that?" Lucas asked.

"The day the feet were found hanging on the wire." Patterson answered. "I wanted her to stay uninvolved in this, I had planned to take care of it. You see, I found out about it within the same week. So, I was going to make the problem go away. However, she became involved and well, I can't walk into his house and slaughter him then hope she finds the surviving victims. Out of necessity, I left a message at the hotel for her this evening, telling her that I thought I knew where August was hiding. I'm here. The SCTU is not."

"Where are you?" Lucas asked.

"I have been trying to make this easy for the SCTU and I have gotten no response. Until you clean house and fix your problems, I'm done. You may deal with August on your own. Tell that leader of yours that if Aislinn dies because of this, I will personally come after all of you." Patterson thought for another second. "And I won't just stop with team members. I will hunt down loved ones as well. I might be old, but I am not incapable."

"I am well aware of what you are capable of," Lucas sighed. "We found your work today, tied to a recliner, his organs strung about his house. We haven't told Aislinn because she doesn't remember George Killian and we aren't sure how it connects to her, we just know that you did it."

"Then I'll tell you, George Killian has been stalking Aislinn since Alaska, killing people to frame her. He tried to kill her in high school in a drive-by shooting, but failed. It took me a while to connect all the dots, but I have nothing but time on my hands and Eric helped."

"You're in contact with Eric?" Lucas asked.

"He reached out after he was sent to The Fortress. He was worried that only Malachi and Nyleena would be looking out for Aislinn. She is capable of getting in her own way and Malachi is both a positive and negative influence on her. So, yes, I have been in contact, sporadically, with Eric."

"I will investigate your claims. I'm guessing you came to me because you knew I wasn't with the team."

"That is correct. I would have gone to Blake, but he has other issues to deal with right now."

"Will you tell me now where August is holed up?" Lucas asked.

"No, you can call it petty, but I have always been helpful to your cases when it was needed and now, when it is needed the most, I don't even rank high enough to have my messages passed along to my granddaughter." Patterson paused. "On another note, I have found your sniper. The SCTU can't go after him, it will look like revenge when you kill him. So I am doing it for you. You may thank me later."

Patterson hung up. He stared at the house. The lights were still on. He had a feeling that August was still awake. Rushing in would be a mistake and he knew it. He could beat August, but August liked dangerous pets and he didn't think he was a match for any predators that might be skulking around the house. He was well past his best days, he didn't think he could break the neck of a boar hog with his bare hands anymore.

Besides, Nyleena had picked up Nina today. He had to return home to carry out his sister's last wishes.

Thirty

Xavier had an oogling buddy. The two stared at the animal skins spread out on special tables in the University of Missouri's zoology department. In reality, they only stared at one skin, the one that Xavier had held up in the basement. He still hadn't told us why he was so horrified to find it in the basement. There were endangered leopards, but tigers were considered more critically endangered if that made sense.

"You were right," Dr. Ritter told him.

"I've seen one before," Xavier said. "In the wild. I spent a summer in Siberia when I was in school."

"For those of us playing the home game," Gabriel interrupted, annoyed by the suspense.

"It's the skin of an Amur Leopard," Dr. Ritter told him. Alarm bells began to go off in my head. "In 2012, it was estimated that there were only about thirty left in the wild. It isn't just critically endangered, it is practically extinct. There's about 170 in captivity that are being used to breed for reintroduction, but so far, no luck. Owning this pelt is very illegal. I'd be very interested in knowing how the person came into possession of it."

"So would I," I told Dr. Ritter. "Let's go find out."

"Um, Ace, there's a problem with that," Xavier said.

"Yeah, I can't beat it out of her because she's old," I was still heading for the door.

"No," Gabriel grabbed my arm. "We don't have her in custody. We don't know where she is."

"Oh yeah," I stopped.

"Do you have any idea where she might be?" Gabriel had turned me so that I was facing him.

"No. I can't imagine the family is protecting her now that Lee is dead and Joe is in custody for killing him. You heard Kyle, crazy is one thing, but murderously crazy is a whole different can of worms."

"What about friends?" He asked.

"I don't know if she has friends. Her own husband called her evil. Does Satan have friends?" I thought for a moment. My back was still tender. I'd already been shot three times and I didn't have a serial killer in custody or my evil great-aunt who was hiding a suspected serial killer. This was not a good week.

"Would anyone in your family know?" Gabriel pressed.

"You seemed to have failed to grasp the concept of my family relations. I talk to Nyleena. Once a year, Nina calls me. I have more contact with The Butcher than I do my family. Although, I guess, technically, The Butcher is my family. I wonder what Lee meant about telling me how my grandfather always knew where I was?"

"Oh boy," John sat down. "Here comes a tangent."

"I don't think so," I told him. "I can guess that Gertrude has been feeding my whereabouts to him, but how did she know? As far as I know, the only people that would have been privy to that information would have been Nyleena and as it turns out, Nina. Nina wouldn't have told Gertrude and Nyleena has about as much use for Gertrude as she does for a two-headed cow. Lee also said that my grandfather had been the murder weapon, not the murderer when it came to my grandmother's death. And that The Butcher had tried to kill me before. Yet, I can't remember an old man breaking into any place I lived to try to kill me."

"This is a tangent," John said.

"No, I don't think it is," I told him. "I think it's all related, literally. What if August and I have more DNA in common than cousins should have? What if Gertrude is pulling The Butcher's strings because August is his son?"

"There goes another fork in the family tree," Xavier giggled.

"Thanks," I shook my head. "My grandmother was killed in the sixties. After August was born. Gertrude does something to wind him up and he goes home and slaughters my grandmother."

"Why not kill Gertrude?" Xavier asked.

"I don't know, because they're siblings or because Gertrude has more on him than just August."

"That might make sense," Gabriel cocked his head to the side. "You don't remember being attacked by The Butcher because you weren't. Grandpa sees that you are like him and he relates to you like a kindred spirit, but he has to keep Gertrude quiet, so he lies to her. He tells her he's tried, but you were too much for him, age is making him slow and weak. He sends the creepy mail because it's his way of keeping in touch with his granddaughter, but to Gertrude, it would appear like he was trying to psych you out."

"But that doesn't help us find Gertrude or August," I sighed. "Or The Butcher for that matter."

"It does make a stronger case for serial killing genes to be hereditary though," Xavier offered.

"That's true. If my grandfather really is August's father, that's a child and a grandchild that has followed in his footsteps. Granted, Eric is more mass murderer than serial killer, but for the sake of argument, I won't split hairs over it."

"Does this help?" John asked.

"Sometimes you just have to follow her logic along," Xavier said. "There is the very real chance that it will lead somewhere."

"If we could somehow let The Butcher know that Gertrude and August were wanted for murder, he might help," I said to Gabriel.

"You want me to start posting their pictures on the news to lure The Butcher into helping us?" Gabriel looked skeptical.

"It might kill two birds with one stone. If my grandfather wants revenge, he'd do what he could to make it possible for us to capture her and her deranged son. While we're working the case of the jaguar and feet," I slapped myself in the forehead.

"That looked like it hurt, a lot." Xavier winced.

"August is missing a foot. Well, not really missing it, we know where it is. He keeps it in a jar. He lost it as a child to a hog. From what I hear, the beast bit right through the bone and started munching on it." I sat down and hung my head. "But there's more to the story than that. He was with my grandfather at the time, he might have been three years old, maybe younger. Lee happened to be nearby. He heard August scream and rushed over. When he arrived, he had a pitch fork. Lee was stabbing the hog when legend says my grandfather grabbed hold of the thing's tusks and broke its neck. The hog let go of August and the foot fell out of his mouth. For some reason, Gertrude kept it. Then August kept it."

"That is a very disturbing story," Xavier said. "I'm not Lucas, but I can pick out four aspects immediately that render it a horror story."

"At least four," Gabriel looked at me. "What's your thoughts on it? True or legend?"

"True," I told him. "I think my grandfather tried to feed August to a hog, I think he got caught and in a psychopathic rage broke the neck of a full grown hog, which says all sorts of things about him. I think August remembers it. And I think it probably was the straw that broke the camel's back and August became a serial killer because of bad genes and childhood trauma. Also, I think I'm an idiot for not thinking of it sooner. I just never believed the story, not really."

"Why do you believe it now then?" John asked.

"Because it explains everything," I answered. "My grandmother was murdered a week later. What better way to wind up a serial killer than threaten to tell his wife about his inbred, illegitimate child that he tried to kill? He might not have been able to kill Gertrude at that moment, for whatever reason, so he goes home, grandmother does something to piss him off, he's already in full psychopath mode and the house gets redecorated in her body parts."

"And now you think you can lure him out of hiding by offering up your aunt and August as bait?" Gabriel asked.

"While we are concentrating on Gertrude and August, because the woman has to know her son is killing all these people, Malachi and the VCU can concentrate on The Butcher," I told Gabriel. "Would you be okay with the FBI taking down The Butcher?"

"If the story is true and my grandfather broke the neck of a hog with his bare hands," I didn't finish my sentence.

I was just fine with that. I might have some of the psychopathic abilities, but I wasn't Malachi

Blake. Malachi could do things that I couldn't. Even as an old man, I had a feeling that The Butcher was probably a force to be reckoned with and Malachi would have a better chance than me. Plus, if he killed Malachi, I'd have to put a bullet in his skull, maybe even six or seven. I was sure he was aware of that fact.

THIRTY-ONE

Within a few seconds of the news airing a photo of my Great-Aunt Gertrude and her possibly inbred and deranged son, tips began to pour in. The switchboard was overwhelmed and crashed at the five minute mark.

However, in that five minutes, we had learned that August being alive was a badly kept secret. All sorts of people knew him, including a grocery store clerk that had sold him groceries a few days earlier and a guy on Highway WW that sold him gas a couple times a month.

I was familiar with the area, my childhood home had been near there. WW sort of ran parallel to Interstate 70. It ran from Columbia to Millersburg and from Millersburg to Fulton. There was a lot of road there. Most of it was still rural, city expansion had gone south, not east. However, some of Columbia's elite had huge mansion estates out there.

August wouldn't own a mansion estate. It was just an indication of how much land was available in the area. The land was worth a ton of money, buying it wouldn't have come cheap. It was also a long way from Hoop-Up where most of the family lived.

However, you didn't stop at the same gas station several times a month, unless it was convenient. John was busy cross-referencing land ownership with names of my family. So far, he'd come up with absolutely zilch.

Malachi was surprisingly composed. He sat on a table in the conference room while I paced the floor. It took about two hours to drive from Kansas City to Columbia. The VCU had made it in under an hour. They were all calm, composed, waiting patiently for a call to come in from the elusive monster that had stalked me for years. My own team was also calm, while John typed furiously on the keyboard looking for a place for August to hide.

My pacing was annoying me, I was sure it was annoying everyone else. However, I couldn't stop. When the tip line had crashed, I had come unglued. Rage had surged into me and the adrenaline was still pumping strong and hard through my veins. I wanted to catch the entire lot of them. They could all go sit with my brother in The Fortress until their skeletons turned to dust.

For this reason, no one spoke to me. No one spoke at all. The only noise came from the heating system and John's fingers clacking across the keyboard. Both seemed extremely loud. The urge to break John's fingers was overwhelming and I kept my hands stuffed in my pockets as I paced to keep from acting on it.

"Why don't you go have a cigarette?" Xavier suggested after a full twelve minutes of me pacing. "And maybe a sedative. I suggest Ketamine."

"You want me to take a horse tranquilizer?" I glared at him.

"Yes, before you kill one of us as a surrogate for your rage," Xavier said.

"I'll go smoke," I grabbed my coat. The door opened.

"The switchboard is back up," Detective Russell told us. "It's still lit up like a Christmas Tree. Crimestoppers has never had this many calls before at one time. We need more operators."

"We'll help," Gabriel stood. "Not you," he pointed at me. "You are definitely not manning a telephone right now. Your soul might be pissed enough to reach through a phone line and strangle the person on the other end."

"That's impossible," I told him.

"Maybe," he gave me a very pointed look. I frowned as the word came to mind. Until meeting

Gabriel, I'd heard the term wendigo before, but I had never really grasped the concept until Gabriel told me a story about his childhood. He believed he had encountered a wendigo while growing up. It was very hard to argue with superstition and even harder when the person making the argument was Gabriel. If it had been Xavier, I would have dismissed it outright, but there was something to the way Gabriel told the story that told me it still haunted him. He truly believed in them.

Malachi and I were deemed unacceptable phone operators and tip screeners. We headed outside. The bitter cold burned my skin as the wind whipped across my face. I lit the cigarette I didn't want. I had never been one to smoke in the cold, it changed the taste of the cigarette.

"Nina believes that Gertrude has somehow been listening to her phone calls with your mother." Malachi said after lighting his own cigarette. Malachi smoked irregularly. He seemed unable to be addicted to anything other than adrenaline. He also chewed, drank, ate things that would never pass between my lips, had random sex partners whose names he couldn't remember, and had charisma that made people like him. The differences between us were vast. The similarities were scary.

"That would explain how he always knew where I was." I stubbed out the cigarette after only two puffs.

"If he kills me, will you avenge my death?" Malachi asked.

"Who?" I returned the question.

"Your grandfather."

"Yes, but not in the way you think."

"You won't kill him."

"I don't know." I thought for several seconds, shivering in the cold. Malachi stepped in closer, blocking some of the wind. "If he kills you, I'll want to kill him. Ultimately, his fate would rest in the hands of Gabriel. If Gabriel gave me the go ahead to kill him, I would. If he said no, then I wouldn't."

"Does Gabriel know he keeps hold of your leash?"

"Yes." I told Malachi. "In this job, someone has to. Nyleena can only do so much. Xavier and Lucas are too submissive to do it. That leaves Gabriel."

"And it doesn't bother you?"

"Not in the least," I admitted. "If left unchecked, I'd be exactly like The Butcher. Nyleena's done a good job, but that was when the monsters hunted me. Now, I hunt them. Do you realize that every time I come in close proximity to one, that's my instinctual reaction? I feel a need to kill them, to rid the world of the evil and chaos they cause. But in doing so, I have to answer to Gabriel. That stops me."

"Answering to Gabriel is more scary than answering to a court or jury?"

"Yes, because Gabriel respects me for who I am." I thought for a moment. "And he likes me. I don't think I understand friendship, not really. I know I like Gabriel, he's an interesting person, easy to talk to, easy to get along with, but real friendship sometimes seems like a foreign emotion. I think I have it with Nyleena and with you, I would also put Lucas and Xavier in that group. You all like me, I have no idea why, but you do. And that's great. I'd die for any of you, but with Gabriel, there's something else there. He is an alpha in his own right, not like you or me, but still an alpha. The fact that most alphas instantly dislike me gives him some power over me. I don't want to disappoint him or get him into a situation that might result in him losing his job as team leader."

"Is that because you like him as team leader or because you don't think you'll adjust as well to another team leader?"

"I believe I like having him as team leader. He's not average."

"He isn't a genius like you or Xavier or Lucas."

"I don't think I'm talking about intelligence. I instantly clicked with Lucas and Xavier, just like I did with you. Gabriel I had to warm up to. I don't normally stay interested in a person long enough to warm up to them."

"Is this some sort of sexual feeling on your part?" Malachi frowned.

"No," I reassured him. Malachi was very concerned about my sexuality. He knew my biggest secret. "It isn't sexual or romantic, I just feel a need to protect him. Some of that is transference, Nyleena really likes him, and so I have to protect him for her. But the other part is just him. He's charismatic, like you, but his is genuine. If I died, I think he would be the third most hurt person by my death. That means something."

"I would be upset."

"Yes, you would be, in your own psychotic way, you'd be devastated and probably start laying waste to entire villages. Xavier and Lucas would be hell bent on revenge, that's how they'd grieve. Gabriel though, Gabriel would truly grieve. He'd shed tears and say a nice eulogy and take care of Nyleena and my mother. He would want revenge, but it wouldn't be his first priority."

"I'd take care of Nyleena and your mother."

"Really? This is about you?" I frowned at him. "Malachi, if a bolt of lightning happens to strike me and suddenly I become interested in sexual relationships, I'll call you first. As I said, my feelings for Gabriel aren't sexual. They're," I paused, realizing exactly what it was about Gabriel that got to me. "He's the brother I never had. He sort of reminds me of Eric, before Eric started killing people."

"Ah," Malachi nodded once. "What you mean is that Gabriel is more of a brother to you than Eric was and you like the sibling banter and feelings associated with it. You had a brother, but the relationship was strained and you missed being a little sister and having a big brother. Gabriel fulfills both of those needs. So, you let him put you on a leash because as your older brother, he has the right to tell you what is right and wrong. He fills the exact same role that Nyleena fills."

"I think so." I bit my tongue. "Nyleena's my sister and you can't tell anyone." I blurted out.

"Good lord, you can't keep a secret to save your soul." Malachi said.

"You don't seem surprised."

"No, I didn't know she was your sister by blood. I'm more appalled that it took you all of five seconds to make the decision that you had to tell me. It's a good thing you aren't involved with national security, we'd be screwed."

"Why aren't you surprised if you didn't know?"

"I am, this is my surprised face," Malachi said.

"Strange, it looks like your everyday face. There is no expression."

"Should I fake it for you?"

"No, the moment is lost. I swore my mother I wouldn't tell anyone. Meaning you can't tell anyone."

"Unlike you, I can keep a secret." Malachi said as Gabriel dashed out the door.

"Holy hell, Ace, you were right. The Butcher just called and told us we should check property records in the name of Tennyson Unger."

"That's strange," I looked at Malachi.

"Yes, it is," Malachi frowned at me. "Are you sure about the name?"

"Positive, why?" Gabriel was now frowning, his excitement replaced with angst.

"Tennyson Unger was my grandfather," Malachi told him. "And I am unaware of any connection between him and the Clachans. Furthermore, he was also a psychopath."

"Your grandfather was a psychopath too?" Gabriel asked.

"Oh yes," Malachi answered. "One day, I'll tell you stories. He's dead, has been for a while. All his property was divided up and sold at auctions. No one in the family wanted it."

I wanted to say more, but didn't. I remembered that summer. Malachi lying on his stomach, unable to roll over because the whip marks on his back were so bad that bone had been exposed. I bit my tongue and Malachi gave me a nod. He must have approved of my sudden silence.

THIRTY-TWO

I had been to the Unger property once as a child. Malachi's mother had insisted on escorts to go clean out her father's belongings. My mother, Malachi, and I had gone with her. She had literally quaked with fear the entire time we were there. After a few hours, she decided it wasn't worth the effort and just sold the house with all the contents still in it.

Tennyson Unger hadn't been a serial killer. He'd been a brutal sadist. From what I remembered, his only pleasure came when he was beating something. The only time I had met him had been at Malachi's house. He'd kicked the family dog and slapped Malachi's younger brother. This had led to Malachi being horsewhipped and his grandfather going to jail for a short time. The incident didn't make Tennyson Unger any easier to get along with, it made it worse. Malachi's family cut complete contact with him. He died alone, with a dog, that he had abused and because Karma is entertained by suffering, it took six days for a neighbor to find him, by then the dog had found he was a decent food source.

The property might have changed hands, but it looked the same. The house was still rundown. It needed more than a few coats of paint. The porch looked dangerous. The shutters were hanging at odd angles or missing completely. The roof had patches on it. The yard was dead, not just dormant for winter, but obviously dead. It was mud, missing the customary dead crunchy grass that happened during a Missouri winter.

The house set about three hundred yards from the road. However, the property itself was massive. Tennyson Unger had been a farmer and he'd been paranoid. A thick grove of trees with a dirt road lead to the fields he had once plowed. There were a couple of barns and out buildings on the property, but I had never seen them.

A large double door with stained windows stared at us. However, the door, like the house, was old and worn. One side was slightly crooked, its weight resting against its companion. If it was locked, the entire thing would probably come crashing down out of the frame if we used brute force against it. Of course, we only used brute force, none of us knew the art of picking a lock.

We didn't force the door. Instead we stood in the cold, waiting for Gabriel to make a decision. We could go storming into the house or we could search around for the outbuildings and see what goodies they contained. Experience had taught us that serial killers with outbuildings were bad. It gave them space to work with less risk of being caught. It also gave them a more secure location to hide their trophies. Cellars were the second worst thing a serial killer could own. Weapons were bad, but it really was all about location.

"Cain, Reece, head down the path and see what you find. Bryan and I will take the house," Gabriel pointed with his head, one hand already on the butt of his gun. I didn't bother with the formality of pretending I might not need it. I drew mine as Xavier and I began to walk.

"I'm starting to enjoy these little treks through the wilderness with you," Xavier whispered.

"I hate woods," I told him. "It's too easy to hide in them." I looked at the barren branches. It was a little harder to hide in winter, but it was still possible. My ears listened for noises other than our footsteps. Gabriel and John could be heard, searching for a way into the house that didn't require them to climb the porch of death.

Xavier drew his gun and put his arm out. I stopped. He pointed. Through the barren trees, I could see a large barn. It was in much better shape than the house. It hadn't been painted, but it just seemed better kept. The doors weren't on this side, instead there was a large heating and air conditioning unit. It was weird finding meters running to a house that still bore blood stains, it was creepy to find a barn with a heating and air unit. Especially one as large as this. It wasn't the normal house model. I didn't know much about heating or air conditioning units, but I'd bet a pizza it was industrial sized.

We took a few more steps and another building came into view. This one was smaller. The clapboard had been painted, it wasn't peeling or fading. It looked like a small barn that had been converted into a house. I frowned and stopped.

"What?" Xavier asked.

"The house is a decoy," I pointed at the second building. "That's his living quarters."

"Why?"

"Would you live three hundred yards from the road if you were theoretically dead?"

"No," Xavier agreed.

"I don't know what the hell is in the barn, but that smaller building is where he lives. We should wait for Gabriel and John."

"How do you keep a jaguar in Missouri in winter? You heat it up," Xavier motioned towards the large unit. "That thing would cook a turkey in a house. Jaguars are tropical. It would stay warm enough."

"Tropical and subtropical," I corrected off-handedly, my attention drawn to the ground. There were no tire tracks, but I hadn't seen a car or truck at the house. A gas station attendant had said he came in regularly to fill up his truck. I took a step backwards, towards a tree. Xavier walked with me, unsure of my intentions, but trusting me. When my back was against the base of a large tree, I slid down it, ending in a crouch. Xavier mimicked me.

"Nothing in the house," Gabriel's voice crackled in my ear. "Not even food."

"Have someone find out if there is a second entrance to this property," I said back. "Also, I think he lives behind the trees. Don't come down the road."

"Where are we going?" Xavier whispered as I stood up.

"To the barn. I bet there's an entrance at the back," I whispered, darting across the path and into the trees. My feet moved on their own, avoiding as much debris as possible. We still sounded like a herd of elephants. I missed Lucas, he could have snuck up on the place quiet as a church mouse.

Gabriel and John joined us at the back of the barn. We had seen and heard them coming. They were quiet, but not silent, it was hard to sneak through the woods, especially in winter.

There was a backdoor. It was a small house door. It looked like it had been added after the land changed hands.

Gingerly, I touched the knob. It was locked. I had a bad feeling about forcing it open. Too much noise when we didn't know what was on the other side or where the occupants of the living quarters were. Gabriel sighed and stepped forward. He produced something that looked like a Swiss Army knife from his pocket. After a few seconds, the doorknob turned. I frowned at him as I pushed it open and entered.

Instinct replaced thought when I entered what could be a serial killer's lair. It did so now. My eyes took in the cage, the smell, the large rocks, the fake cave, the lush trees and bushes, but my mind didn't process all of it. Instead, my free hand grabbed my Taser. A shadow darted past me.

I yanked the door shut before anyone could follow me. It slammed hard in the frame. Another shadow moved. Outside, I could hear the men moving, shouting. The door slamming gave us away. I backed up against the cold steel door that I knew we shouldn't have opened. The first shadow was fast, moving at incredible speed as it shot past me. My brain kicked in. I had just shut myself in a cage with two jaguars. I couldn't make out the second, it stayed in the shadows, but few things could share a space with a jaguar. I was betting this was a mother and her offspring. I was in her territory and she was not happy.

It leapt at me, coming from my side. My arm swung and the Taser prongs shot out of it. The creature let out a whimper as it fell limply to the ground, twitching. The next sound was human, a loud scream, I shifted my attention. Outside the cage was a young girl, she looked to be around eight. Her hands were bound above her head and she dangled a few inches off the ground.

A low growl and movement caught my attention. The creature nearly blindsided me, hitting my arm still. My Taser skittered across the floor and I tumbled to the ground with it on top of me. I put my gun to where I thought the head should be and stopped. The eyes were human. The teeth that clamped onto my arm were also human. They were dull and tore at the skin instead of puncturing it. She gnawed at my wrist.

Her hair was long, dirty, and matted. Her face and body were scarred. She was completely nude. I understood the human teeth marks suddenly. I punched her in the face with my other

hand. Her hands tore at me, digging into my sides.
I punched her again, this time her teeth loosened
and she let out a guttural noise that didn't sound
human.

I dropped the Beretta. She wouldn't know
how to use it and I didn't think shooting her was
the answer. Twisting beneath her, I gained leverage
and flipped her over onto her side. She grunted,
but kept attacking. I punched her in the face again.
Her nose broke and blood began oozing from her
mouth. This time when she bit me, her front teeth
dislodged from her gums and became imbedded in
my arm.

"Damn it!" I screamed at her, rolling over
and on top of her. I pushed up on her chin, forcing
her head back. My other hand attempted to secure
her wrists. Her ability to fight me off was startling.
I planted all my weight on her chest and moved my
hand to her throat. My fingers tightened, her face
began to turn red. She stopped digging at my side
and clawed at my hand. I didn't let up, but I had a
free hand now. I dug out handcuffs and put one on
a flailing wrist.

This was the worst thing I could have done.
She freaked out. Her hands no longer clawed at me,
trying to get me to release my grip on her throat.
They now searched for my face and long nails raked
down the side of cheek. The red began to turn a

mottled purple. I was hoping she'd pass out soon. She didn't. Her instinct to survive kept her fighting. I finally released my grip, worried I'd strangle her. She gasped, gulping in air, while trying to throw me off of her.

I grabbed hold of the handcuff and yanked it, feeling her arm give at the socket. My hands stung as I twisted around and slipped the other cuff onto her ankle. Her free hand dug into my hair and scraped down my back. I jumped off of her. She wiggled on the ground, trying to free herself and attack me. I reached down and grabbed a handful of hair, bringing her close to me.

"I don't know if you understand me, but if you do, stop fighting. I'm not here to hurt you," I told her. She stared back at me, her body becoming motionless. "My name is Aislinn Cain, I'm a US Marshal."

She grunted at me. I hoped like hell she understood me. I stood back up, picked up my gun and holstered it. As I grabbed my Taser, she bit my leg. The prongs hit her in the back and I felt the surge of the electricity as it danced up my leg. Saliva is a great conductor of electricity. It wasn't enough to make me flop, but it tingled. It caused her to bite down harder, my leg was probably the only thing that kept her from biting off her tongue or slamming her jaws together hard enough to break out more teeth.

I stopped the flow and looked at her. Slowly, I realized I recognized her. Horror crept over me. August Clachan was going to die.

THIRTY-THREE

Xavier came in through the front of the barn. He looked terrible. Blood flowed from his forehead and ran down his face.

"Get me out of this cage," I said very quietly.

"Oh," Xavier frowned. "Let me tend to the girl first."

"Now, Xavier."

"I don't think you can kill him, he's in custody." Xavier began untying the little girl and identifying himself. She cried as her arms fell to her sides. Her pain was second to her terror at the moment. It would change when she discovered she was safe.

I had bound the jaguar with zip cuffs and the woman in the cage with me wasn't going anywhere. I stood very close to the bars. Gabriel brought in August. John brought in Gertrude.

"Let me out," I told Gabriel. Gabriel looked at me, then at the woman on the floor, then back at me.

"I can't," Gabriel told me. "Not until both suspects are secured." This really meant protected.

"Let me out," I repeated.

"Go out the back," John said. I had forgotten about it. Gabriel looked like he had just choked on a bone. He made a gagging noise.

Once outside, I didn't walk to the front of the barn, I ran. August consumed my thoughts. I wasn't just feeling the calm, I was filled with rage. More than I had ever experienced before. The door swung open hard, slamming against the outside wall of the barn. John and the little girl rushed past me, away from me. Gertrude and August weren't so lucky. Gabriel had a firm grasp on August and was standing in front of him. Xavier had backed my great aunt up, almost touching the bars. For a moment, I wished I had released the woman in the cage.

"Get away from him, Gabriel," I growled.

"I can't let you kill him in custody, Ace," Gabriel told me.

"That woman in there is feral, Gabriel. Feral. She's been a prisoner in this barn since she was three years old. She can't speak. She doesn't walk upright. She's battled jaguars all her life to stay alive and god only knows what this son of a bitch has done to her. Just walk away, Gabriel, just walk away. We'll tell everyone that I went into the barn and found myself alone with the two suspects and the kidnap victims, no one will ever know."

"How do you know she was three?" Xavier asked.

"Because that woman is Vera Callow," I spat at him. "August has been keeping her as a pet since she was three when he kidnapped her."

"Are you sure?" Gabriel asked.

"Callow had a very particular shade of blue eyes. In the pictures of Vera, she had them too. That woman has them. It's her."

"You sick fuck," Gabriel suddenly reached back and slammed August into the bars of the cage. "You kidnapped a child and forced her into cannibalism? I ought to give you to the jaguar and your prisoner." He slammed his head against the bars again. Blood began to run down the cold metal.

"Gabriel," Xavier let go of Gertrude and grabbed hold of our boss. Gabriel drew back, like he was going to hit him and stopped.

"I'll take Gertrude out," Gabriel looked at me. "Xavier will escort out August." He paused. "However, I would like nothing more than to let you have him."

"Then let me," I told Gabriel.

"I can't, Ace."

"To hell with the law," I told him, taking my Marshal creds out of my pocket and tossing them on the floor at his feet.

"It isn't about the law," Gabriel moved in very close. "If you kill him now, in this state, you may never come back and I don't want to lose you. We've lost too much lately anyway."

"Why don't you guys just get a room?" Gertrude snorted. "And don't think I'm not going to tell everyone that she tried to kill August or that you beat him up while he was in handcuffs."

"Tell them," Gabriel spat at her. "Tell them I Tasered you too." With that, Gabriel pulled his Taser and shot my aunt with it. Her body crumbled into a heap and she made mewing noises.

"I think everyone needs medical attention," Xavier said. "Including the little girl and John."

"Oh shit," I felt the calm slip away. "I must have scared her to death."

"You scared me to death," Xavier quipped. "If you ever look at me like that, I'm fleeing."

"It was deserved," Gabriel looked at August. "He should die, slowly and painfully. If we still did executions, I'd pull the switch myself."

"That's why we don't have them," I said. "If the profession of executioner still existed, we wouldn't have had botched executions and we wouldn't have had the controversy with continuing them. Since it's an extinct profession, we now have The Fortress."

"With friends inside," Gabriel added. I didn't point out how twisted it was that Gabriel had immediately thought of my "fan club" inside The Fortress. I had thought it, but we had never encountered a killer that made Gabriel want to torture them. He might want revenge from time to time, but that was different.

"What do we do about her?" I asked, pointing into the cage.

"Do you want to take her out and control her?" Xavier asked. I noticed again that he looked like he'd been in a brawl.

"Not really," I said. "What happened to your face?"

"I was attacked," Xavier scowled. "By a freaking capuchin monkey. Who trains a capuchin to be an attack monkey?"

"I offered to go first," Gabriel looked at my great aunt. "You know, we have a few minutes. I can't leave Aislinn and Xavier unsupervised. John will be getting back-up out here, but let's face it, it's going to take a while. So, let's talk."

"I have nothing to say," Gertrude answered, sticking her chin into the air and turning away from him.

"I think you do, here's your one-time offer. We won't report you as assisting a serial killer, we'll just process you for fraud. This means that you'll go to jail for a year or so, but it won't be in The Fortress. In exchange for this very generous deal, you're going to tell us how The Butcher kept tabs on Aislinn and you're going to tell us where he is," Gabriel told her.

"Go fuck yourself," my great aunt responded.

"Wow, that was very unladylike." I spoke in long, drawn out tones. "Here's where you should be brought up to speed. He has never actually attacked me. Also, we are going to collect August's DNA and prove that you and your brother are his parents. This says all sorts of weird things about you by the way..."

"He is not August's father!" Gertrude looked horrified. "He did try to feed August to a hog, but not because he's his father. That's not just absurd, it's disgusting."

"Lee said he was," I told her.

"Lee is wrong," she huffed at me. "August might not be Lee's son, but he certainly isn't my brother's."

"Then who is his father?" I asked.

"That is none of your business," she sniffled ever so slightly. Bells went off in my head.

"You don't know, that's why my grandfather tried to kill him." I shook my head. "That's what Nina has over you."

"You don't know what you're talking about."

"Yes, I do," I looked at my great aunt a little differently for a moment. Nina once told me that during the 1960's she went to a party. Someone slipped something in her drink and she woke up nude in a strange bed. She always claimed she went alone, but I hadn't believed her. Now, staring at Gertrude, I realized that I had been right. They had gone together. I was willing to bet they had both been drugged and raped. Gertrude's had resulted in August. "So, you told an unstable man that you had been raped and August was the result and he tries to kill the child. When that fails, he redirects his rage at his wife and slaughters her."

"Nonsense," Gertrude said.

"Fine, but I'm making sure to run August's DNA through CODIS and any other databases on the planet to see if there's a match." I told her.

If she was going to say something it was interrupted by the arrival of paramedics and sheriff's deputies. There was even an FBI agent, not

Malachi or a member of the VCU, but a different one that I hadn't seen yet.

"Hey!" I shouted at a paramedic that was nearing the cage. "Be careful. She seems to be feral. I'd suggest full restraints. She's been injured, but treating her will not be easy. I'm not even sure she understands language."

"That will make it hard to identify her," the sheriff's deputy closest to me said.

"Her name is Vera Callow. She went missing roughly twenty years ago. I'm not sure how much family she has left. Her uncle is dead, her father committed suicide within a few days of her uncle dying. I don't know about her mother or if she had siblings." I looked at Vera. She wouldn't know any of them and in some ways, it would be better to tell her family they'd found her body. She'd been turned into a wild animal, living off human flesh and whatever else August gave them to eat.

THIRTY-FOUR

Gertrude Clachan and her son, August Clachan, were facing a lot of charges. They'd be tried for trafficking in exotic animals, importing critical endangered animals, kidnapping, holding Vera Callow hostage for twenty years, animal abuse, assault, and sexual assault, but only one would matter; serial murder. They'd found nearly two hundred feet in August's house.

During the last twenty-some years, he'd been doing a lot of travelling and abducting homeless people, hitchhikers, vagabonds, runaways, and anyone else that was easy prey. After the abductions, he'd bring them back to the barn and start feeding them to Vera and his assortment of jaguars. He'd taped all of it.

Gabriel excused me from watching any of the videos. Instead, I had worked with Xavier to collect DNA from August and Gertrude. When Gabriel and John emerged from the room, Gabriel once again looked like he could kill someone. John was white as a ghost.

Malachi and the VCU were headed to Maine. What my grandfather was doing in Maine was beyond my comprehension. It seemed far more likely that he was living in Kansas City. Especially since we had figured out that August had mailed several of The Butcher's letters and packages during his hunting trips.

Vera Callow was being taken to the Fulton State Hospital for the Criminally Insane. She kept trying to eat people. There, they would attempt to socialize her and get back some of her humanity. I wished them the best of luck, I didn't think it was possible. However, I did ask her doctors to keep Xavier appraised of her situation. I had killed my abductor, but there was still a smidge of a feeling that she was a kindred spirit. I wanted to be kept informed.

I had been shot three times. None of them by our serial killer. I felt like that was an accomplishment. I'd also had my ass kicked by a feral human woman, but she hadn't killed and eaten me. Now, she had eaten the chunk of flesh she tore from my wrist, they found it when she threw up at the hospital. It was still another win.

If my great aunt or August would spill their guts and tell us everything, it would be even better.

Neither was talking. There were a lot of unanswered questions and I didn't like that. We had discovered that Gertrude had supplied the DNA sample for the body originally thought to be August's, from a hair brush. Other than that, we only knew that August was a serial killer and his mother had known about it.

Beating them with phonebooks had crossed my mind, but Gabriel had nixed it. Even though it looked like he wouldn't mind taking a swing or two at both of them.

I sat in the conference room, staring out the window. It was snowing again. The roads were nearly deserted. In a few hours, we'd be leaving Columbia. When I got home, I had another great aunt waiting for me, ready to spill all the family secrets that she knew. This wasn't much comfort. I felt annoyed.

Xavier came into the room, hitting my feet as they rested on the table. Not hard enough to knock them off, but enough to make me readjust my position.

"Stop sulking," he said.

"I'm not sulking," I told him. "I'm very annoyed. We have a lot of bodies. It is going to take months to sort them all out, if we ever sort them all out. We have a serial killer that isn't talking, a mother of a serial killer who knew about it and isn't talking. I hate loose ends and this case has a lot of them."

"It happens. The key is focusing on the positive."

"Vera Callow is most likely damaged beyond repair."

"I wasn't talking about Vera. I was talking about Joanie."

"Who is Joanie?"

"The little girl, strung up in the barn, Vera's next meal. Her name is Joanie Cole. She's seven years old, a straight-A student, an avid participant in sports and according to her parents, very good at math."

"I'm still waiting for you to get to the positive."

"Are you so far gone that you don't realize she's alive?" Xavier narrowed his eyes and frowned.

"So, she's alive. She'll be scarred for life. She'll need a ton of therapy and if she's really lucky, she'll eventually be able to live on her own. And why the hell did he abduct a girl? He'd been taking teen boys, not little girls, as of late."

"Ace, she's seven. Yes, it will be rough, but she's alive. She'll bounce back. And she's here."

"They brought her here for questioning?" I asked, appalled. God only knew how long she'd been suspended from the ceiling, waiting to die. She should be in a hospital.

"No, her parents brought her here."

"Bad parenting."

"Ace, she wants to thank you, personally, for saving her life. The cage was unlocked, you never tried the door. We didn't either, but Joanie says a little while before you burst into the cage, August came in and unlocked the door. I'm letting them in."

Before I could stop him, the door opened. The little girl entered, along with her mother, father, and a teenaged brother. I stared at the brother.

"I wanted to thank you," the little girl stepped forward. "For saving me and all."

"It was my pleasure," I told her, tearing my gaze off the boy. "I'm glad you are safe and unharmed."

"You're very pretty," the girl said to me. "Earlier, you were scary, but now you're pretty."

"Earlier, you were scared and in pain, now you're safe, it changes how we see things," I lied through my teeth. "Joanie? Would you mind staying here with my friend, Xavier, while I talk to your parents for a second? And you can just call him X, Xavier's so hard to say."

Joanie giggled. She might get out of this with only a little bit of scarring.

"Sure," she said.

"I'm going to leave your brother too," I told her, standing up. In the hallway, I tried not to glare at the parents. They hadn't done anything wrong, I was just tired and irritated. "I have a question, I've been wondering for a while why he abducted Joanie..." I pursed my lips unsure how to phrase my question without being very blunt. Sometimes I could be diplomatic.

"We reported her missing yesterday," her mother broke down, sobbing hard enough to make her shoulders heave.

"Tommy and Joanie were getting some stuff from Wal-Mart yesterday. The man tried to abduct both of them, but Tommy says both he and Joanie were fighting with the man. Tommy, being the bigger of the two, got away from him. Joanie didn't. Tommy's small for his age, he's nearly seventeen, but he was able to fend off the abduction and call the police immediately." The father told me.

"He did a good job," I assured the parents. "Joanie and Tommy are both safe. Joanie will need therapy and lots of support to get over this incident. Hopefully, it will bring her and her big brother closer together. He'll be her most valuable asset as long as she doesn't become angry with him."

"You say that like you know from experience," the mother composed herself.

"We deal with serial killers all the time, I've seen cases similar," I lied, again. I had been speaking from my own experience. Eric hadn't been there for me after Callow. I had become angry with both my siblings, feeling like it was their fault even though I had known it wasn't. It was one of the reasons I wasn't close to my family. I blamed all of them. The cycle of violence had started centuries ago, I had just been another victim of it and it was their fault. It sounded good. I had actually distanced myself from my family simply because I didn't want to be around them. But it was the perfect excuse.

"Do you think she'll be okay?" The mother asked.

"I'm not a therapist, I don't know for sure, but she seems to be fine right now and that's a good sign. She's young, she might bounce back without so much as a hitch in her step or she might require special attention as she grows older and deals with all the mixed feelings involved."

"Mixed feelings?" The father asked.

"This is really something you should speak with a therapist about. I have seen kids spring back from things much worse, but I've seen them crumble from things that weren't that bad."

"How bad was this?" The father asked.

"Do you know the circumstances of the case?"

"Only that she was abducted by a pedophile," he answered. I frowned, suddenly needing Gabriel. The family would find out when it hit the news that their daughter was nearly cannibalized by a feral woman and eaten by a jaguar for the perverse pleasure of a serial killer. However, I didn't think I was the right person to tell them. "Is that not correct?" The father pressed.

"Um," I shifted. "He wasn't a pedophile in the traditional sense. He's a voraphile, Joanie's age didn't interest him all that much, she was just easy to catch."

"I'm sorry, I don't know what a voraphile is," the mother told me.

"Well," I searched for the words.

"A voraphile is someone that achieves sexual arousal through the fantasy of eating or being eaten," Lucas walked into the hallway. I nearly jumped out of my skin I was so happy to see him. I willed my feet to stay in one place and not run to the giant.

"What do you mean 'eating or being eaten?'" The father sounded suspicious. The mother looked like she would faint.

"In this particular case, the suspect moved out of the fantasy world and could only achieve arousal by watching his 'pets' eat a human being. One of his 'pets' was actually a woman that he had kidnapped when she was only three. He kept her caged with jaguars and she became feral. The suspect was particularly interested in watching her consume the humans he captured for her to eat." Lucas told them. "However, that is not your concern now. I believe your daughter's name is Joanie. I've talked to a few therapists and they will take her case." Lucas handed them cards. "She does not need to know any of this information. She believes she was going to be mauled by the jaguar. She doesn't know that the jaguar and the human were going to eat her. She doesn't need to know. Neither does your son. In reality, you should all seek treatment with a licensed professional."

"This is our resident psychologist, Dr. Lucas McMichaels," I introduced Lucas.

THIRTY-FIVE

"What are you doing here?" I asked after Joanie and her family had left.

"I'm here to conduct psychological evaluations. I'm useless in the field, but I can sit in a chair and ask questions with the best of them."

"Great! I'm very happy to see you."

"I can tell from the frown on your face." Lucas said. I touched my lips. I was frowning. I tried to smile and failed. "Give it some time, you've been through a lot from what I hear. Your cousin holding people hostage and feeding them to others is pretty gruesome. Finding Vera Callow alive and feral is also gruesome. The fact that you didn't kill her despite being attacked, requires some thought."

"Why? She was a victim."

"That's the reason it needs some thought." Lucas looked at me. "You identified with her, maybe not on some great cosmic level, but you saw her as you saw yourself at the time of your abduction, as a victim."

"I have never been a victim," I told him.

"Yet, you identified her as such. You must have had some feeling for her."

"You're here to evaluate me," I sighed.

"I wish," Lucas also sighed. "John says Gabriel wanted to give the suspect to you to kill, but didn't."

"You're here to evaluate Gabriel?" I asked.

"Sort of," Lucas answered cryptically. "Don't worry, I've already formed my opinion and Gabriel is as sane as he is going to get. He certainly hasn't slid further off the deep end. Everyone has something that bothers them more than others. You dislike bombers. Xavier dislikes snipers. I harbor a deep-seeded hatred of necrophiles. I think we found Gabriel's."

"Cannibalism?"

"No, voraphilia. It's a very broad term, but most voraphiles either want to be eaten themselves or they want to watch as someone or something eats another person. On rare occasions, they want to do the eating, but as I said, it's rare. I imagine John harbors a particular hatred for certain types of killers, we just haven't seen it yet. However, I'm giving Gabriel very high marks for not turning

August over to you. Xavier told me why he didn't do it."

"Something about pushing me over the edge."

"Yes," Lucas said. "Killing in self-defense is one thing, in cold blood is another. Gabriel saw the distinction and realized that if you started killing in cold blood, it wouldn't stop. So he curbed his urge to save you."

"That's..." I frowned. "I don't know."

"Nice, sweet, thoughtful, any or all of those would work. Like a true friend, he put your needs before his own desires."

"I believe I've had this conversation already," I frowned harder. "Malachi thinks I am romantically interested in Gabriel."

"Malachi is just terrified that he isn't the biggest, baddest man in your life anymore. He doesn't really believe that, he just can't figure out how he fits into your world and he needs to fit. It's less about you and more about himself."

"Well, he is Malachi."

"He is and you accept that in him. Malachi has always thought of himself as your guardian angel, now you have a few more and he isn't sure how much he's needed. It's worse with Gabriel because while you are friends with Xavier and me, Gabriel seems to fulfill the role of big brother.

Malachi deliberately misinterprets the connection to give him some righteous indignation. He isn't sane enough to fulfill the role of big brother, but he could fulfill the role of lover should you ever decide to break your vow of chastity."

"I think of you as my big brother."

"I know, but I'm not a big brother like Gabriel is. Gabriel goads you and I don't. That's more sibling rivalry. It works for both of you. Gabriel needs someone to help keep his sanity. You give him power, control, a friend, a sister, and an ear when he needs to talk. As long as we all continue to fulfill our roles in the group, the group is harmonious."

"Power, control, blah, blah," I told Lucas. "He keeps me on a leash so I don't become more of a predator than I already am."

"And it works. I can't do that for you. Xavier certainly can't. Gabriel has his role. I have mine. Xavier has his. You have yours."

"You didn't mention John."

"That's because I don't know John's yet. Currently, he's an antagonist. He stirs the pot a little too much. We aren't as by the book as he would like and it's a problem. One I hope he sorts out soon." Lucas began to walk away.

"Hey," I went after him. "What exactly is my role?"

"You fill many," Lucas looked at me. "You can be the damsel in distress, the sister we all need because our own families don't understand us, the friend that can listen to our woes, as long as we don't mind you telling Nyleena or your mother, or you can be the monster that rips apart the bad guys with your bare hands and then rushes to our side to make sure we are alright."

"I think I'm mostly monster," I told him.

"You are, but like most monsters, you can hide in plain sight."

"People keep pointing out that I'm a terrible friend."

"You aren't a terrible friend, you just don't do secrets. Given your family, on both sides, I would be more surprised if you did keep secrets. In your mind, secrets are dangerous and maybe, evil."

I let him go. I hadn't considered that. I did consider secrets to be bad. Secrets led to grandfathers butchering grandmothers and then stalking their grandchildren. Secrets had let a serial killer go free for at least twenty years. Secrets had resulted in my being kidnapped by Callow and held in a closet while I thought about ways to kill him.

As I walked slowly, pondering my dislike of secrets, Gabriel came into the hall. His jaw was clenched, his face red. He saw me and his face softened.

"What's up, Kemosabe?"

"Ace," Gabriel took a deep breath. "It's Nyleena."

"Where?" I looked around.

"There was an incident. She's in the hospital."

"Incident? What sort of incident?"

"She's been shot, witnesses say an older gentleman walked up to her and Nina as they got out of a car at a restaurant. Nina was killed. Nyleena was shot in the face. She's alive, but just barely."

I couldn't breathe. My knees gave out under me and only Gabriel catching me kept me from hitting the floor. I had to get to her. It was the only thing I could think about. I had to get to Nyleena.

THE BUTCHER

He had followed his sister from Nyleena's apartment to the restaurant. The car had crisscrossed through the city as they made stops at different places, getting different things. How much stuff could one person need?

Finally, they pulled into the parking lot of a restaurant. He parked in the free spot directly behind them. He got out and waited, his legs were sore from being in the car that long. Age had brought muscle spasms and cramps. It had slowed his walk, but only a little. Lines had formed in his face, his hair had turned grey at the temples, but not on the rest of his head. A feat considering he was nearly eighty-seven.

However, he'd kept in shape. A small paunch had formed at his mid-section from too many TV dinners, but that was it. No arthritis or dementia, no diseases associated with aging had set into his body. He was slim and not bad looking for a guy his age. The ladies at the VFW's Friday Night Bingo swooned over him.

The women emerged. The younger one fussing over the movements of the older. He watched his sister for a second, wondering whether to call her name or not. He opted not to. Instead, he drew a gun from a holster on his waist.

"Excuse me," he said, grabbing both their attention. The gun fired. The younger woman collapsed, blood flowing from her cheek. Bubbles formed as the air escaped her sinus passage. His sister looked shocked. He didn't know why. He fired at her. She crumbled to the ground.

He walked over, straddling her as she lay bleeding and put a second bullet into her head. He sighed, relief washing over him, he'd done as she asked. He waited another second before getting back into his car and driving away.

The VCU had taken the bait, tracing the call to some place in Maine. He'd been right outside the police department when he'd made the call. He'd watched his favorite granddaughter rush out with her team to track down his sister and her wretched son. He'd watched Malachi Blake leave with his team of federal officers. He'd even waved at the younger man.

The secrets might not have been kept, but he was sure Aislinn and Nyleena wouldn't tell. And if

Nina hadn't told them, they'd eventually figure out the connection with Tennyson Unger.

Now, he had other business to attend to. Business that would require him to cross the state again. He'd gotten a lead on the sniper that Aislinn was desperate to catch. A friendly visit to the man wouldn't hurt, at least it wouldn't hurt him. It might hurt for the sniper.

EPILOGUE

Aislinn had flown back to Kansas City three hours earlier. Nyleena was in a coma, but alive. Gabriel would know where to find her. In the meantime, he had something else to deal with. Lucas sat across from him in the conference room. They should have already left Columbia, but Lucas had brought damning information that delayed their leaving.

Not only had The Butcher killed Nina and critically injured Nyleena, he had been trying to pass messages along to Aislinn the entire time. Gabriel had hung up with the hotel less than thirty minutes ago. John Bryan, their newest member, had ordered all her messages and calls be routed to him. It was problematic to screen her messages and calls. It was a huge fucking deal that he had failed to pass that information along to anyone. They could have wrapped up the case the day the plane touched down if he had given the information to Gabriel or Xavier.

Xavier came into the room. They hadn't told him anything except to be there at four. It was two minutes to four, he was early for Xavier. The mood was somber and Xavier fidgeted uncomfortably. He said nothing though, waiting for the fourth member to come in.

At a minute past four, John joined them. He took a seat and immediately mistook the somberness as grief for Nyleena, a woman he didn't know very well. Gabriel cleared his throat. These were serious allegations that might go beyond the SCTU. He was waiting for one more to join them.

However, the fifth wasn't showing up. He was late. The minutes ticked by, Xavier fidgeted more and more. Lucas was calm. Gabriel was not. His hands kept clenching and unclenching.

"What's this about?" John asked after a half hour.

"Just a few more minutes," Gabriel checked his phone. A text message appeared. He sighed and clasped his hands together. This was going to be tricky. He needed Malachi to do his job and not let his personal impulses control him. Sometimes, Malachi needed help with that. Gabriel hoped Lucas, Xavier and himself were up to the task. Especially since Malachi was in a heightened state of psychopathy due to the shooting of Nyleena. He might not have a personal attachment to her, but she was Aislinn's life line, transference ran both ways.

Any semblance that Malachi was a healthy, sane, well-adjusted thirty-four year old male, was completely lost when he walked into the conference room. He had completely dropped the mask that he wore all the time. His face was devoid of emotion, but his nostrils flared when he breathed, his heartbeat was strong enough to make the pulse in his neck visible, tendons stood out on his forehead, creating ridges, his eyes were alive, vividly green and containing nothing short of the fires of Hell within them. His body screamed that he wanted nothing less than to bathe in blood. None of them wanted to guess what he was thinking, they were sure it involved pain, unbearable pain that would make eternity in the hands of demons seem like a pleasure cruise.

He didn't walk, he stalked into the room. The door banging loudly as it bounced off the wall with his opening it and slamming closed from the momentum. He moved to stand behind Gabriel, his rage too consuming to allow him to sit down.

Xavier didn't know what was going on, but he knew it wasn't about Nyleena. John squirmed under Malachi's searing gaze.

        "We were informed that Aislinn Cain received four messages from The Butcher, Patterson Clachan, while we were working this case. The first one arrived at the hotel a few hours after us. We also know that she didn't receive these messages and that they contained the identity of the killer. Can you explain why you directed the hotel staff to have all her messages sent to you as well as any phone calls she received?" Gabriel asked John. John squirmed a little more.

        "Someone died because she didn't get that message," Lucas spoke calmly to John. "That was vital information. It doesn't matter that it came from a serial killer, you had no right to keep that information from the team."

        "Or pretend to be in command so you could dictate what messages one of my Marshals received." Gabriel added. "Now, we are giving you the chance to explain yourself. Special Agent Blake is here to act as a witness."

        "You're all crazy," John snorted. Malachi growled. It was low. More predator than human, John didn't even know humans could make those noises. He felt it rumble in his chest.

        "That's not going to help you," Lucas said.

        "Marshal Cain has been helping a serial killer avoid justice for a long time." John said. "She has repeatedly been in contact with Patterson Clachan over the years."

"We know," Gabriel said. "She reports all contact to Special Agent Blake because he's in charge of the investigation into The Butcher."

"How can you justify allowing your Marshals unit to be in contact with a known serial killer and pedophile?" John shouted.

"The Butcher is not a pedophile," Lucas answered. "Patterson Clachan has no gender preference for victims, but he does have an age preference. During his years in Europe, it was Nazi soldiers and occasionally, a civilian when soldiers were in short supply. Back in the states, he kills both men and women, but they tend to be people he thinks has slighted him in some way. George Killian tried to kill Aislinn Cain when she was in high school in a drive-by shooting and has since been following her and killing to frame her. Nina Clachan asked Patterson to kill her, so that she wouldn't suffer through the end stages of her cancer. His next target is the sniper that killed Michael Giovanni. Unfortunately, he knows more about the killer than we do and he was unwilling to share that information because he felt slighted that Aislinn wasn't responding to his messages. He attempted to kill August Clachan when August was a child, but that was because Tennyson Unger raped

August's mother and August was the by-product. He never sexually abused any of the people he killed. He likes to kill, but it does not give him a sexual rush. It gives him a feeling of control and power."

"He raped and murdered my daughter!" John shoved his chair away from the table.

"No, he didn't," Malachi frowned at John. "Unless you found your daughter with her organs removed and nailed to different pieces of furniture in your house, Patterson Clachan didn't kill your daughter and he certainly didn't sexually assault her. He considers rapists and pedophiles to be the lowest of the low."

Gabriel turned the full weight of his stare at John. "I don't know why you thought Patterson Clachan killed your daughter, but he didn't and your personal vendetta not only cost a life, but endangered the safety of this unit. You are relieved of your duties and will be turned over to the FBI to be prosecuted. Do you understand?"

"If it wasn't Patterson Clachan, who was it?" John demanded. "My daughter was raped then butchered."

"No, your daughter was killed and then raped," Gabriel told him. "Your information is wrong. In your mind, she might have been butchered, but in reality she was stabbed seventeen times. That is nothing compared to what Patterson Clachan does to his victims."

Malachi produced a photo and put it on the table. George Killian, split from navel to chin, sat in a chair. The torso cavity was devoid of everything. Blood had soaked into the chair so heavily, that it dripped from the bottom.

"That is what Patterson Clachan does to his victims when he can't think of a more 'poetic' way to kill them, like breaking their legs and leaving them to be eaten by their abused dogs, like he did with Tennyson Unger."

All heads turned towards Malachi. He had forgotten they didn't know that or that Patterson Clachan had an MO. He had known for years that Patterson Clachan was The Butcher. He had kept it secret because of a letter he'd received telling him that he had personally taken care of Tennyson Unger and that their family no longer had to worry about the old devil who had done things worse than raping Gertrude Clachan.

Two VCU agents came into the room and took John into custody. They were alone. Malachi knew what came next. He had slipped up. Aislinn was making him soft and forgetful at times.

"Would you like to elaborate, Special Agent Blake?" Gabriel reminded him of his job. Malachi was an old pro at lying, it was one of the benefits of being a psychopath.

"When Aislinn first started receiving letters from The Butcher, I did as well. They stopped after only a few, then after the funeral of Tennyson Unger, I received my final letter from him. He knew that Tennyson had molested my younger brothers. I didn't know it was Aislinn's grandfather and I didn't know how he knew about it. The only people that knew were my mom and Aislinn's mom. In the letter, he stated that he had incapacitated Unger by breaking his legs and then left him to be eaten by his mutt. Since I was glad he was dead, I burned the letter. Now that I know about Gertrude Clachan tapping Nina's phones, I understand how Patterson Clachan found out about it. I wasn't an FBI agent at the time, I hadn't even graduated college yet. I should have turned it over, like Aislinn did, but I was young and I didn't want my brothers to be humiliated by it being revealed to others."

"And the MO?" Gabriel asked.

"Michael and I were keeping it secret. If Aislinn had found it in the database, she would have known her grandfather was The Butcher. The powers that be are in the dark about it, as well. There are things about our jobs that they neither want nor need to know. With Aislinn, it was a matter of protection, she questions her humanity enough without having to wonder how many killers her family has produced. His favorite targets are pedophiles. He really doesn't like pedophiles."

"Tennyson couldn't abuse you sexually, so he did it physically." Lucas said slowly.

"Yes," Malachi answered. "Aislinn doesn't need to know that, either."

"Aislinn doesn't like secrets," Lucas said. "With good reason."

"No, she doesn't," Malachi agreed. "And she's about to get more answers than she ever wanted."

"Why?" Xavier asked.

"Patterson Clachan is about to make his final stand," Lucas looked at Xavier. "He told me he had a list, when he finishes the list, he'll let Malachi take him into custody. He won't turn himself into us, he's afraid of what Aislinn will do. Nyleena was an accident, but one that Aislinn is going to have trouble ignoring, even when Nyleena wakes up."

"Do we know any of his other targets?" Malachi asked.

"I think we can safely add Joe Clachan, August Clachan, and Gertrude Clachan to the list. Can you think of anyone else that has slighted Aislinn or her family?"

"That's a long list considering what Patterson sees as a slight. You can add John Bryan." Malachi looked at them. "As a matter of fact, with the exception of Nyleena, Ace's mom and her immediate family, and us, I'd say everyone is a potential target."

"Patterson felt guilty for shooting Nyleena in the face like he did. He said he didn't mean to do it," Lucas told everyone. "He says it was supposed to be a through-and-through to her shoulder. She was going to bleed, maybe have a broken collar bone, nothing more, but she turned and Patterson fired into her face by accident. He specifically shot Nyleena with a .22 though and Nina with a .9mm. His intentions were obviously different."

"A psychopath with a conscience." Gabriel sat back down.

"It gets worse," Malachi told him. "Patterson doesn't really have a conscience like you do, he has one like Aislinn does. It's fake, completely created by Nina and Lila. He feels bad about Nyleena because he knows he is supposed to, because Nina and Lila would have told him to feel bad about it. Now, they're both dead and he's wounded, because he's lost his connection with Ace and Nyleena."

"Wounded?" Lucas asked.

"If Aislinn were ripped out of my life, I would suffer some serious side effects. He killed

Lila, sure, but not because he wanted to, I think he wanted to kill Gertrude, but Lila was there. That's why he disappeared. It wasn't fear of going to jail, it was fear of never getting revenge on Gertrude. Nina always stopped him. Nina's gone. In a perfect world, Aislinn and Nyleena would fill the void, but it isn't a perfect world and with the loss of those women, so goes his grip on whatever control he had."

"So, he didn't just kill his sister, he killed his touchstone," Lucas said.

"Yes," Malachi answered. "He wouldn't have killed her if she hadn't made him promise to do it."

"Psychopaths need contact with their touchstones," Lucas said.

"No, they don't. They just need to know they are around if they need them. I don't have to talk to Ace. I can hear her voice in my head. Ace hears Nyleena's. Ace requires more contact than I do, because I am not trying to be a sociopath. I just need to know that Aislinn Cain is alive for me to keep some of the darker parts in check."

"Like the urge to kill," Xavier said.

"I'm not a killer," Malachi answered. "Death is interesting, the power of life and death is a thrill, and I have no problems making the decision, but that isn't what my psychopathic urges are about."

"You're a sadist," Lucas said.

"I don't torture people because Ace tells me it's wrong, even if they want it." Malachi admitted. "Pain is my world. Death would be accidental in that situation. And before you go over thinking that statement, mixing pain and pleasure does not always mean sex. Sometimes, it's about control and feeling invincible."

"You're a true sadist, not a sexual sadist," Lucas gave a soft whistle. "That is truly rare."

"You would have made a great inquisitor," Gabriel said.

"I would have been one of the best," Malachi answered.

ABOUT THE AUTHOR

I've been writing for over two decades and before that, I was creating my own bedtime stories to tell myself. I penned my first short story at the ripe old age of 8. It was a fable about how the raccoon got its eye-mask and was roughly three pages of handwritten, 8 year old scrawl. My mother still has it and occasionally, I still dig it out and admire it.

When I got my first computer, I took all my handwritten stories and typed them in. Afterwards, I tossed the originals. In my early twenties, I had a bit of a writer's meltdown and deleted everything. So, with the exception of the story about the raccoon, I actually have none of my writings from before I was 23. Which is sad, because I had a half dozen other novels and well over two hundred short stories. It has all been offered up to the computer and writing gods as a sacrifice and show of humility or some such nonsense that makes me feel less like an idiot about it.

I have been offered contracts with publishing houses in the past and always turned them down. Now that I have experimented with being an Indie Author, I really like it and I'm really glad I turned them down. However, if you had asked me this in the early years of 2000, I would have told you that I was an idiot (and it was a huge contributing factor to my deleting all my work).

When I'm not writing, I play in a steel-tip dart league and enjoy going to dart tournaments. I enjoy renaissance festivals and sanitized pirates who sing sea shanties. My appetite for reading is ferocious and I consume two to three books a week as well as writing my own. Aside from introducing me to darts, my SO has introduced me to camping, which I, surprisingly, enjoy. We can often be found in the summer at Mark Twain Lake in Missouri, where his parents own a campground.

I am a native of Columbia, Missouri, which I will probably call home for the rest of my life, but I love to travel. Day trips, week trips, vacations on other continents, wherever the path takes me is where I want to be and I'm hoping to be able to travel more in the future.

http://www.facebook.com/hadenajames

hadenajames.wordpress.com

@hadenajames

Newsletter